THE FINAL PLAY

Also by Shelly Ellis

The Branch Ave Boys
Know Your Place
In These Streets

Chesterton Scandal series
To Love & Betray
Lust & Loyalty
Best Kept Secrets
Bed of Lies

Gibbons Gold Digger series
Can't Stand the Heat
The Player & the Game
Another Woman's Man
The Best She Ever Had

Published by Dafina Books

THE FINAL PLAY

A Branch Ave Boys Novel

SHELLY ELLIS

KENSINGTON PUBLISHING CORP.

www.kensingtonbooks.com

DAFINA BOOKS are published by

Kensington Publishing Corp.
119 West 40th Street
New York, NY 10018

All Kensington titles, imprints, and distributed lines are available at special quantity discounts for bulk purchases for sales promotion, premiums, fund-raising, and educational or institutional use.

Special book excerpts or customized printings can also be created to fit specific needs. For details, write or phone the office of the Kensington Sales Manager: Kensington Publishing Corp., 119 West 40th Street, New York, NY 10018. Attn. Sales Department. Phone: 1-800-221-2647.

Dafina and the Dafina logo Reg. U.S. Pat. & TM Off.

ISBN-13: 978-1-4967-2467-0
ISBN-10: 1-4967-2467-4
First Kensington Trade Paperback Printing: November 2019

ISBN-13: 978-1-4967-2468-7 (ebook)
ISBN-10: 1-4967-2468-2 (ebook)
First Kensington Electronic Edition: November 2019

10 9 8 7 6 5 4 3 2 1

Printed in the United States of America

To Andrew and Chloe,
to Mom and Dad, and
to Aunt Rachel and Greatgrandma,
you're always there in some shape or form in my heart.
Thanks for being who you were and who you are.
You will always be important to me.

Acknowledgments

I say it all the time . . . Even though splashy debuts get a lot of attention in our industry, I wish there was more praise for authors who have staying power. Climbing the summit and publishing your first book is hard. No doubt about that. There's a lot of focus on how to break into the industry, from books to blogs to podcasts. But few will tell you that staying on that summit you just climbed or continuing to have a viable career as an author can be even more challenging. There isn't much "how-to" advice in that area—just lots of trial and error.

I marvel at the authors who have written dozens and dozens of books and still keep their audiences or grow them. I'm amazed at how they manage to come up with amazingly creative story lines and memorable characters. I remember looking at my parents' bookshelves when I was younger, seeing paperback after paperback with names like Nora Roberts, Stephen King, Dean Koontz, Francis Ray, and Terri McMillan on the covers and along the spines. I would think, "Man, I wish I could do that! I hope that's me someday." I'm not a Roberts, King, or McMillan, but I'm proud of my little sumthin' sumthin' I've done with my writing. I know it hasn't been an easy journey and I've gotten help and lots of encouragement along the way.

The Final Play marks the release my fifteenth full-length novel. (I've written eleven full-length novels under Shelly Ellis, two under Shelly Stratton, and two under L.S. Childers.) It's also the closure of my fourth series. I couldn't have gotten this one done without the support of my husband, Andrew, and our daughter, Chloe, who played quietly to herself or on her Kindle to give me time to create. I also couldn't have done it without my lifelong cheerleaders—Mom and Dad. I also want to thank my wordsmith and editor, Esi Sogah, and my agent and counselor, Barbara Poelle. And thanks to an unsung hero, Rebecca Cremonese, production editor at Kensington Books. Rebecca and I have worked together on numerous novels. She handles all my page proofs. She's the last line of defense to keep my writing from looking crazy and I appreciate all the work she does.

I have a long list of writer friends and readers (though frankly, I think every reader is a potential writer at heart) who I commiserate with daily. If I missed one of their names, I'd feel guilty so I will say to the writers, "You know who you are. I love you. Thanks for sharing in the joy and misery that is being a writer. You're all talented and I wish you the best and most success." And to the readers who have supported me in the past and continue to support me: Thank you, thank you, thank you! You complete the circle and make me feel like a rock star.

Chapter 1

Derrick

"Hey! Hey!" someone shouted, making Derrick Miller lurch awake.

He opened his eyes and squinted against the bright morning light. He dazedly looked around him, wondering why he had fallen asleep in his car and not his bed. He looked down at himself. And why was he still wearing his tuxedo?

The pounding in his head wasn't helping him focus. It was like a jackhammer was trying to beat a hole through his skull. His mouth was dry, too. His neck, back, and shoulders ached after sitting up in the driver's seat for he had no idea how long.

"Look, man, you can't be sleepin' here! This ain't no damn hotel!" a muffled voice shouted at him.

Derrick turned slightly in his seat to find a security guard standing at the driver's-side door, rapping his knuckles on the glass. The guard—a squat, fat, elderly man in a too-tight uniform—was scowling at him and sending spittle flying at the window.

As Derrick stared back at him, he finally realized where

he was. He had fallen asleep in his Nissan in the same parking garage he had parked in last night. After he had left the education gala, after his girlfriend, Morgan, had walked out on him—probably for good—he had decided to lick his wounds and stay huddled up in his car. Derrick had been too drunk to drive home. He hadn't wanted to make his bad evening worse with a car accident or getting pulled over by Metro Police for a DUI.

He had already dodged being sent to jail last night. There was no need to take the chance again.

"I'm tellin' you, man. If you don't move this car, I'm callin' the cops!" the guard shouted. "I'm not playin'!"

Derrick held up his hands and nodded groggily. "I'm leavin'. I'm . . . I'm leavin'. Just . . . just give me a second to get . . . get myself together. Okay?"

He tiredly scrubbed his hands over his face and turned on the engine. He threw the car into reverse and pressed the accelerator, making the car heave back and the guard jump out of the way to keep from getting hit or his toes run over.

"Damn! Watch it! You tryin' to kill somebody?" the guard yelled.

Derrick didn't answer him. Instead, he continued to back out of the parking space, though he did so more carefully this time. He looked up and followed the EXIT signs, pointing his car in the same direction as the yellow arrows overhead until he finally reached the gate that would take him out of the garage onto a Northwest D.C. street that was already teeming with morning traffic.

As Derrick made the slow drive back to his apartment building, the events of last night came rushing back to him in lurid detail. The more he remembered, the more he cringed.

In one night, he had not only managed to lose the opportunity to get badly needed funding for the Branch Avenue

Boys' Youth Institute where he was executive director, but he'd also lost his girl . . . his love, Morgan. And he had done it all because of misguided jealousy and fury—all because he had found out his ex, Melissa, was now dating his *former* best friend, Jamal.

Now sober, Derrick realized how insane he must have looked last night to everyone in that ballroom as he yelled and cursed. He could still hear the echoes of the screams from the crowd around them as he punched Jamal in the face in a fit of rage near the hotel's elevators.

Did he regret what he'd done? He certainly regretted the aftermath. He did love Morgan and hadn't wanted her to think otherwise. He had wanted to make a good impression on John and Eliza Mayhew—the wealthy couple whom Morgan had arranged for him to meet at the gala in the hope that they would donate money to the Institute. Derrick hadn't wanted to squander either opportunity. But how was he expected not to lash out, to not feel anything about Jamal's betrayal? He was only human; any red-blooded man in a similar situation probably would have done the same damn thing. Derrick just wished he hadn't done it so publicly. He wished Morgan hadn't been there. He shouldn't have been so reckless or stupid.

When he arrived at his apartment building twenty minutes later, he pulled into a vacant space, slowly opened his car door, and staggered onto the sidewalk. His head was still pounding. He still felt like he needed sunglasses to keep out the morning sun. A couple of minutes later, he shoved open his front door, revealing an eerily quiet apartment.

He didn't expect Morgan to be here, even though she had moved in with him briefly. They were both supposed to move into their new apartment in a few weeks in Brookland, near Gallaudet University. It would've been the first place they had gotten together.

Morgan's lease at her apartment had ended earlier than his. She had been staying here until their big move.

Until I fucked that up, he thought morosely as he closed the apartment door behind him.

Derrick had managed to lose two women and a cat in less than six months. He was certain of it now: He was horrible at relationships.

He walked down the hall to his bedroom, removing his tie from around his neck and his jacket along the way. After he'd stripped off all of his clothes, he looked at himself in the bathroom mirror, pulling back his dreads and securing them with a rubber. Derrick hadn't been the one hit last night but his eyes were puffy, probably from the lack of a good night's sleep. Fatigue was all over his mahogany-hued face. He flexed his sore hand, climbed into the shower stall, and adjusted the shower head from the last time Morgan had used it, making it accommodate his tall height. He felt the hot blast of the water, hoping to wash away the frustration and shame he felt. Derrick emerged from the bathroom thirty minutes later, having brushed his teeth and taken some aspirin. When he did, he heard a thumping sound in his bedroom. He walked down the hall and found Morgan hunched over one of the drawers, shoving some of her clothes into a duffel bag. She was no longer wearing her gown from last night but a T-shirt and shorts. Her curly hair was in a loose bun atop her head.

He leaned against the door frame as he watched her. It was obvious she was unaware he was standing there because she went about her task without even giving him a glance.

He had been through this before when Melissa had packed her things and moved out after she found out he had been cheating with Morgan for months. But watching Morgan go through the same ritual, hurt even more. This was supposed to be the start of something new and fresh.

This was supposed to be the relationship he had finally gotten right. There was no tug-of-war with Morgan like what he'd experienced with Melissa even in their best of times because, though they'd loved each other, they were too different at heart. With Morgan, everything fell into place—and he had ruined it.

His phone rang, snapping her attention, making her turn around to look at his cell that sat on one of the night tables. When she did, her eyes landed on Derrick and she held up her free hand.

"I don't wanna talk," she said as the phone rang again. She returned her attention to her packing. "I just wanna get some of my shit and get the hell out of here. I'll come back for the rest later. Okay?"

"I didn't hear you come in."

"You weren't supposed to," she muttered.

"Where are you staying?"

She didn't answer him. Instead, she continued to pack.

"Morgan, don't do this, baby! Look, I know what I did last night was fucked up," he began, tightening the towel around his waist and walking toward her. "But I want you to know . . . I *need* you to understand that it wasn't be-cause I want to get back with Melissa. I know that's over between us. I just—"

"The only reason why it's over between you and Melissa is because *she* left *you*, Derrick," Morgan said icily. "I was the consolation prize—the backup. I always was. I know that now. And the only reason you're upset I'm leaving is you'll be alone. But you'll find another girl. Men like you always do. Another sucker will come along. Don't worry!"

"You aren't a sucker and you weren't the consolation prize, damn it! I really do lov—"

"I don't want to hear it anymore. I'm tired of your bull-shit and your lying! You're wasting your breath!" She glanced at his phone again. "You should probably answer that. It keeps ringing."

The ringtone continued to fill the bedroom. He grimly pursed his lips and stepped around her to answer his cell.

"Yeah?" he said after pressing the green button.

"Mr. Miller," Gary, one of the security guards at the Institute answered, "sir, I'm glad I caught you. We've got a situation up here."

Derrick frowned. "What's wrong? Did something happen? Is it one of the boys?"

At those words, Morgan halted. She turned and looked at Derrick.

In addition to being his girlfriend, Morgan was also an instructor at the Boys' Institute. She taught woodworking and was one of the favorite teachers of most of the boys enrolled in the rehabilitation program. She had embraced the underprivileged teens, ignoring their troubled pasts and seeing them for who they were at their core. It was one of the things Derrick loved most about her.

"Something happened?" she whispered, narrowing her green eyes.

He shrugged helplessly as he listened to Gary on the other end.

"Yeah, it's one of the boys. He's disappeared," Gary finally explained.

"Who?"

"Cole Humphries, sir. We checked the dormitories, all the classrooms, the basketball court . . . everywhere, and we can't find him. One of the kids said he thinks he saw Cole sneak out last night, but it's not on any of our security footage. We don't know where he went."

Derrick grimaced.

Cole was one of his more troubled students. He had been working for one of the biggest drug kingpins in D.C., Dolla Dolla, before one of his crimes had landed him at the Institute. He'd even been holding and transporting drugs and money for Dolla Dolla at the school, until Derrick and Morgan had confronted him together and put a stop to it. Cole had promised them that he would no longer work for Dolla Dolla, that he would clean up his ways. Now Derrick wondered if he had been telling them the truth.

"Okay," he murmured. "I'll be in soon. I'll start making phone calls to see if I can track him down."

"Okay, sir," Gary said before hanging up.

"What's wrong?" Morgan asked as Derrick lowered his cell phone back to his night table.

"Cole's missing."

"*What?* Did he run away?"

"Looks like it," he said, yanking his towel from around his waist and tossing it to the floor. He strode to his dresser and began to gather underwear and socks.

She dazedly shook her head. "But why would he . . . I don't understand."

"I don't either, but I have to find him before the cops do." He stepped into his boxer briefs. "He's going to be in violation of his sentence for leaving the Institute like this. He could get sent to jail."

Though the boy had been a thorn in Derrick's side pretty much since he'd arrived at the Institute, he didn't want to see Cole go to prison. Putting a young man in a cell with older, hardened criminals who had committed much worse crimes than him would only make Cole worse, not better. And honestly, Derrick saw a little of his young self in Cole—the false bravado, the swagger. Those were the same traits that had landed Derrick at the Institute twenty years ago, before he'd learned the error of his ways.

"I'll help you," Morgan said, making him pause and stare at her in surprise.

"Huh?"

"I said I'll help you find Cole! I'll talk to some of his friends at the Institute. Maybe they'll tell me why he would leave . . . where he went. He could be at his mom's house, but he might not. What if he went back to Dolla? What if something happened and he just had to *go*, Derrick?"

Derrick was considering that, too. Maybe Cole hadn't run away from school, but was fleeing from something else . . . or *someone* else.

"The boys trust me. They might tell me stuff that they won't tell the rest of you," she insisted.

"You don't have to do this."

After all that he had put her through, she would still be willing to help him?

"I know. But I care about Cole and what happens to him."

He stared at her for several seconds before slowly nodding. "Okay. Thank you."

"Let's be clear though. This ain't for you. *We're* done." She pointed at herself then him then back again. "This is for Cole." She zipped her duffel bag closed and threw the strap over her shoulder. "I'll wait for you in the living room while you get dressed," she said.

He watched silently as she walked out of the room.

Chapter 2

Jamal

Jamal Lighty opened his eyes to light streaming through the bedroom blinds, surprised to find himself in bed alone. Melissa must have woken up before him, but he hadn't even felt her stir or leave. He must have been sleeping pretty hard. Not surprising, considering the night they'd both had.

"Lissa?" he called out. "Lissa!"

No one answered.

He pushed himself up to his elbows and stared tiredly around the empty room. His gaze landed on the calico cat perched at the end of the mattress, staring at him with the unflinching gaze of an Egyptian sphynx.

"Hey, Brownie," he mumbled in greeting to Melissa's cat, smacking his lips and wincing at the sour taste in his mouth. "What's up? Where's your mama?"

The cat answered him by purring softly and walking across the feathery duvet, before head-butting him in the bare chest. Jamal laughed and rubbed Brownie's head and flank. He was rewarded with more purrs. After a minute, the cat flipped onto his back, offering him his tummy for a rub.

"Let's table this for now. We'll continue after I pee, okay?" he said to Brownie before tiredly crawling off the bed and walking to Melissa's en suite bathroom.

He flicked a switch near the door and winced at the bright light coming from the vanity mirror. He then looked around him again.

Her bathroom was as clean as her bedroom, with dark granite countertops, white subway tile, and chrome finishes. Body gels, perfumes, makeup, and hair products were all neatly arranged. He examined a few bottle labels and glanced in the mirror, catching a glimpse of himself. He winced again at his reflection.

He stared at his wheat-colored face. Under his five-o'clock shadow, a purple-hued bruise had started to bloom along his jawline where Derrick had punched him last night, and one side of his lip was cut and swollen. He probably should have iced it to prevent the swelling, but he'd been admittedly too preoccupied with other things last night to think about tending to his injuries.

Other things, he thought with widened eyes and rubbing his hand over his curly head. That was an understatement.

His mind flashed to images of him and Melissa humping for dear life on her sofa and her living room wall. The frenzied passion of their first tryst had caught him off guard, to say the least. He still wasn't convinced it wasn't some angry revenge fuck on her part. She'd wanted to get back at Derrick for cheating on her; sex with his former friend was one of the best ways to do it. Jamal wondered if that explained her absence this morning. Maybe she had woken up regretting what she had done and was patiently waiting in her living room for him to get dressed and get the hell up out of there. Well, he wouldn't linger much longer if that's what she wanted. He'd had a good time; it seemed like she had, too. He had feelings for her but he knew how this went; sometimes feelings aren't requited. He'd have to accept this was where their ride ended.

Jamal turned, raised the toilet seat, used the bathroom, and washed his hands. He threw water onto his face a few times, hoping to get rid of the last remaining cobwebs of sleepiness before his drive back home. He planned to grab his clothes from the bedroom floor and dress, leaving his shower for when he got back to his own apartment. But first, he had to get this stale taste out of his mouth. It was driving him crazy. He glanced at her toothpaste and toothbrush near the faucet.

Nah, can't use those.

Sure, they'd slept together, but using someone's toothbrush seemed like a level of intimacy that went beyond even sex.

He bent down and opened one of the doors of the cabinet beneath her counter and quickly found a bottle of mouthwash. He removed the lid, tossed some of the minty liquid into his mouth, closed his eyes, and gargled. When he opened his eyes again and spit the froth into the bathroom sink, he found Melissa standing in the bathroom doorway, leaning against the door frame, grinning at him.

"Mornin'," she said, casually twirling the belt of her blue silk robe while one sienna-hued leg dangled out seductively. She was all dimples this morning with a broad smile. She'd taken out her twists from last night and now piled her golden red coils atop her head in a loose bun. Melissa was practically glowing.

"H-h-hey," he stuttered, turning around to face her,

wiping mouthwash from his lips with the back of his hand. "Good . . . good morning."

"How was your sleep? It had to be good. You didn't get up even when I took a shower. You were still snoring."

"Oh? I . . . uh . . . I guess I was really tired."

"Sorry I wasn't here when you woke up. I was in the kitchen with my earbuds on, grading papers. I'm way behind this week. I see you found your way around though." She gestured to the bottle he held.

"Oh! Oh, yeah! I . . . uh, I found it in the cabinet," he said nervously, setting the bottle back on the counter and screwing the lid back on. He shoved it onto one of the cabinet shelves then shut the door, feeling his cheeks flush with heat.

He should've known the morning after with Melissa would be awkward, though he seemed to be the one who was nervous, not her.

"I wasn't looking through your stuff though," he explained. "I just wanted . . . you know . . . the mouthwash."

"I didn't think you were, Jay."

"I hope it wasn't . . . umm . . . that I didn't . . . I hope it wasn't too presumptuous, is what I mean."

She laughed, shook her head, and strolled toward him. "Using my mouthwash wasn't presumptuous. *This* definitely is though," she said, lowering her hand and wrapping it around his dick while staring boldly into his eyes. She raised her mouth to his, placing butterfly kisses on his lips, as she began to stroke him.

Jamal felt dual sensations of shock and sexual pleasure. He started to harden in her hand.

So Melissa hadn't regretted last night; instead, she wanted a repeat, and he was more than happy to oblige her.

He slipped his tongue inside her mouth and tilted back her head, deepening their kiss. She fell back against the counter as he undid the belt at her waist and shoved the panels of her robe open, tugging the garment off her shoulders and letting it pool at her feet on the bathroom floor. She was naked underneath. One hand snaked to her breasts while the other went between her legs. She spread them wider, raising one leg and wrapping it around him as he shifted his kisses from her mouth to her neck. She moaned at his touch, moving her pelvis against his hand.

"You're gonna have to stop, Lissa," he panted against her ear a few minutes later.

"Why?" she asked, increasing the tempo of her stroke.

"'Cuz I'm gonna cum in your hand," he grunted.

"And what's wrong with that?" she asked with an impish smile just before he pulled her hand away.

"Because there's a lot more I want to do to you before that happens," he whispered. He eased her out of the bathroom back into the bedroom, kissing her again.

He noticed out of the corner of his eye that the bedroom door was closed and Brownie was absent. *Good*, he thought. He'd give the cat the rubdown he'd promised later. For now, all his attention was focused on Melissa.

He had told her the truth; there was a lot more he wanted to do to her this time around. The sex last night had been good, but way too fast. He'd urged himself to savor the moment but that was hard to do when the whole thing had lasted all of ten minutes. He wanted to take his time with Melissa for their second round.

They landed sprawled on her bed with lips still locked. It took almost Herculean strength to wrench his mouth away. He spied the box of condoms sitting on her night table. In their fervor, they had skipped using one last night. They wouldn't again. He quickly put one on and came back to her. He shifted his mouth to her breasts and she started moaning again as he ran his tongue over the dark nipples. He descended lower, kissing his way down her rib cage and stomach, licking her navel, and finally he spread her legs wide. He tested the wetness with his fingers first and he instantly felt her tense, saw the muscles flex along her thighs and her stomach. He began to rub her there, watching as she squirmed and whimpered. He was utterly fascinated.

For years, Melissa had not only seemed out of Jamal's reach as Derrick's girl, but also seemed to exert an almost magnetic power over him from afar. It had been a battle sometimes not to stare at her when she smiled or draw close to her when she spoke, to not make it obvious to the rest of the world how he really felt about her. But she was no longer out of his reach. Her body was responding to his control. He could touch her, kiss her. He wanted to taste her, too.

He removed his hand and lowered his mouth between her thighs, throwing both her legs over his shoulders. She tasted how he thought she would: as sweet and wet as a peach. As he licked and sucked, her moans turned into shouts, then screams. She yelled his name and cursed. Her legs began to wobble. Her toes curled. Just before she came, he centered himself between her thighs, steadied her hips, and plunged forward. He pumped his hips rhythmically while looking down at her, feeling her tighten around him, watching as pure ecstasy washed over her face while she orgasmed, screaming something that didn't sound quite like the English language.

Seeing her like this, watching her writhe beneath him, he wanted to come then, but he held back. He wanted to make this last even longer if he could.

He spread her legs wider and rubbed her clit again, even as he plunged, even as she begged him to let her catch her breath.

"Wait! Damn it! Shit!" she yelled. "Oh, God! Oh, God!"

Despite her protests, Melissa began to buck underneath him again, moaning and whimpering as she did it. She started clawing at his back, digging her nails into the flesh. Her bucking became almost convulsions as she closed her eyes. She screamed again when the second orgasm rocked her.

Jamal felt her tighten around him, and what little control he had, he lost this time. He braced himself for the rush and let out a long, guttural groan as he came. He slumped on top of her, twitching, jerking, and moaning as the last waves of pleasure ended.

Minutes later, he pulled out of her and rolled back onto the mattress.

They both stared at the ceiling in silence until Melissa did a slow clap, making him cock an eyebrow at her.

"Why are you clapping?"

"Because you are really, *really* good at this!" she exclaimed with widened eyes. "Shit!"

They both laughed, waiting for their heart rates to return to normal.

"Thanks. So are you." He lazily rubbed the soft skin along her inner thigh, and kissed her bare shoulder. "You sound surprised though."

"Surprised by what?"

"That I'm good at this."

"Not surprised but . . . how should I put it?" She wiped the sweat from her forehead with the back of her hand. She blew a gust of air between her inflated cheeks then licked her lips. "All those years I knew you, I never took you for the type. You know?"

That pronouncement made him frown. "No, I don't know. What *type*?"

"A headboard banger . . . a 'make you speak in

tongues' type. You know what I mean, Jay!" She nudged his side playfully with her elbow.

The truth was, he usually wasn't that type. None of his past girlfriends ever would have described him that way. He usually was a lot more reserved in the bedroom, but with Melissa he felt inspired. He wanted to try damn near everything he could imagine and had fantasized about for the past twenty years—if she'd let him.

She turned onto her side and beamed at him. "You're always so quiet and reserved. But it's always the quiet ones, isn't it?" she said, bringing her mouth to his, kissing him slowly, toying with his lips. Jamal kissed her back. It didn't take long for the kiss to deepen and for the screams to start up again.

Several hours later, Jamal stepped into the lobby of his apartment building, sipping coffee from the metal to-go mug Melissa had given him.

A goofy smile was on his face. He should be exhausted, but he was still surfing on the high of serotonin and endorphins, though he knew the crash would come soon.

Jamal had just left Melissa's apartment after four rounds of loud, uninhibited lovemaking, topped off with breakfast in bed and a nap in between. Thank God for the runs he did three times a week. It'd built up his endurance. If it hadn't been for all that cardio training, he never would've made it out of there alive. But even if he'd died today, he would've died a very happy man.

"Good morning," he now said to one of his neighbors—an elderly black woman in a pink tracksuit and matching visor, who lived on his floor.

"I think you mean good afternoon, young man," she said, staring at him warily as he passed her.

He paused, pulled up the sleeve of his tuxedo jacket, and glanced down at his wristwatch, surprised to see that it was already after two o'clock. "You're right! It is afternoon, isn't it?"

Time flies when you're having a good time, he thought wryly before continuing to the elevators.

"Are you all right, sweetheart?" the old woman asked, eyeing him.

He paused again and turned around to look at her. "Sure. Why?"

"What happened to your face?"

Jamal raised his hand to his chin, gingerly touching the bruised skin. He had almost forgotten about it. It had to look ghastly by now though, all purple and swollen.

"Oh! Uh, I fell down last night while I was walking home." He forced a chuckle. "I'm clumsy sometimes."

The old woman sucked her teeth and shook her head. "You young people and your drinkin' and your carryin' on . . . You should be more careful!" She pointed a gnarled finger at him. "I hope you weren't driving! Could've gotten into a car accident and hurt somebody."

"No, I wasn't driving, ma'am."

"Humph," she grunted before turning back toward the lobby's gold revolving doors, muttering to herself as she adjusted her visor.

Jamal finally reached the elevators, where he saw a boy in a hoodie sitting on the marble bench. He looked to be no more than sixteen or seventeen. He paused from reading his cell phone to look up at Jamal, who was pressing the up button. Jamal nodded at him in greeting before taking another sip from his coffee.

As he waited for the elevator car to arrive, Jamal wondered what Melissa was doing right now. She said she was supposed to meet her best friend, Bina, for lunch and then come back to her place to finish grading papers and work on her fourth-grade lesson plan for the week. He wondered when she would get back home. Maybe he should call her later, ask if she wanted him to stop over again tonight.

No, don't do that, he warned himself.

They'd literally just said goodbye to one another less than an hour ago. He didn't want to seem overeager, or worse, come off like he was harassing her. But it was hard to shut out those flashes of her bucking underneath him as they made love, or the saucy lick she did before bending over and hooking her hands onto the headboard. He could remember the outline of her face as she stared up at the ceiling while they talked, and the way she threw back her head and laughed at his joke before biting into a strawberry, feeding him the rest. He had licked the juice from her fingers as he gazed at her, entranced, like she'd cast some spell over him.

Because she has *cast some spell over me.*

Jamal closed his eyes, blowing air through his inflated cheeks. "Goddamn," he whispered.

It was bad enough that he had already fallen hard for Melissa, and he still didn't know if his feelings were reciprocated. He was no longer in the friend zone, but he still couldn't say if they were more than just fuck buddies. He had to get his emotions in check, because if he didn't watch out, he could easily become addicted to this woman. And who the hell wanted to be a strung-out junkie constantly looking for his next fix?

He opened his eyes when he heard the *ding* signifying that the elevator had arrived. The doors opened and he stepped inside. He noticed that the boy sitting on the bench stood and walked onto the elevator car with him.

Jamal pressed the button to take him to the eleventh floor. The boy leaned in front of him and pressed the button to the thirteenth floor. They both rode up in silence.

As the elevator ascended Jamal continued to drink his coffee. He glanced again at the teenager. He was a bit taller than Jamal, which wasn't surprising. Being five feet, seven inches, Jamal had long ago reconciled himself to the fact that most men were taller than him. The teen was a couple of shades darker and slight in build. The hoodie he wore looked about two sizes too big for his slender frame. Jamal wasn't sure why the teen was wearing a hoodie at all. He had to be hot in it; it was almost eighty degrees outside today.

The elevator dinged again and the compartment came to a stop. The doors opened and Jamal stepped onto his floor, reaching into the pocket of his rumpled tuxedo jacket for his keys. He noticed right before the doors closed that the boy also hopped out. Jamal glanced over his shoulder at him.

"Pressed the wrong button, huh?" Jamal said.

The boy shrugged.

Jamal continued on his way to his apartment, but as he walked, his euphoria from spending the morning in bed with Melissa was quickly being replaced with a growing sense of unease. The boy was following him—he could feel it. He'd felt this way before, back in 2001 when a few dudes in his neighborhood had decided to jump him and rob him, stealing his money and his brand-new sneakers as he walked home from school.

But it won't happen again today, Jamal resolved.

He was older, wiser, and more aware. He could try to fight him off if it came to that, but Jamal knew he had never been much of a fighter, hence Ricky and Derrick covering his ass for so many damn years. Besides, the boy could have a weapon. He suddenly came up with another plan. As he walked, he began to fiddle with the lid on his metal coffee cup, twisting it open. When he neared his apartment door, he paused to remove the lid. He inserted his key into the lock and eased the door open by an inch. He felt the teen drawing closer and closer, bearing down on him. Jamal whipped around and hurled the coffee inside of his cup at the boy, scalding him, making him scream out in surprise and hold his face.

"Oww!" the boy yelped. "Oww! It burns! My eyes! Why'd you do that?"

Jamal cringed. *Shit*, he thought.

Maybe he had misjudged this.

"Sorry, I-I . . . I thought you were . . . you were gonna rob me," he said feebly before taking a step toward him.

The boy continued to groan, blinking furiously.

"This was my mistake. I'm sorry. Look, you'll be okay. I've got some Neosporin and bandages in my . . ."

His words trailed off when he noticed the grip of a handgun peeking out of the pocket of the boy's hoodie. Jamal took a step back. His blood ran cold.

The boy lowered his hands from his face and looked down, following the path of Jamal's gaze. He then looked up again, still blinking. Their eyes met.

"No," Jamal whispered, shaking his head, realizing what was about to happen. He staggered back toward his apartment door.

"I'm sorry. I don't wanna do it, but I gotta—or he's gonna hurt my moms," the young man muttered almost helplessly. "I don't wanna do it, but I gotta!" He then reached for the gun.

Jamal watched, frozen, as the young man pulled out the handgun and raised it. Time seemed to slow down and speed up simultaneously. The teen steadied his arm, aiming for Jamal's head. His finger went for the trigger. Jamal threw the entire coffee cup this time, hitting the boy in the chest, throwing off his already shaky aim. He shoved open his apartment door and slammed it shut, but he wasn't fast enough. One bullet fired as he secured the deadbolt then another blasted through the wood, sending splinters and shrapnel flying in its wake, stinging his arm and shoulder. Jamal ran, ducking for cover behind his foyer wall while the boy kept firing. Jamal scrambled on all fours down the hall to his bedroom and shut the door behind him.

He waited on the floor behind his bed for the sound of more gunfire. One minute passed, then another. He didn't hear anything else; just the sound of his own breathing and the blood whistling in his ears.

What the fuck, he thought. *What the hell just happened?*

That wasn't the robbery he'd been anticipating. The boy hadn't demanded anything—not even his money or his gold watch. And before he fired, he'd said he *had* to do it. It was like he'd come there just to kill Jamal.

"But I'm still alive. I'm still alive," Jamal whispered, grabbing the edge of the bed and pushing himself to his feet.

When he did it, he cried out in pain, clutching his shoulder and dropping back down to his knees. He breathed in short bursts through his clenched teeth, whistling softly. When he pulled his hand away from his shoulder, he saw blood on his fingertips. He pulled back the lapel of his tuxedo jacket and looked down to find the whole left side of his white shirt was soaked in blood.

"Oh, shit," he whispered. "Oh, shit! Oh, shit!"

He'd said if he died today, he would die a happy man. But he hadn't meant that literally.

He reached down and pulled his cell phone from his

pocket. He dialed nine-one-one, leaving little red smudges on the glass screen. He brought the phone to his ear.

"Hello, nine-one-one, what is your emergency?" the dispatcher answered.

"Hi . . . uh . . . hi, umm," Jamal began in a trembling voice, wondering if he was going into shock, "a guy followed me to my door and . . . and shot me."

"I'm sorry. Can you repeat that, sir?" the dispatcher said. "What happened to you?"

"I've . . . I've been shot."

Chapter 3

Ricky

I wonder if she'll eat anything.

That was the thought that crossed Ricky Reynaud's mind as he removed the McDonald's bags from the passenger seat and slammed closed the door to his Mercedes. He carried the paper bags along with a few others—two from Target filled with clean clothes, underwear, and anything else he thought a pregnant woman might need—across the motel parking lot to the room where they were paying sixty-five dollars a night to stay. He was the only person out there, the lone black man in black t-shirt and jeans, trying his best to seem as inconspicuous as possible and blend into the roadside landscape, but it was a challenge with Ricky's 6-foot-2-inch frame and a face most would describe as handsome.

Though Simone hadn't touched any food since last night, Ricky suspected the cheeseburger and fries he'd gotten her would still remain untouched even though it was well past lunchtime. Simone, the mother of his unborn son, probably didn't have much of an appetite after witnessing her family getting slaughtered.

Ricky inwardly shuddered at the memory of discovering Simone's mother dead on her living room floor hours ago. Simone's sister, Skylar, had died in his arms, gasping for air as she choked on her own blood. If he had only arrived there an hour earlier, he may have been able to save them all, to avert them from being killed by one of Dolla Dolla's goons. He may have been able to spare Simone the agony that left her crying herself to sleep, but he hadn't. Instead, he had arrived in just enough time to rescue only Simone, and whisk her away to safety before even more men could arrive to finish the job the first dude had started.

Ricky had to focus on that victory, or the losses and the odds now stacked against them surviving this whole episode would overwhelm him.

He reached the motel room door and glanced over his shoulder at the sleepy Virginia roadway. He didn't see a cop car, which was a good sign. He was sure the cops had discovered the bodies back at Simone's place by now though, and that Simone was missing. But if the cops found out he was with her, that he had left D.C. in violation of the terms of his release, he could go to jail. He wasn't ready to return to the city just yet. He had to make sure she would remain safe. He had to be sure that Dolla Dolla, his former business partner, wouldn't get to her. Ricky just didn't know how he was going to accomplish that. Until then, they would have to lie low. They would stay hidden in the hotel until he could figure this all out. Ricky contemplated making a call to his boy, Derrick, and see if he could offer some advice or help. But what should he tell him? Where would he even begin? So much had happened in a short amount of time.

Ricky set down his bags to pull out his room key. He knocked gently before unlocking the door. "Simone, it's me," he said. "I picked up some stuff for you, baby."

She didn't answer him.

He nudged the door open, revealing a small room filled with a queen-sized bed, dresser, television, and night table. The walls were stark white and the décor was dated, with a burgundy, paisley-patterned bedspread and curtains, and particleboard furniture made to look like carved oak. The flat-screen television was on, filling the room with the sound of the laugh track from a *Friends* rerun that was now playing. Ricky looked around for Simone, but she was nowhere in sight.

"Simone?" Ricky called out again as he carried the bags inside and set them on the dresser. He shut the hotel door behind him. "Baby, I'm back! I brought you something to eat. You hungry?"

She still didn't answer him.

He glanced at the bathroom door, which was closed. Light from inside shined from beneath the bottom edge. He could hear the steady whir of the ventilation fan. Simone was in there. She had to hear him, so why wasn't she answering him?

For a split second, he wondered if maybe he shouldn't have left her alone that morning to get food and supplies. He should have realized the grief from losing her sister and mother simultaneously was too much and she just couldn't handle it. After all, she had been willing to sacrifice him, to make a devil's bargain and jeopardize his freedom in order to save Skylar—and now her sister was dead. Maybe Simone had done something to herself. Maybe she had tried to kill herself with God knows what while he was gone. His stomach dropped at the thought. His hands shook.

"Simone!" he shouted, grabbing the door handle and twisting it. He charged into the bathroom. "Simone!"

"*What?*" she yelled, looking startled.

She had been lying naked, soaking in the motel room's bathtub with a washcloth over her eyes. When he stormed into the bath, she instantly sat upright, sending water splashing onto the tiled floor. She clutched her rounded belly protectively.

"Fuck!" he shouted, slumping onto the toilet seat with relief, making the towel that was sitting on the lid fall to the floor. He dropped his head into his hands. "Shit!"

"What's wrong?" she asked, now frowning.

This was the second time he'd braced himself for losing her, only to find her alive and well. But he should've known better. He should've remembered that Simone had made him a promise that she would never do anything to sacrifice their baby. She would never end her life if it meant ending their son's.

"You damn near gave me a heart attack, girl," he mumbled, raising his head to look at her. Her nutmeg brown skin stood out in stark contrast to the white bath bubbles. Her protruding stomach, now etched with the first signs of stretchmarks, and her full breasts bobbed above the water. "You scared the shit out of me! I thought something was wrong, Simone. Why didn't you answer me? I've been calling you!"

She shrugged. "I'm sorry. I guess I was just . . . out of it."

He nodded. Considering what she'd been through in the past twenty-four hours, her being "out of it" was understandable.

"I thought sitting in a warm bath might help me feel a little better. That it might help calm me down," she whispered, sinking back against the tiled wall. "It's not working though."

"Something like this is gonna have to take time, baby."

"I don't think there will ever be enough time to forget what happened to them," she said, closing her eyes again. They were still swollen and red from all her sobbing from last night. "I think about how I could've stopped it. I think about what I could've done. When I heard he was arrested and finally going on trial, I figured he would get desperate. He would start taking out witnesses who could testify against him. I knew Skylar was probably on his hit list, so we left D.C., but that wasn't enough." A tear trickled down her cheek. "I should've started before that . . . *way* back . . . before she'd even met Dolla. I should've started when Mom and I first saw signs that Skylar was on the wrong path, that she was screwing around with coke and Molly. Maybe then they'd still be alive. I should've set her up with a counselor or a psychologist or—"

"Don't," he said. "I told you that I played that same 'I should've' game with my sister. It leads nowhere."

His sister, Desiree, had also fallen into a life of drugs and prostitution, like Skylar, a decade ago. Desiree had been killed at a young age as well.

"I wanted to save her, too, Simone, but I didn't. I tried my very best, but she was going to do what she wanted. Skylar was the same. You know that."

"I know that. But that still doesn't make the pain go away," she whimpered, lowering her head like she was about to start crying again.

He rose from the toilet seat and fell to his knees on the wet tile. He reached out to her and placed a comforting hand on her shoulder only to have her whimper turn into a low moan. He yanked his hand away and watched as she reached out and clutched the side of the tub in a white-knuckled grip. She clenched her teeth and leaned forward.

"Simone, what's wrong?" he asked, staring at her, bewildered. "What's wrong, baby?"

She didn't immediately answer him. She continued to groan and whimper for another minute until finally, the noises stopped. She let go of the edge of the tub and fell back against the tiled wall again. She turned to look at him. She gave a shuddering exhale.

"That's the other reason why I got in a warm bath. I thought it might stop the contractions. I've been having these bastards all morning," she said.

"*All morning?* Why the hell didn't you say anything?" he cried. "You have my cell. You could've called me while I was out! I would've come back."

"I've been under a lot of stress, Ricky! I thought they were Braxton-Hicks contractions, that once I calmed down a little they might go away—but they're not." She pursed her lips. She looked and sounded exhausted. "They're doing the opposite. I haven't been counting, but it . . . it feels like they're starting to get closer together."

"So you're in labor? *Right now?*"

She nodded and rubbed her belly again. "It looks like it."

Shit, he thought.

So much for them lying low. There was no way he could handle the delivery of their baby by himself. The chapters of *What to Expect When She's Expecting* that he'd read weren't going to get him through such a big task. He could feel panic tighten its grip around him again.

"Then I have to take you to a hospital."

"No," she said, shaking her head. "The cops will find out you're here. They'll arrest you."

"But we have to go! Shit! You can't deliver our baby in a motel bathroom!"

"Of course not, but I wasn't going to deliver in a hospital anyway. Remember? I wanted a natural childbirth. That's what I planned. We just have to call my midwife. She'll know what to do."

"What's her number?" he asked.

A couple of minutes later, Ricky was listening to a phone ring on the other end of the line. Simone wasn't sure if the number was correct. She usually kept it in her cell, which was still back at her house. For their sake, he hoped her memory was better than she thought it was.

"Hello?" a woman answered.

"Umm, is this Mary Biles?" he asked, pacing the hotel bedroom. "The . . . the midwife?"

"Why yes, this is she!" the woman replied cheerfully. "How can I help you?"

"My girlfriend, Simone Fuller, has . . . uh . . . well, she's going into labor and she told me that I should call you."

"You're Simone's man? You're Ricky, aren't you? So you're the one I've been hearing so much about!"

Ricky stopped pacing. He went silent. He hadn't known Simone had spoken about him to someone outside of her family. Their relationship had been a secret from the beginning: Simone, the patrol cop, and Ricky, the criminally-adjacent businessman who was in Dolla Dolla's pockets. She must trust this woman a lot to have mentioned him to her.

"Well, I'm glad to hear you'll be here to make it for the birth, after all," the midwife said. "She's a little early. By about a week and a half, I guesstimate without giving the calendar a look-see, but babies come when they want to, don't they?" She chuckled. "Let me gather my things. I'll be there in forty-five minutes . . . maybe forty if I speed a little."

"No! No! Uh, we're . . . we're already on the road," he lied, glancing at the bathroom door. He swore he could hear her groaning again. It must be another contraction. "Can we come to you? Simone said you aren't far from where we are now."

"Well, how far apart are her contractions, honey? She might not deliver for hours. She has plenty of time to get back to her place. I generally prefer a woman to have her baby at home, in her own environment," the older woman rambled. "They find it more comforting to—"

"Please," he said desperately, "she wants to come to you."

Mary, the midwife, grew quiet on the other end of the line. "Okay, honey, if that's what she wants," she finally said, to his relief. "Bring her in. I'll start setting up for her now."

"Thank you. Thank you so much, ma'am! We'll see you soon," he said before hanging up.

Chapter 4

Derrick

Derrick sat behind his desk with his arms crossed over his chest while Morgan sat in one of the chairs facing him. Beside her was Jayden, a fifteen-year-old with a wide afro and chin and cheeks inflamed with pimples. He stared down at his lap, chewing his nails and jittering one leg restlessly.

"Tell Mr. Derrick what you told me, Jayden," Morgan said.

The security staff and Derrick had questioned most of the boys who were either friends with or in the same dorm as Cole, but they still were no closer to finding the teenager. Even his mother said he hadn't run to her house when he'd disappeared, and she had no idea where Cole could have gone instead. Morgan had secretly pulled aside a few of the boys to question them again. Most had kept mum, but Jayden hadn't. That was why he was now in Derrick's office with the door closed. He kept glancing at the door, looking like he just wanted to escape, like he wanted to be anywhere but here.

"Go ahead, son," Derrick urged, leaning forward in his desk chair.

"I don't wanna be a snitch," Jayden whispered with his eyes still downcast.

"I understand." Derrick nodded. "But we're trying to help Cole, not hurt him. We want to bring him back to the Institute. If the cops find him before we do, he could get arrested, and where he's taken after that is up to the judge. I don't want it to come to that, Jayden."

Jayden stopped chewing his nails. His knee stopped bobbing up and down. He finally raised his eyes to look at Derrick. He sighed. "Cole had to do it. He had to go. He said shit . . . I mean *stuff* would go down if he didn't," he said in a voice barely above a whisper.

"What stuff?" Derrick persisted.

Jayden anxiously glanced at Morgan, who nodded, encouraging him to continue. "He said that if he didn't leave and meet up with some dudes he used to work for, that they were gonna . . ." He sucked his teeth. "Basically, they were gonna do somethin' to him and his mom . . . to his little brother and sister."

"*Do something?*" Derrick repeated.

Jayden dipped his chin in a quick nod. "He was scared. He was scared if he didn't go, they would do what they said they were gonna do. He didn't wanna take the chance. He said since he stopped working for them, that they weren't sure if he was a snitch now. If he would tell the po-po what was goin' on. He had to prove that he was still down for them, that they could still trust him."

Derrick suspected he knew who "them" was: Dolla Dolla and his crew.

"What did they want him to do?"

Jayden shrugged. "I don't know. He wouldn't tell me. I don't think he knew either, but he was supposed to meet some dude somewhere up in P.G. to find out. That's where he was headed last night, but I don't think he's still there."

"Are you telling us the truth?" Derrick asked. "Are you telling us everything you know, Jayden?"

Jayden nodded again, looking solemn. "Yes, sir."

"Okay. Thank you, Jayden. You can head back to class," Derrick said.

He and Morgan watched as Jayden opened the office door and walked out of the room.

"So it's what we thought it was," he said as the boy shut the door behind him.

"Yeah. Cole is back to being mixed up in all that shit." She shook her head in exasperation. "Do you really think that son of a bitch threatened to hurt Cole and his family?"

"I don't see why he wouldn't. Dolla Dolla has done it before. He's not known for being the most forgiving when he thinks someone may double-cross his refrigerator-lookin' ass."

"Damnit," Morgan mumbled. She slouched back in her chair and began to crack her knuckles, a gesture she always did when she was lost in thought.

Watching her, he went soft on the inside. He could tell she was stressed out about Cole—probably even more so than him. He wanted to rise from his chair, walk around his desk, and rub the tension out of her shoulders. He wanted to kiss her frown and worry lines away from her brow and cheeks and tell her they could only try their best and things like this were out of their control. But he had broken her heart one too many times. She was done with him. He would have to keep those thoughts, caresses, and kisses to himself.

"What do we do now?" she asked. "P.G. is a big county. He could be anywhere, Derrick."

He threw up his hands helplessly. "I have no idea."

"So we just . . . *what*? Keep waiting?"

His cell phone began to buzz and he glanced at the screen. His eyes widened when he saw the phone number, and he grabbed it and raised it to his ear.

"Who is it?" Morgan asked.

"Cole's mom," he said, holding a finger to his lips as he pressed the green button to answer. "Hey, Mrs. Humphries. Did you finally hear from Cole?"

"My baby! My baby! Oh, Lord!" she cried. He heard sobbing and hiccupping on the other end, making his stomach drop to his sneakers.

Oh, hell, Derrick thought. *What happened now?*

"Mrs. Humphries, what's wrong?" he asked. "What happened to him? Is Cole okay?"

She finally sniffed. "The police called," Cole's mother croaked on the other end of the line. "They . . . they arrested him this afternoon."

Derrick closed his eyes and sank back in his chair. It wasn't the best-case scenario, but at least the boy wasn't dead.

"I know that's upsetting," he said, trying to pacify her. "But if Cole is in police custody, he's not wandering—"

"He shot somebody!" she screamed. "The cops said he followed a man to his home and tried to rob him. They think he wouldn't give Cole what he wanted, so Cole shot him. My boy shot another human being, and now they don't know if the man is gonna make it!" She let out another tortured sob.

Derrick sat shell-shocked as he listened to Cole's mother. Morgan squinted at him, confused by his stunned silence.

"What? What is she saying?" Morgan whispered frantically.

"My boy could get charged with murder, Mr. Miller," Cole's mother continued. "He could go to jail *forever*, and I don't . . . I don't understand. *Why?* Why would he do something like this? He's gotten into trouble before, but shooting someone? This isn't him!"

"Do you know what station they took him to?"

"No," Mrs. Humphries said, sniffing again. "They won't . . . they won't call me back. They won't tell me anything."

"Okay," Derrick said, rising from his chair. "I'll make some calls. I'll find out and I'll call you back."

"All right," she whimpered before hanging up.

"You look like you were just hit by a bus, Derrick," Morgan said. "What the hell happened?"

Derrick took a deep breath. "The cops have him. Cole may have killed someone."

"*What?*" she shouted, shooting to her feet. "Oh, Jesus!"

"I gotta find out where he is. Figure out what the hell happened. I have a few contacts in the Metro police that I work with. Maybe they can help. Can you give me a few minutes to make some calls?"

She nodded limply. "Sure. Sure, what . . . whatever you need," she murmured before staggering out his office door.

For the next half hour, Derrick called every cop he had ever worked or argued with in the course of running the Institute, hoping he could get more info on Cole. Finally, he got one on the phone who was willing to talk to him, to help him.

"Thanks for doing this, Sergeant Mitchell," Derrick said.

"Yeah, yeah, yeah," the gruff cop muttered over the phone. "So what's the perp's name?"

"Cole Humphries. He's a student here."

A long pause followed, along with the sound of clicking computer keys. "Yeah, they brought him in about three hours ago," Sergeant Mitchell murmured. "He's still in holding."

"What's the charge?"

"At this point, attempted murder that could be bumped up to first-degree murder if the victim dies . . . attempted robbery, possession of a weapon during the commission of a crime of violence . . . yada, yada, yada. This is some heavy stuff. It looks like your kid is going away for a long time, Derrick."

Derrick's heart sank.

"And I'll say something else . . . when that kid aims to commit a crime, he aims high," Sergeant Mitchell murmured.

"What do you mean?"

"I mean . . . I could be wrong, but I'm lookin' at the name of the victim in the records and it . . . it looks like it's Jamal Lighty. Ain't he high up in the mayor's office? The deputy mayor or something?"

At those words, Derrick swore the wind was knocked right out of him. "Who . . . who did you say?"

"I said Jamal Lighty. He's the guy your kid might've killed. Can you believe that?"

Derrick didn't respond. He was too shocked to utter a word.

Chapter 5

Ricky

"Is this your first, too, Ricky?" Mary Biles asked with a knowing smile.

"Huh?" Ricky said, adjusting the cool washcloth on Simone's forehead as she lay on her side in the king-sized bed in one of Mary's guest rooms.

Simone gritted her teeth and groaned through another contraction, squeezing his other hand like she was trying to squeeze juice from a lemon, crushing the bones in his fingers. He tried not to wince. It hurt like hell, but she was in much worse pain than he was.

"I said, is this your first baby?" the elderly white woman asked, pulling up a wooden rocking chair on the other side of the bed. "I know it is for Simone. I was wondering if it was for you, too."

"Uh . . . uh, yeah," he answered shakily.

At least, he thought it was. He was pretty sure that out of the many relationships and one-night stands he'd had in his thirty-one years, this was the first baby he'd ever made. And he was eagerly awaiting his first son's arrival. Maybe that's why he was so nervous. Maybe that's why in the nine hours since they had arrived at Mary's house, he seemed incapable of doing anything right—or Simone made him feel that way. He'd been trying to coach her through her labor, but nothing he did seemed to help her.

"Stop," Simone muttered when the contraction finally waned. She shoved his hand and the washcloth away from her. "Just stop!"

She then let go of his other hand and turned onto her other side on the mattress, closing her eyes as she exhaled.

"Okay, if you don't want the damn washcloth, then what *do* you want? Huh?" he asked impatiently. "More ice cubes? You want me to rub your back?"

"No," she whimpered, sounding a lot like a sullen child at that moment. "I don't want anything. Nothing, all right?"

That wasn't true. He knew she wanted her mother and her sister right now.

Because he'd had to stay away to not draw Dolla Dolla to her, Simone's sister and her mother were the ones who had taken her to her Lamaze classes, purchased baby clothes and diapers, and helped her set up the nursery. They were the ones who were supposed to coach her through this. Now they were dead, and he was starting to feel like an unsuitable replacement.

"I just want this to be over and done with," Simone said between clenched teeth. "God, I want it to stop!" she cried.

He looked pleadingly at Mary. "Are you sure you can't give her anything? Nothing for the pain?"

Mary shook her head. "We have to let this run its course. Women have been doing this without the assistance of drugs for millennia. We're stronger than you think. Birthing mothers always hit the point where they think they can't go any further, but they always do. She can handle it. Trust me. And a natural childbirth is what she wanted. She was adamant about that. Weren't you, Simone?"

Simone moaned in reply as she was struck with another contraction. They seemed to be coming back to back now. Mary leaned toward her and held her hand. "Don't forget your breathing, dear. You're doing fine."

"No, she's *not* doing fine! She's fuckin' miserable! What if she can't do it?" he persisted. "Shit! She's been in labor for more than twelve hours. She's exhausted. Can't you see that? Maybe we should take her to a hospital. Maybe they could give her some—"

"Shut up!" Simone shouted, making him stop short. "Just shut up! Go somewhere, Ricky! Anywhere! Please? I don't need to hear you arguing. You're not helping!"

He gritted his teeth and balled his fists at his sides.

"Why don't you take a little break," Mary whispered, rubbing Simone's shoulder. "I'll take over for a bit. We'll be fine."

Ricky tossed the washcloth onto the night table, turned, and stalked out the bedroom.

He walked down the hallway, through a beaded curtain into a kitchen that was filled with knickknacks, that had an array of potted plants on the counters and windowsills.

Part of him wanted to hop in his car and drive away. *To hell with this shit*, he thought. He'd risked his life for her, saved her, and now she was treating him like this?

The other part wanted to charge back into the bedroom and yell at Simone. He wanted to shout at her that he was only trying to help.

In the end, Ricky did neither. Instead, he sat at the kitchen table, slumped forward in his chair, rested his elbows on his knees, and closed his eyes—trying to get his roller coaster of emotions under control.

"Everyone handles pain and stress differently," Mary called out twenty minutes later.

Ricky sprung upright in his chair. He opened his eyes and looked around him dazedly. He must have dozed off, which wasn't surprising. He'd only had a few snatches of sleep since yesterday. He had been coasting on an adrenaline high for so long. He guessed he was long overdue for a crash.

He stretched and yawned.

"She doesn't mean what she says," Mary explained, walking to the kitchen sink with a plastic bowl. She lowered the bowl into the stainless steel sink and turned on the water to rinse it out. She then took the bowl and walked toward her fridge. She laughed. "I wouldn't take it personally."

"I'm not taking it personally," he muttered, wiping sleep from his eyes.

"Oh, men and your pride!" She snorted as she pulled out a tray of ice cubes and loudly shook the ice into the bowl. "Yes, you are! But let me tell you, most fathers get their feelings hurt during delivery. You aren't unique. That's part of the process, too."

He eyed the old woman. Her gray hair was long and scraggly, like bleached straw. She wore an oversized T-shirt, cargo shorts, and pink Crocs with mismatched socks. She looked like one of those homeless women you saw hanging out in front of grocery stores with carts filled to the brim with junk.

Yet, there was something reassuring about her. He didn't know much about her medical abilities, but the eccentric old woman seemed kind. She had a comforting air about her that made him understand why she would cater to pregnant women and usher babies into the world. He now understood why Simone had chosen her for her midwife.

"You love her and you hate seeing her in pain. I get it," Mary continued.

She was right. It wasn't just seeing Simone writhe and

groan hour after hour that ate away at him; that part was bad enough. But he also knew about the emotional pain she'd suffered last night and was still experiencing. It seemed like a double whammy to endure physical agony, too. Couldn't Simone get a break?

"But she's gotta go through it to get the baby out, Ricky. It's nature's way. It doesn't look, feel, or sound good, but it's perfectly natural." She tilted her head and beamed. "And I just checked her. She's dilated nine centimeters. The last centimeter will be here before you know it. The baby should be out soon. Come in when you have yourself back together, when you're ready. Despite what she said, we're gonna need your help with this."

He gradually nodded again.

After Mary left, he rose to his feet and staggered to the sink. He turned on the faucet and splashed his face with cold water. He stared out the window for a couple of minutes before walking through the beaded curtain and back down the hall to be by Simone's side.

The labor dragged on for almost another hour before Mary announced, "You are ready to push, my dear." She pulled her hand from between Simone's legs and removed her latex glove. "You are fully dilated. It's showtime."

Ricky felt simultaneously excited and terrified. He gazed at Simone, whose brow and T-shirt were soaked in so much sweat that her curly pixie hair was pasted to her brow and her shirt clung to her like a second skin. She had been grunting and whimpering, crying and moaning through the pain. He found it hard to believe that she would have the strength to sit up, let alone deliver their baby, but it didn't look like she would have much of a choice.

"We can do this any way you wish, sweetheart, but I find many women prefer to bear down in a kneeling position. Let gravity work to your advantage. It'll be like taking the biggest, best poop you could imagine! Your man can hold you from the front while I handle the back end," she said cheerfully. "Onto your knees, honey." She pointed to Ricky. "You sit on the bed in front of her, Ricky. Wrap your arms around her waist and hold her. Bear her weight as she pushes."

Ricky did as she ordered. He helped Simone get on her knees between his legs then sat on the bed, facing her. He wrapped his arms around her waist and she wrapped hers around his shoulders.

"One second, folks," Mary said. "Let me get everything in place."

He watched over Simone's shoulder as Mary fiddled with supplies on her night table.

"I'm scared, Ricky," Simone whispered against his ear, drawing his attention. A lone tear trickled down her cheek. She sniffed. "What if I can't push him out?"

"Don't be scared, baby. I'm here. I got you," he whispered before kissing her neck and rubbing her back. "I promise. And you'll do fine. You heard what Mary said: Your body was meant to do this."

She let out a shaky breath.

"Speaking of bodies . . . I think it's funny as hell that you're gonna deliver him this way." He smiled. "I mean . . . isn't this the position that got us here in the first place?"

She let out a laugh that quickly turned into a moan that had her clinging to his shoulders.

"All right," Mary said, getting into position behind her. "As soon as the next contraction starts, I want you to push with all your might, sweetheart. You hear me? And don't forget to breathe!"

Within seconds, Simone was pushing. Each time, he and Mary counted off simultaneously to let her know how long to push. Each time, Simone would grunt or yell.

"One more! One more, Simone!" Mary cried. "One more big push, honey. Your boy's almost here!"

Simone did as Mary ordered and this scream was the loudest. It sounded like a screech. Ricky swore his ears were ringing and probably would be hours from now.

"There!" Mary said and Ricky heard the baby's cries next. Mary held his son aloft. She grinned. "Take a look at your baby boy, Mommy and Daddy!"

Ricky lowered Simone to her side. They both stared dazedly at the slimy, crying infant that Mary held. He was pink and tiny. He wriggled and pumped his little fists with each wail.

I'll be damned, Ricky thought with awe. *I'm a daddy now.*

"Would you like to cut the umbilical cord, Ricky?"

He gradually nodded.

An hour later, the cord had been cut and Simone was stitched up. The sheets had been changed. Simone, who could barely lie down without moaning hours earlier, had taken a quick shower and was now wearing a fresh tank dress and nursing their son. She wasn't in agony anymore. She looked dog-tired, but happy. For once, she looked happy.

Ricky ran his hand over his son's crown, feeling the dark curls against his fingertips.

"So what are you going to name him?" Mary asked, breaking into the moment.

"Well, I'm . . . I'm not sure," Simone said, looking at Ricky again. "I don't think we ever decided. I mentioned Darius. You said you liked the name Shaun. We also said Miles sounded good."

"Miles," Ricky said with a nod. "That sounds about right."

Ricky had traveled many miles to find Simone, to track her down. He'd traveled even more to make sure Simone and his son were safe, and he would travel to the ends of the earth and back to make sure they stayed that way.

"Miles," she repeated, then nodded. "I like it!" She

then looked down at their son and smiled, holding him close as he continued to nurse, oblivious to the conversation around him. "Welcome to the world, Miles."

When Ricky woke up the next morning, he blinked and looked around him, trying to assess once again where he was. He wasn't in his bed at his condo or in a bed at the motel.

He could hear the faraway sound of the morning news and the smell of bacon sizzling. He raised his head from a pillow and looked to his left. Simone was reclined against a stack of pillows, nursing Miles again against the backdrop of the morning light. Ricky grinned, realizing he must have fallen asleep on the guest bed not too long after Simone had given birth.

Watching Simone and Miles now, he swore he had never seen anything so beautiful.

"Well, would you look at that?" Simone whispered down to their son. "Daddy is *finally* awake."

"How long have I been out?" he asked, sitting upright and stretching, listening as the vertebrae in his spine cracked.

"About *six hours*. You managed to snooze through two feedings," she said, side-eying him.

Ricky chuckled. Of course, he'd slept so hard. Surrounded by so much peace and contentment, who wouldn't?

"Meanwhile, Mommy fell asleep at one point with a baby still connected to her breast," she murmured before gently rubbing the spiral of dark hair at the crown of Miles's head.

"I'll rock him back to sleep after he's done feeding," Ricky offered.

He'd only had the chance to hold his son once since his birth. He yearned to do it again.

"I'd love that, but I'd love food even more. I think

Mary is cooking breakfast. Do you mind bringing me a plate?"

He nodded and rose from the bed. "Bacon and eggs coming up, baby."

He strode out of the bedroom, down the hall, and through the beaded curtain leading to the kitchen. Mary stood by the oven with a spatula in her hand, watching the mini portable TV she had on the kitchen counter as she cooked.

"Good mornin'," he said, as he walked toward her. "Smells good! Simone was wondering if she could have some of . . ."

His words faded when his eyes zeroed in on the expression on Mary's face. She had gone deathly pale. Her mouth was hanging open and her eyes were wide; she looked horrified.

His gaze shifted to where her focus seemed to be, which was on the television screen. He saw footage of Simone's house surrounded by yellow police tape. He saw police officers wheel out three gurneys with black body bags that likely contained Simone's mother and sister and the body of Melvin, the man Ricky had killed.

Mary whipped around to face Ricky, still clutching the spatula.

"Oh, my . . . oh, my . . ." she cried hoarsely. "What is going on? What . . . what happened to her family? Why are they dead?"

He held up his hands. "It's okay. You don't have to be scared. Just let me explain."

"Did you do that?" she screeched, brandishing her spatula at him like it was a knife. She seemed less like a homeless woman and more like an escapee from a psych ward at the moment. "Is that why she couldn't give birth at her house? Did you kill them?"

He shook his head. "No, I di—"

Ricky didn't get to finish. Mary went rushing across the

kitchen, reaching out for the cordless phone that hung on the wall near the refrigerator. She was going to call the police; he was sure of it, and all the effort he had made for him and Simone to stay hidden would be destroyed.

Luckily, he beat her to it and grabbed the receiver before she could. He slowly shook his head. "Don't do that, Mary."

"You stay away from me! You just stay away!" As she backed away, she swung the spatula at him, slapping him in the chest, making him wince.

"What is all this yelling about?" Simone asked, strolling into the kitchen, cradling Miles to her shoulder. "Is everything okay?"

"No, it is not okay!" Mary shouted. "Simone, are you this man's prisoner?"

"His prisoner?" Simone repeated. "Why would I be his prisoner?"

"Did he kill your family? Has he threatened you, sweetheart?"

Simone went quiet. She looked at Mary, then Ricky, then Mary again. "He hasn't hurt or threatened me. He didn't kill my family either. He *saved* me. I might be dead, too, if it wasn't for him."

"*What?*" Mary asked. "What the hell have you gotten yourself into, girl? What did you bring into my house?"

"You have nothing to worry about." Ricky held up his hands again. "Just . . . just put down the spatula and sit down, and I swear, we'll explain everything, okay?"

Mary looked warily at them both.

"Mary, please," Simone said, and Miles began to wail.

He watched as Mary slowly lowered the spatula to her side. "Go ahead and tend to the baby," she said to Simone before eying Ricky. "Meanwhile, you better start explaining." She pointed up at him. "And I mean pretty damn fast, buddy boy, or I'll tackle you down and grab that phone right out of your hand!"

He pursed his lips. Her bravado didn't scare him. He had her by about a hundred pounds and thirteen inches, but he admired her courage. Ricky debated on what parts of the tale he should leave in or keep out, and finally decided to just tell her everything—well, almost everything.

"Okay, I'll explain, but it's a long story," he began.

Mary eyed him. "I've got time. Start talking!"

Chapter 6

Jamal

Jamal slowly opened his eyes, surprised to find his mother gazing down at him, hovering mere inches away from his face.

"Oh, my baby! You're alive! Oh, honey! You gave your mama such a scare!" she drawled before leaning down to kiss his brow.

Jamal blinked and slowly looked around him.

The last memory he had was of being slumped on his bedroom floor, holding a balled-up bedsheet against his wounded shoulder, trying his best to stop the bleeding from his gunshot wound. But even the sheet was soaked with blood by the time the paramedics had arrived.

"Are you still with us, Jamal? Can you hear me?" a male voice had called to him, shining a penlight into his eyes, making him flinch.

"Yeah, I hear you," Jamal had answered. Or he thought he had.

It probably actually sounded a lot more garbled to the EMTs.

His eyelids had grown heavy. He'd been losing the battle to stay conscious before they arrived. Once he saw the uniforms, his body had given out.

"Shit! We're losing him," another voice had said just as Jamal's head thumped against the hardwood floor.

But they hadn't lost him. He was still here. That was evident from the room he now found himself in.

It was obviously a hospital room and he was obviously in a hospital bed. Several vases filled with bouquets of roses, carnations, and Asiatic lilies filled the space, along with Mylar balloons of all shapes and sizes. His mother hovered over him protectively, patting his cheek.

He noticed a petite, blond nurse stood at the foot of his bed in short-sleeved green scrubs.

"Welcome back to the world, Mr. Lighty," she said, brightening her pretty face with a smile. "I'm Samantha, though you can call me Sam. I tell all my patients that. Less syllables makes it easier to say." She chuckled. "I'll be your nurse during this shift. The doctor said your surgery went well. We called him and told him you're awake now. He should be in shortly to explain everything in more detail."

"Thanks," Jamal said.

He noticed as he spoke that his throat was a little sore. The drugs, which undoubtedly included a cocktail of painkillers, were also making him a little groggy.

"I told my son about livin' in this godforsaken city!" his mother interrupted, kissing his brow again. "That's why I moved back to North Carolina to leave all this fightin' and shootin' behind. My blood pressure can't take it! I told him that he should have left with me."

Jamal rolled his eyes. He had just woken up and he felt tired already; his henpecking, melodramatic mother could exhaust him so easily. It was one of the reasons he had no intention of ever moving anywhere close to her home in North Carolina.

"When the cops called me and told me you were shot, Jay, my heart almost jumped out of my chest." She fell back into a brown pleather chair beside his bed and patted a buttery hand to her skinny bosom. "I almost died, baby!"

"No, *I* almost died. *You* just freaked out," he said dryly.

He noticed out of the corner of his eye that Nurse Sam was laughing silently as she tapped something into the computer tablet she held.

"*You hear that?*" his mother asked Nurse Sam. "You hear how he treats his mama? He's picking at me even though I took the first flight up here to be with him!"

"Stop talkin' about me like I'm not here, Mama—or like I'm deaf," he mumbled.

"Yes, he can be ungrateful sometimes, but I still love him. And I'm glad he's better," she continued like he hadn't said anything. She turned back around to face him. "I'm glad you survived this, baby. I don't know what I would've done if you hadn't." She leaned forward in her chair. "You know it was all over the news: the shooting and the arrest. People were shocked to hear the deputy mayor got shot in his own apartment building."

Nurse Sam raised her brows. "*You're deputy mayor?*" She glanced around his hospital room. "That would explain all the balloons and flowers! I just thought you had a big family."

Jamal shook his head. "I'm not deputy mayor anymore."

After Mayor Johnson had had the reporter Phillip Seymour at the *Washington Recorder* murdered for sniffing too close around his dirty business dealings, Jamal couldn't stomach working for him any longer. Under Melissa's advice and guidance, he had finally worked up the courage to quit—whatever the consequences might be. He wondered if he was suffering those consequences now.

"You aren't the deputy mayor anymore?" his mother asked, looking genuinely shocked. "When did that happen?"

"Last week."

"Why didn't you tell me, Jay?" his mother cried.

Jamal gave a side glance at the nurse, who was staring at them, still looking amused. "Mama, do we have to talk about this right now?"

"Well, anyway, Jay used to be deputy mayor," his mother said to the nurse, sounding dejected. Jamal had taken away prime boasting fodder that his mother could lord over his aunts and uncles at the dinner table back in North Carolina, whose sons in comparison were unemployed or in jail for overdue child support. "He was in the business department."

"Planning and economic development," Jamal corrected.

"Impressive," Nurse Sam said with a nod, making her blond ponytail bob up and down. "I thought you looked familiar. I've seen you on TV a few times, haven't I?"

"Maybe," he murmured, and tried to shrug, but noticed his left shoulder was now in a sling.

"Don't be shy about it, honey!" his mother insisted. "Being deputy mayor was a big deal and I bet you'll even become mayor one day—even though that boy tried to take away your chance before you could even try! The police caught him, you know? They said he'd been hiding in the stairwell, running between floors before the police tracked him down. He never even made it out of the building." She slowly shook her head. "He's only seventeen years old. Can you believe that? What on earth would make a young man follow someone to his door and shoot him? I blame poor home training!"

And I blame something very different, Jamal thought.

He suspected Mayor Johnson was behind it. Jamal had run afoul of the mayor when he announced that he was tired of keeping the mayor's secrets and he was quitting city hall. The old man had promised that Jamal would pay a heavy price, though Jamal wasn't sure at the time if he would go through with his threat. Now he realized it had been foolish not to take the mayor seriously. It seemed too random that the boy had targeted Jamal and the boy had insisted before shooting him that he had to do it, that he had no other choice. This was a hit—a targeted hit.

And I wrote a check to that son of a bitch to give him back all the dirty money he gave me, Jamal thought with disgust.

"Well, I'm going to check on my other patients," Nurse Sam said. "Don't hesitate to let me know if you need anything, Mr. Lighty. Your call button is right here." She leaned forward and pointed to a blue button on one of the hospital-bed brackets. "You can reach me or the nurses' station that way."

"Thanks," he said, smiling.

She nodded again and walked out of the hospital room.

"She seemed nice," his mother said when they were alone again.

"Don't all nurses seem nice?"

"Oh, no! You should've met the nurse who tended to your grandmother when she had a double mastectomy. As mean as the devil, honey!" His mother paused and looked down at her purse that sat in the chair beside her. "This thing won't stop buzzing."

"What thing?" he murmured tiredly.

"Your phone!" She reached into her purse, pulling out

his cell. "The hospital said that you were holding it when they took you into the ambulance. They had to pry it out of your hands. They gave it to me when I got here." She wiped the screen with a Kleenex before handing it to him.

He frowned as he looked down at his phone. Even through there were smudges of blood on the screen, he saw a list of calls and text messages that he'd received in the past twenty-four hours. About a third of the calls were from Melissa. Without even thinking he pressed the button to automatically call her back and raised the phone to his ear.

"Jay, I don't think you're supposed to use cell phones in here," his mother chastised.

She pointed to a sign on the wall with an illustrated cell phone and a red X drawn through it, but he ignored her and listened to the ringing on the other end of the line.

"Jay!" Melissa shouted. "Oh, my God! Is that you?"

"Yeah, it's me," he said, smiling again. His chest instantly warmed at the sound of her voice.

"Shit! You scared the hell out of me! I've been seeing all this stuff on the news and . . . and I tried calling and texting you, but you wouldn't answer. I was so worried. I couldn't even concentrate in class. I bet the kids think I'm crazy! Are . . . are you okay? I know you're alive but . . . are you okay? You're talking, so you must be okay, right?"

He laughed. "I'm alive and I'm okay, I think. I'm awake and out of surgery. I think I'm in one of the recovery wards at the Washington Hospital Center," he said, judging from the signage he saw around his room.

"Can I come see you? Can you accept visitors?" she asked.

"Sure!" His face was a full grin now. "Of course, you can come see me. You know that!"

"Okay, I'll leave school right now. I'll tell the principal

it's an emergency and ask my assistant to take over. I should be down there in a couple of hours. All right?"

"All right. See you soon." He hung up.

"Who was that?" his mother asked, narrowing her eyes at him.

"A friend," he muttered, not eager to tell his mother all of his business at the moment. He continued to scan his text messages.

"Sounded like a lot more than a friend to me," she mumbled.

He didn't comment.

An hour and forty-five minutes later, Melissa arrived with a bouquet in one arm and a small grocery bag in the other. She strode into the hospital room, looking as beautiful as ever with her coils in a bun atop her head, wearing a button-down pink shirt and black pencil skirt—her fourth-grade teacher attire. She made for a very sexy teacher, in his opinion. Though Jamal was in a sling and a hospital bed, he wanted to reach out and peel off that pencil skirt that hugged her curves in all the right places.

"Melissa! Is that you, girl?" his mother shouted, rising from her chair when Melissa entered the room.

"Mrs. Lighty! Oh, my . . . I haven't seen you in such a long time! How have you been?"

Melissa set the bag and the flowers in an empty chair and the two women embraced.

His mother had known Melissa back from the early days when she would occasionally tag along with Derrick, Jamal, and Ricky. She still saw her every couple of years when the guys hung out together.

When we used to hang out, Jamal thought forlornly, remembering their old friendship.

"I've been doing good," his mother said as she took a step back and gazed at Melissa. "And you look as pretty as ever! You're gonna look so nice in your wedding dress, honey! Have you picked it out yet? You and Derrick finally settle on that wedding date?"

"Mama," Jamal said warningly.

Melissa's smile disappeared. She lowered her eyes.

"Oh, they've been engaged for a while now, Jay! I'm not the only one asking." She patted Melissa's shoulder. "I know you probably get tired of people quizzing you, honey. Just know that I'll be looking forward to that invitation in the mail if I can't convince my son to take me as his plus-one."

Melissa cleared her throat. She slowly raised her eyes from the linoleum-tile floor. "Actually . . . umm . . . Dee and I . . . well, we broke up, Mrs. Lighty. We did a few months ago."

"Oh," his mother said, looking crestfallen. "Oh, no! I'm so sorry to hear that!"

Melissa shrugged. "It's okay. It just wasn't meant to be. I'm fine with it though. Really!"

"But you two were together for *so* long!" His mother went silent. Alfreda Lighty, who usually couldn't stop talking, for once in her life looked unsure of what to say next. "Well, honey, I'm . . . I'm glad that you and Jay have stayed friends. I hope he's supporting you through all of this." She grabbed Melissa's hand and squeezed it. "Breakups can be hard. I hope Jay is making you feel better."

Melissa smiled again. "Oh, he is! *So* much better! I can assure you of that." She then gave him a conspiratorial glance.

Jamal thought back to the sex marathon they'd had only two days ago and knew Melissa was thinking about it, too. He almost snorted at their inside joke, but caught himself.

"Well, I was gonna head out to get some lunch. I'll let

you two catch up for a bit and when I come back, I want you to tell me everything you're doing now and how your family is doing, Melissa." She squeezed her hand again and then looped her purse over her shoulder before walking out of the hospital room.

When she left, Melissa turned to face him. "You've been having a rough couple of days, huh?"

"Tell me about it!" Jamal chuckled.

She reached for the bouquet and grocery bag sitting on one of the pleather chairs. "I brought you flowers." She surveyed the room. "But it looks like you have plenty of those. I also brought you some white cheddar popcorn— your favorite! I figured no one else would think to bring that."

"No, no one else would," he said, loving her even more for such a simple but thoughtful gesture. "It's perfect." He patted a spot on the bed beside him. "Come up here and share it with me."

She frowned as she walked closer to the edge of the bed. "*You sure?* Is that even allowed?"

"Yeah! Just lower the bed rail."

She did as he told her, following the instructions to lower the hospital bed's rail. She climbed onto the bed, sitting near his side. She ripped open the bag of popcorn and offered it to him.

"Can you feed it to me?"

He still had use of one of his hands, but he liked the idea of her feeding him again. He licked the cheddar off her fingers as she placed it in his mouth, making her giggle before she popped a couple of pieces into her own mouth.

"So what kinda bum-ass luck do you have, to get punched one night and robbed and shot the next day?"

He shook his head as he chewed. "It had nothing to do with luck. I wasn't robbed. That kid *wanted* to kill me."

"Who the hell would want to kill you, Jay?"

"I can think of someone . . . and I'll tell the police as soon as I get out of here."

She fed him another kernel. "Is this the stuff you didn't want to tell me about? The stuff you said could have goons coming after me?"

He nodded. "But I think it's okay now."

"*You think?*"

"The kid made his attempt and failed. He was arrested. They're probably questioning him. I don't think the person who did this will risk trying it again. It's too hot for them right now."

"But they might."

"I don't know."

"Should you get protection . . . a police guard, then? Will you have to start carrying a gun?"

"I don't know, Lissa. I hope not."

"Jesus," she whispered, raising her hand to his face, running her fingertips along his brow and bruised cheek. Her feathery touch made his heartbeat kick into overdrive. He was sure she could hear it beeping on his monitor. "This is crazy! You know that, right? You could've been killed!"

"I'm well aware."

"And you aren't even sure if you're safe now. This might not be over. God, you're making me a nervous wreck! What am I going to do with you, Jay?"

Love me as much as I love you, he wanted to say, but didn't because he knew how sad and desperate it sounded.

"Don't die on me. OK?" She leaned forward and brushed her lips against his. "I'm gonna be pissed if you die."

"I'll try not to." He stared at her full lips. "So can I get a real kiss?" he asked hopefully, making her giggle again. "I know I'm in a hospital bed and hooked up to IVs, but I swear I can take it!"

She leaned forward and kissed him again, running her tongue over his bottom lip this time. He wrapped his hand around the base of her neck to hold her against him, opening his mouth and meeting her tongue with his own so the kiss could deepen, forgetting the hospital room, and the nurses, doctors, and patients outside his doorway. Alone with Melissa, he forgot the world around them.

Chapter 7

Derrick

When the steel doors to the elevator opened, Derrick stepped onto the hospital floor—and immediately wanted to step back onto the elevator.

He didn't want to do this. He didn't want to have to walk into Jamal's hospital room with his hat in his hand, ready to eat a giant helping of humble pie, especially only two days after punching Jamal in the face in front of almost a hundred people. But that is exactly what he would have to do today.

Derrick needed to talk to Jamal about Cole. He had to explain that the boy's own life and the life of his family had been under threat when he'd shot Jamal, and that was the *only* reason why he'd shot him. Maybe, if Derrick explained Cole's predicament well enough, Jamal would have sympathy for his plight. Maybe then Jamal would convince the prosecutor not to be so hard on the boy and seek a lesser penalty than what usually came with an attempted murder charge.

And beyond the stuff about Cole, Derrick knew he and

Jamal had their own unfinished business to settle. They had been friends once. He, Jamal, and Ricky had been as close as brothers for nearly two decades—but within the past year that had all gone haywire. Jamal getting shot and almost killed was a reminder that time was guaranteed to no one. Derrick didn't want to waste it fighting and arguing.

Derrick made the slow trek down the hall to the recovery ward, taking a deep, steadying breath as he did it. The cops had told Derrick what ward Jamal was in, but he didn't know Jamal's hospital room number.

He halted in front of the octagonal-shaped nursing station where several nurses in green scrubs stood around talking, laughing, or staring down at clipboards.

"Uh, excuse me," he said, drawing one of the nurses' attention—an Asian woman with her hair in a bun.

She turned to him and smiled. "Yes! How can I help you?"

"I'm looking for Jamal Lighty. I know he's on this floor, but I'm not sure which room."

She nodded and turned to a chart that was posted next to a computer on the counter. "That would be room 2455, sir."

"Thanks," he said before strolling down the corridor. He passed a few rooms before arriving at room 2455, practicing what he would say along the way. When he finally reached the open door, he raised his hand to knock on the metal frame, but halted when he caught view of the interior of the hospital room.

He saw Jamal sitting up in his hospital bed, reclining against pillows with his shoulder and left arm in a sling. Jamal was surrounded on all sides by bouquets of flowers and balloons with messages that said "Get Well" and "Thinking of You!" Melissa was sitting on the edge of the bed, leaning toward him, whispering something. The two laughed, and she leaned forward and gave him a light kiss.

Jamal said something more, wrapped his free hand around the base of her neck, and kissed her again, tugging her closer so that the kiss could deepen.

Watching them, Derrick swore he saw his vision go red. He gritted his teeth. He clenched his fists. He felt his heartbeat accelerate.

Despite all his regrets for lashing out at Melissa and Jamal at the education gala, despite him insisting to Morgan that he didn't want to rekindle his relationship with is ex, Derrick was still flooded with rage. He wanted to charge into the hospital room, yank the couple apart, and start punching Jamal all over again. He wanted to take the vases filled with flowers that sat on his hospital tray and along the windowsills and throw them at the wall and Jamal's head.

But the rage was nothing compared to the sense of betrayal he felt watching Melissa and Jamal kiss with a passion and ease of a couple who had done it many times before. That part was indescribable. She used to be his fiancée. Jamal used to be his boy. How long had they been doing this? When had their relationship started? Had there been an undercurrent of attraction flowing between them for years and he'd been oblivious? Had they been flirting or even hooking up with each other behind his back the whole damn time?

Fuck this shit, Derrick thought bitterly. *Fuck the both of 'em.*

Within an instant, he forgot the entire reason why he had come to the hospital. Derrick just wanted to get off that floor, through the hospital's automatic doors, and far away from here before he did something stupid or something else violent. He backed away and turned on his heel. By the time he reached the elevators, he was at a near run.

Derrick didn't know how he'd made it back to his car

in the parking garage. His journey was a blur of red-tinged fury. He could have bumped into a few people along the way—he couldn't say—but at least he hadn't hit anyone.

As soon as he climbed inside, Derrick closed his eyes and lowered his forehead to his steering wheel, taking several deep breaths, willing himself to calm down. When he finally felt the rage ease its grip on him, he heard his cell phone chime.

"Shit," he murmured, contemplating letting the call go to voicemail.

He didn't want to talk to anyone, not in the state he was in, but it could be another emergency. Maybe something else had happened at the Institute.

What else could go wrong?

Derrick grumbled, leaned back from the steering wheel, and tugged his cell from his pocket. When he did, he saw Ricky's number on the screen. He hadn't talked to him in the past couple of weeks. Ricky seemed preoccupied with something, which wasn't surprising, considering how much drama he had going on in his life since his arrest in December.

Derrick pressed the green button and raised his phone to his ear. "Yeah, what's up, man?"

"Shit, Dee, I'm so glad you answered! I thought you might be busy and I wouldn't catch you. You got some time?"

"Yeah, I got a few," he said, looking around the hospital parking garage. "What's up?"

"I got a favor to ask you, bruh."

Derrick shook his head, still trying to mentally drown out the memory of Melissa and Jamal kissing in the hospital room. "Now is not a good time, Ricky. I've got a lot of shit going on and—"

"I've got a lot of shit going on, too, Dee. More than

you could imagine. Trust me! And this is a favor I *need* for you to do. I wouldn't trust anyone else to do it."

Derrick frowned, not liking how desperate his friend sounded. "What's wrong? What happened?"

"I gotta explain when you get here. I'm not a fan of saying incriminating shit over the phone."

"*Incriminating?* What? What the hell did you do now?"

"Look, I just need you to go to my place and pick up some things for me. You still got the spare key I gave you, right?"

"Yeah, back at my place," Derrick said warily. "But you told me to use it only in case of emergencies. Is this an emergency?"

"You could say that. I need you to go to my wall safe in my home office. I'll text you the code to get in it. But I need you to take everything out of there and bring it to me, and I mean *everything*, Dee. Don't leave anything in there. That part is important."

Derrick's frown deepened. The more he heard, the more suspicious he became.

"*So* after I get all your shit, where am I supposed to bring this stuff? Where are you?"

"I'm in Chancellor. It's not too far from Fredericksburg. I'll text you the address, too."

"*Fredericksburg, Virginia?* Nigga, that's over an hour out of the city!"

"Yeah, it's a scenic drive, too. You should like it," Ricky said with a laugh.

Derrick grumbled again.

"Look," Ricky began, sounding somber, "I know it's a long drive, Dee, and I'm asking you to do a lot. But again, I wouldn't ask you to do this if it wasn't important. I'll explain everything when you get here, but for now, you're gonna have to trust me. Okay?"

Derrick closed his eyes. He had trusted Jamal once, too. He had thought their trio would hold each other down forever, and it hadn't turned out that way.

But Ricky ain't Jamal, he thought. And just because one of his boys had betrayed his trust, that didn't mean the other would.

"All right, man. Give me some time to do this shit. I probably won't be there until the evening."

"Thanks, Dee. You my nigga! You know that, right?"

"Yeah, I'm your nigga," Derrick said tiredly. "See you in a few hours." He then opened his eyes and hung up.

Chapter 8

Derrick

There hours later, Derrick pulled onto a black asphalt driveway bordered on both sides by ceramic geese and toads, garden gnomes and tulip-shaped mini windmills. The two-story house was made from cedar planks and had a wide wraparound porch with a railing decorated with potted plants and brass wind chimes that swayed gently in the afternoon breeze.

Derrick reached for the duffel bag sitting in the passenger seat. He hesitated for a few seconds over whether he should bring it with him, but decided to grab it anyway.

When Ricky had asked him to bring everything that was inside his wall safe, he had anticipated the thick stack of hundred-dollar bills that he'd discovered along with the envelope filled with credit cards under false names. What he hadn't expected were the three handguns—a Magnum and two Glocks—and several clips that Ricky had been storing there, too. When Derrick saw them, his blood ran cold. He instantly got a better idea of what kind of mess Ricky had stepped into, and he suspected it had something to do with Dolla Dolla. All bloody roads seemed to lead back to that man.

Derrick shoved open the car door and climbed out. When he did, the screen door to the house swung open and slammed shut with a thwack. A petite white woman with long gray hair stepped onto the porch with her hands on her hips.

"Who are you?" she barked. "Why are you on my property?"

Derrick hesitated again. He glanced at the number on the wooden mailbox. This was the address that Ricky had given him. So who was this woman?

"It's okay, Mary," he heard Ricky call out.

Derrick saw his boy step into the doorway. He was smiling. A slumbering infant in a short-sleeved onesie and diaper was perched in Ricky's arms.

Ricky didn't look like a man who needed three guns and ammo; he didn't look like he needed anything. He seemed perfectly satisfied.

"He's the friend I told you about," Ricky continued to casually explain to the old woman as he patted the baby's back gently. "He's okay. He's just here to help."

"*Help?*" she muttered ruefully before shaking her head, sending her long, ratty ponytail swaying. "I'm terrified to think what he's about to help you do, but I'll stay out of it. I'll keep my word," she said, easing past Ricky and stepping back inside the house.

Derrick shut the car door and climbed the porch stairs. "Who was that?"

"That's Mary. Don't mind how she acts—she's cool. She delivered my son."

"*Your son?*"

"Yeah, I told you Simone was pregnant. She gave birth yesterday." Ricky pointed to the sleeping infant cradled against his chest. His smile widened into a grin. "Meet Miles."

"Oh, shit," Derrick whispered in one exhalation as he stared down at the infant. "You're a father?"

"Yeah, I know," Ricky said with a chuckle. "I never thought it would happen, either. Though I'll be honest. With how many women I've bagged over the years, it should've."

"Congrats, man," he said, giving Ricky a fist bump.

"Thanks!" Ricky turned around and gestured Derrick forward with his free hand. "Come inside. Did you bring the stuff?"

Derrick sighed and held up the duffel bag. "Yeah, I brought it. But I hope you don't use this shit, bruh."

Ricky paused in the doorway. His smile disappeared. "I hope I don't have to, but I will if it comes to that."

"This is some serious shit, Ricky. I know you've run with these types of dudes in the past, but this ain't you. We're fighters, not shooters."

"Not anymore," Ricky said, adjusting as the infant began to squirm.

"Huh?"

"I said not anymore," he repeated as the baby began to whimper softly. Ricky met Derrick's eyes. "I've done what I had to do to protect me and mine, Dee. And I ain't scared to do that shit again."

Derrick squinted at him. "You mean you . . ." His words drifted off as it settled in. He realized exactly what Ricky was saying. "You can't mean that you—"

"I mean let me hand Miles over to Simone. It sounds like he's hungry, and we need to talk. Come on."

Derrick nodded as they stepped into a cluttered living room filled with a hodgepodge of furniture. They walked through it into a brightly lit kitchen.

"Hey, I heard him all the way down the hall," a female

voice called out as Derrick pulled out a chair at the kitchen table.

Derrick turned to his right and saw a woman in a loose-fitting sundress striding toward them. She had a pretty face, large, almond-shaped eyes, and glowing nutmeg-hued skin. Her short curly hair flopped along her forehead and ears as she walked.

So this is the mysterious Simone, Derrick thought.

This was the woman who Ricky had fallen in love with, who had turned his life upside down, and had him doing things that Derrick never would have thought in a million years he would do.

"Yeah, I think he's shouting for dinner," Ricky said, lowering Miles from his chest and cradling him lovingly. He kissed his son's forehead and handed over the squirming infant to his mother.

"He's *always* hungry," she said with a laugh before turning to Derrick, extending her free hand. "Hi, I'm Simone. It's a pleasure to meet you, Derrick. Ricky has told me so much about you."

"And he's told me a lot about you, too," Derrick said, shaking her hand.

"Yeah," she said, cupping Miles against her chest, "and I bet there were plenty of four-letter words involved."

"Never, baby," Ricky said slyly, shaking his head.

"Yeah, right." She stood on the balls of her feet before kissing his cheek. "I'll go feed Miles. It was nice meeting you, Derrick."

"Nice meeting you, too," Derrick called after her.

The two men watched as she walked out of the kitchen. Derrick gave a side glance at Ricky, studying him as he watched Simone. Ricky had a soft look about him, a glazing of the eyes that let Derrick know Ricky was still firmly in love with that woman. He was in love with her and his son.

"I don't get it," Derrick announced, making Ricky turn

around to face him. "If you have all this now, why would you risk it by getting mixed up in some shit?"

Ricky narrowed his eyes at him. "You really think I wanna get mixed up in it? I had no choice, Dee! I got dragged into it, and I'll see this shit through to the end," he said ominously.

"How did it even start?"

Ricky loudly exhaled and scrubbed his hand over his face. "You want the quick and dirty or long version?"

"Whatever one you feel like telling."

Ricky shrugged. "I'll start with the shorter one, and go from there."

So they both sat down and Ricky finally told him. He told him about how he'd heard Dolla Dolla confessing that he'd placed a hit out on Skylar and the other girls who he used to trick out. Dolla Dolla didn't know that Ricky had been in touch with Simone, Skylar's sister, the whole time. Ricky had tried to warn Simone and Skylar about what was coming, but had not reached them soon enough. Melvin, the hitman Dolla Dolla had sent, had already taken out Skylar and their mother, Nadine, and barely missed shooting Simone by the time Ricky arrived. Ricky killed Melvin and left the house with Simone, assuming that if she was the only living witness to the hit, Dolla Dolla would strive even harder to make sure the next hitman finished the job the next time around.

"And I can't let that happen, Dee," Ricky confessed at the end of his story. "I know if the detectives . . . the Metro cops figure out I'm out here . . . that I'm out of the city, they could send my ass back to jail. But I don't even care. I've gotta protect them. Dolla's on a rampage! He's not gonna stop until they're all dead."

Derrick nodded. "I know. Simone and her family aren't the only ones he put a hit out on. He tried to take out Jamal, too, for some damn reason."

"*Jamal?* Jamal who?"

"What do you mean, Jamal who? Jamal Sinclair Lighty! The dude we grew up with. Our former homeboy turned punk-ass bitch."

Ricky's face went blank. He slowly shook his head. "I don't get it. Why the hell would he wanna kill Jay?"

Derrick shrugged. "Your guess is as good as mine. But I know the kid who shot him. He was working for Dolla, and he said Dolla pressured him to pull the trigger."

"Damn!" Ricky fell silent. After a few seconds, he started tapping the kitchen table, like he was tapping a piano key. "You know what? Now that I think about it, the night that I was at Dolla's place, Mayor Johnson was there. Jay works for him, right? Dolla mentioned that Johnson wanted him to 'take care' of somebody who crossed him. You think it was Jay they were talking about?"

"Could be." Derrick shrugged. "Jay knew Johnson was dirty. He told me himself. Maybe Johnson realized Jay had found out and wanted to keep him quiet. That would be a good way to do it."

"Does Jay know all of this though? I know we're not tight with him anymore, but it feels messed up to not tell him . . . to not warn him."

Derrick sucked his teeth. "You can tell him. I ain't got shit to say to that nigga."

"Don't be like that, Dee! You're taking this holding-a-grudge shit way too far! He's still—"

"Jay is fucking Lissa, Ricky! I can't let that shit slide."

Ricky went silent again. This time he seemed genuinely stunned. "*Jay is fuckin' Lissa?*" He choked out a laugh. "You're kiddin', right?"

Derrick shook his head. "No, I'm not. I told you that he made that big confession to her about how he loved her and how she should dump me, back in December."

"Yeah, but you said that Melissa said he was drunk! That he was talkin' out of his ass!"

"Well, he wasn't. He meant every damn word."

"That still doesn't mean they're fuckin', Dee!"

"I saw them out together a few days ago. They seemed real cozy. I confronted them about it and I couldn't get a straight answer out of her or him on what's going on between them."

"You confronted them? *How?*"

Derrick sucked his teeth. "I beat the shit out of him."

Ricky closed his eyes and chuckled. "Oh, damn. You ain't right. You know Jay don't fight like that."

"Fuck him, man!" Derrick said with a dismissive wave, refusing to feel any more guilt for the beating he'd given Jamal. "Anyway . . . when I stopped by his hospital room after he got shot, to warn him about the very shit we're talking about now, she was in the room with him. He damn near had his tongue down her throat, Ricky, and she wasn't pushing him away. They're together now. That nigga went behind my back and started fuckin' my ex . . . the woman who I thought I was gonna marry."

Ricky sat back in his chair, crossed his arms over his chest, and sighed. "But you didn't want her, Dee. You have to admit that. You cheated on her. You already moved on."

"So that gave him the right to do the dirty shit that he's doing now?" Derrick challenged, feeling his heart rate pick up. "That gave him the right to stab me in the back like this?"

"No, it doesn't. But—"

"But nothing, Ricky! If there was anybody he could've gone after, why did he have to shoot his shot with her? Why Melissa? He knows what she meant to me."

Ricky didn't answer him. What could he say? He believed in loyalty just as much as Derrick did. Loyalty among their crew—whether they were beefing or not—was paramount. Melissa was a woman who should've remained out of Jamal's reach, just like Derrick would never think of pursuing the dozens of women Jamal and Ricky had had serious relationships with in the past. Jamal broke a code when he started dating Melissa, and for that, Derrick would never forgive him.

"And let's keep it real. Jay's always been a jealous motherfucka," Derrick said. "That nigga always wanted to be us. He's never had any swag. Now this is his chance to get what I had. He's just doing this shit to be petty. That's the only reason! To rub it in my face."

Ricky shook his head again. "I don't know, man. That doesn't sound like Jay."

"Maybe not to you. But it damn sure sounds like him to me. I saw it with my own eyes. Anyway . . . it is what it is," Derrick muttered. "I still don't have shit to say to him. If you want to hit up Jay and talk to him, be my guest. But he and I are done."

Ricky held up his hands. "Whatever way you wanna handle it. I feel you."

Thirty minutes later, the two men strolled back onto Mary's front porch, watching as the sun began to set.

"Thanks again for doing this, Dee," Ricky said.

"Hey, despite all the crazy shit you've made me do over the years, you know I got you."

Ricky and Dee dapped then embraced. Ricky pulled away and slapped his shoulder.

"So this is where you're stayin'?" Derrick asked. "I should come here if I need to find you?"

Ricky shook his head. "Nah, we'll hole up somewhere else, but it's not far from here. Mary is renting it to us. She said she's willing to help us, but we just can't stay here. This is where she works. Clients come in and out. We understand."

"So when are you coming back to D.C.? You can't stay here forever, man. The cops are gonna figure out you're not in town anymore."

"I don't know." Ricky shoved his hands into the pockets of his jeans. "I haven't decided yet. I'll stay as long as I need to. Until I can figure this shit out."

"Stay in touch though."

Ricky nodded. "I will. You be careful headin' back to D.C. You know how these rednecks drive out here."

"And you just be careful *period*, Ricky. I mean that shit! I know you wanna protect your family, but you can't do that if you're dead."

"I know," Ricky said, nodding solemnly.

Derrick turned and walked down the stairs back to his car. He took one last glance over his shoulder at his friend. He waved goodbye, opened the car door, and climbed inside, hoping to God it wouldn't be the last time he would ever see Ricky again.

Chapter 9

Jamal

"I put a big pot of beef chili in the fridge, baby," Jamal's mother called from his kitchen. "And I made you some lasagna. To bake it, all you have to do is pop it in the oven, set it on three-seventy-five, and it should be done in forty-five minutes. It should last you all week."

"Okay, thanks, Mama," Jamal said, pushing himself up from his sofa.

His mother looked around his apartment then glanced at his arm, which was still in a sling. "Are you sure you don't want me to stay longer, honey? Because I can."

He shook his head.

"But I don't like leaving you alone up here by yourself, especially before your shoulder has healed all the way," she said with a wince, adjusting her purse.

He shook his head. "I'll be fine, Mama. Really."

You've been here long enough, he thought with exasperation, but didn't say it aloud.

His mother had been staying with him for the past three weeks, since he had been released from the hospital. Though she had tried to help him during his recovery, that "help" quickly became more of an annoyance.

His mother had hovered over him and babied him. She'd rearranged all his kitchen cabinets and the refrigerator, and he had to kick her out of his bedroom when he caught her trying to rearrange his underwear drawer. She'd done all his laundry and cleaned his apartment from top to bottom, which he would have appreciated if she hadn't muttered the whole time that if he had a woman in his life, such cleaning would be taken care of by her.

He didn't know what Donna Reed–version of a girlfriend his mother believed was out there who wanted to clean after him and cater to him, and he didn't bother to ask.

"Am I gonna die before you get married . . . before I have *any* grandchildren, Jay?" his mother had lamented one night over dinner, finally fed up with him. "Tell me now if that's the case, honey. I'd just like to prepare myself!"

"I just turned thirty-two three months ago, Mama. What's the rush?"

"What's the rush?" she'd cried. "Your cousin Tyrone was a father of four by the time he was twenty-three!"

"And Tyrone is up to his neck in child support payments and angry baby mamas. What's your point?"

His mother had sucked her teeth in reply before finishing the last of her collard greens.

But even though she annoyed him, his mother's presence offered a distraction from the anxiety that plagued him constantly now. When Jamal was alone in his apartment or when he walked to the local Starbucks to grab a cup of coffee, he would be struck by panic attacks. They would come out of nowhere, sweeping over him and dragging him under like a tsunami. He'd simply be walking along, minding his business, and his heart would start racing. He'd have shortness of breath. He'd get dizzy and have to sit down.

Jamal knew why he was having the panic attacks. Even though the cops had arrested the boy who'd shot him, he knew the men who were behind it were still walking the streets. He'd tried to tell the police as much, but they wouldn't listen.

"So you're saying the mayor . . . *Mayor Johnson* is behind your shooting?" the detective had asked during his interview the second day he was in the hospital.

Jamal had nodded. "When I told him I was quitting he threatened to have me killed. Within a week, the shooting happened. It doesn't sound like just a coincidence to me."

"But you said the argument between you and the mayor got heated, right? Maybe it was just an idle threat, Mr. Lighty," the detective had said. "Maybe all of this really was just a coincidence. I mean . . . he's *the mayor*! Why would he put out a hit on you and use a seventeen-year-old kid to do it? Wouldn't he have a lot to lose? What makes you think he would take such a risk?"

Because he's done it before, Jamal had thought, but kept the thought to himself.

He knew the mayor had been behind the reporter Phillip Seymour's murder earlier that year. The old man had admitted as much to Jamal. But if Jamal admitted that he'd known the details behind the unsolved murder and hadn't breathed a word to the cops, he might face some jail time himself. So he let the issue drop. He let the detective laugh off his worries. Meanwhile, he still kept a wary eye over his shoulder just in case Mayor Johnson made another attempt on his life. But that worry had morphed into paranoia. It was obviously starting to screw with his head.

Jamal now watched as his mother walked to his front door, where her rolling suitcase stood. "I still don't feel comfortable doing this, Jay. I don't like leaving you alone like this."

"I'm a big boy, Mama. Don't worry about me. I'll be fine. Besides, the sling will be gone in less than a week. That's what the doc said. I'll survive."

But he could tell from the look in her eyes and the expression on her face that she was very worried. She looked like she was five seconds away from taking off her sweater, dropping her purse on his coffee table, dragging her suitcase back into his study, and declaring, "That's it! I'm staying!"

"Go on," he said, using his free hand to unlock and open the door. "The Lyft driver is waiting for you downstairs, Mama. Don't miss your flight."

She leaned forward and kissed him on the cheek, despite whatever reservations she might have. "I'll call you when I get back in North Carolina, Jay. You be careful now. All right?"

He nodded.

"I love you, baby," she said, reaching for the suitcase's handle. She dragged it behind her as she stepped into the hall.

"Love you, too," he said.

He watched his mother until she walked down the corridor and boarded the elevator. She waved one last time before the metal doors closed on her stricken face. He then turned and closed his front door behind him.

Jamal strolled into his living room, and looked around him. He waited for the panic to set in. One minute passed, then two. After fifteen minutes, the panic still hadn't encroached. He was relieved.

"Maybe it's finally disappeared," he whispered, then reached for his cell on his coffee table. He typed a text to Melissa.

Haven't seen you in weeks. What have you been up to? Are you free today?

Within minutes, she texted him back.

Melissa: I'm at a school event but it ends at 5. Want to meet up after that?

Jamal: Sounds like a plan. Can you come here to my place?

Melissa: Maaaaaybe. You gonna feed me?

Jamal: How does lasagna, wine, and salad sound?

Melissa: That works! I'll be there a little after 6. Gotta clean up here first.

He grinned down at the phone screen. He was finally going to see Melissa again.

That had been the other downside of having his mother staying with him for damn near a month: no sleepovers. Melissa hadn't been to his place and he hadn't been back to hers since the morning he'd been shot. She'd call on occasion and ask him if he needed anything, while his mother loudly shouted her hellos in the background, but Melissa had remained scarce.

Jamal now understood the old adage "absence makes the heart grow fonder," because he missed Melissa—a lot. It wasn't just the sex that he longed for, though he definitely desired a repeat of their sensual marathon. He missed her smile, her laugh, her smell, and everything else that made up Melissa Stone.

When the hour that she was supposed to arrive drew closer, Jamal placed his mom's dish of lasagna in the oven. He already had a bottle of merlot chilling in the fridge and had started to remove the fixings for a salad when he heard a knock at his front door. He glanced at the clock on the microwave. It was only five fifteen. Had Melissa left the school event early?

He walked out of the kitchen and into his foyer. He looked through the peephole in the front door and saw a twenty-something black dude in cornrows standing on his welcome mat.

"Yeah?" Jamal called, feeling an undertow of disquiet pull at him.

"Food delivery," the man called back.

"I didn't order anything. You've got the wrong apartment!"

He watched as the guy raised a large paper bag and glanced at the receipt stapled on it. The guy shrugged. "It says this is the right address. This is where I'm supposed to deliver it."

"Look, man," Jamal repeated, feeling the familiar grip of anxiety wrap itself around him, "I didn't order any food. I've got no reason to lie."

"Then maybe somebody else in there ordered it," the guy called back.

"There's no one else here!"

"Can't you just open up the door? If I gotta bring this back, I gotta eat the cost. Just open up! Look at the receipt and see it for yourself."

Jamal started to wonder if this was another trap—another hit attempt by Mayor Johnson. The dude on the other side of the door wanted to hurt him, wanted to kill him. He started to slowly back away as his heart began to race.

"*Hello?*" the guy shouted. "Hello?" He pounded his fist against the door, making the frame rattle.

Jamal could feel a vise tightening around his lungs and his throat. He couldn't breathe. The world around him began to swirl and he got dizzy. Jamal reached out for the wall to steady himself but he was losing his footing. He slumped to the floor as the pounding at the door continued. He felt like he was dying all over again. He felt like he needed to escape, but there was nowhere to go. He was all alone. He closed his eyes as he trembled, praying for the episode to be over.

Jamal didn't know how long he stayed on his hallway's hardwood floor, breathing deeply, sweating buckets, but he was shaken out of his stupor when the smoke alarm went off. He blinked and gradually made it to his feet. When he staggered down the hall back into the kitchen, he saw smoke rising from the oven.

"Shit," he muttered, then rushed toward the oven door, coughing through the smoke.

When Melissa arrived at his apartment five minutes later, both the living room and kitchen were filled with smoke, but, thankfully, the beeping had stopped. He swung open the front door. When she saw him, she gaped.

"What the hell . . ." she murmured, squinting at him. "What the hell happened to you?"

He loudly grumbled and threw out his arm that wasn't in a sling. "I burned dinner. I'm sorry."

"Yeah, I can smell it," Melissa said with a slow nod as she followed him inside and shut the door behind her. "But I'm not talking about dinner. I'm talking about *you*." She reached out and ran her hand over his shirt. "You're soaking wet, Jay! You look like you took a shower with your clothes on. Do you have a fever or somethin'?"

He looked down at himself. "I just . . . give me a few minutes while I change my clothes, okay?"

She gradually nodded. "Okay."

When he returned to the living room fifteen minutes later, wearing a T-shirt and drawstring basketball shorts, he found Melissa reclining on his couch, watching television. The remote was in her hand. She sat upright when he entered the room.

"You're back!" she said with a smile.

"Yeah, I'm sorry again about dinner."

"No apologies needed. Lucky for you, I had a big lunch," she joked when he walked around the sofa and took the cushion beside her. She turned off the television and leaned her elbow against the sofa cushion, propping up her head. She nudged his knee with her own. "You still didn't tell me what happened though. Why were you sweating like that? What the hell did I stumble into, Jay?"

He shook his head, preparing to tell her a lie, to give an excuse, but he could feel her assessing him with those dark, penetrating eyes. He took a shaky breath. "I was . . . I was having a panic attack. That's why I burned dinner."

"*A panic attack?* Are you sure?"

He nodded. "I've had a few of them since . . . since the shooting. I was hoping I was getting better, but I guess not. The cops didn't believe me when I told them who I thought was behind it. It wasn't that kid. I *know* who it was—but they didn't believe me. So in the back of my mind I keep thinking, what if it happens again?"

She reached out and placed a hand on his shoulder. "I didn't know you were going through this. You should've said something!"

"What were you supposed to do if I told you?"

"I don't know!" She dropped her hand from his shoulder. "Recommend a good therapist? Be your panic attack buddy to talk you back down?"

"Thanks," he said dryly and gave a morose laugh. "The worst part is, I can't even find peace in my own damn home! Every time I walk down the hall . . . every time I step in my bedroom, I think about the moment that I got shot. That shit pisses me off! A person should be able to lie in bed without feeling like they're dying, right?"

"So then you need to go back to the cops. You've got no other choice."

"Go back to them and tell them what, Lissa? I already told them I didn't think the kid was working alone. I told them who I thought was behind it. The detective literally laughed in my face."

"I don't know, but you need to make them listen. You can't live like this!"

She was right. He couldn't. But how was he supposed to convince the detective differently?

"I wish you would tell me what you're tangled in. It might help. That's what friends are for, right? Offloading stuff."

He stubbornly shook his head.

"But—"

"No, Lissa! You're better off not knowing. Trust me."

The last person who had found out about Mayor Johnson's dirty dealings had ended up dead. An attempt had been made on Jamal's life, too. The only person who had managed to remain unscathed was Derrick, and Jamal suspected that was only because he had no connection to Derrick anymore.

If he told Melissa the truth and it got back to the mayor, her life would be in danger. He was sure of it, and he couldn't stomach the notion of something happening to her.

"I don't like being kept in the dark," she said. There was a harder edge to her voice.

Kept in the dark . . . He knew she was talking about Derrick and how he had carried on an affair behind her back. It had broken her heart to find out the truth.

"I know. But I'm not doing this to lie to you or hurt you. I'm doing it to *protect* you," he argued.

"Different reason. Same result, Jay."

"I'm not blowing you off. I'm not dismissing you," he whispered. "I would tell you the truth . . . I *want* to tell you, Lissa, but I can't. I just can't! If that means you being pissed at me—so be it. At least you're safe. That's all that matters."

Melissa raised a hand to his cheek. "You're really not gonna tell me, are you?"

"No," he said firmly.

"Fine." She lowered her hand. Her body language changed; she shifted away from him and went stiff. She stared at the blank screen of his television. "Have it your way, but I thought we were here for each other. I thought you trusted me."

"We *are* and I *do*," he assured her, reaching out for her with his working arm, drawing her close again. "And if I really had it *my* way, Lissa, things would be very different."

He wouldn't feel like he was a hunted animal. He would've quit his job as deputy mayor months ago before it all went left. If he had his way, Melissa would be his woman, not his "friend."

But you can't always get what you want, he thought.

"Do you believe me?" he asked.

She nodded.

"Do you trust me?"

She nodded again. "Yeah, I do."

She gazed into his eyes, leaned forward, and kissed him. It was like a salve. It didn't take all his anxiety and apprehension away, but it came close. Jamal kissed her back, sliding his tongue inside her mouth. They kissed for several minutes until she pulled away.

"Well, I obviously can't fix whatever is going on with you, and I don't think I can banish your panic attacks," she said, as she stood from the sofa and tugged her shirt over her head, revealing the black lace bra underneath, "*but* I can definitely give you a more positive association for your bedroom." She tossed her shirt to the hardwood floor. "Come on."

Jamal quickly pushed himself up from the sofa and followed her out of his living room. "You'd be willing to do that?" he asked, now grinning.

She nodded as they strolled down the hallway. She unclasped her jeans and lowered the zipper. "I think I could make the sacrifice."

He looked down at his sling. "We gotta work around my arm though. Do you mind?"

She laughed again, turned to him, and lowered her hand so that she was cupping his dick though his drawstring shorts. At her firm touch, he instantly felt a twinge. His heart began to race for a very different reason. "As long as everything below the waist still works, we're good, Jay."

She then turned and strolled into his bedroom, pushing her jeans down her hips. He wasn't far behind.

Chapter 10

Ricky

It was the best of times, it was the worst of times . . .

Ricky remembered reading that line in a book in high school, but he hadn't paid attention in English class long enough to recall the title or the author.

It was one of those dead white dudes, he thought absently as he changed his son's soiled diaper, learning from a previous pee mishap to get the diaper on first before he started fiddling with the tabs to seal it closed.

The line from a book seemed appropriate for his life right now. It was the best of times and the worst of times for him. For the past month, since Miles's birth, Ricky teetered between the best he'd felt in months—maybe *years*—and a growing sense of foreboding, like storm clouds where gathering in the distance, getting bigger and bigger, closer and closer, ready to dump rain and lightning on his head.

"All right, big man," he said, gently patting Miles's round tummy and snapping closed his striped sleeveless onesie. "I think we're good."

Miles gurgled in reply as he gazed up at Ricky with

wide doe eyes like his mother's, making Ricky smile. Ricky lifted him from the changing table and carried him from their bedroom down the hall to the eat-in kitchen.

Ricky wished their lives could stay like this. Their little family was suspended in a protective bubble of domesticity—a life Ricky hadn't had since his grandmother and sister were alive.

Mary regularly brought Ricky, Simone, and Miles enough food, household items, and baby supplies with the money Ricky gave her so they rarely left the house they were renting from her. They also didn't get any visitors besides Mary. She had stopped by a few times in the past few weeks, once to take Miles to a pediatrician in town who agreed to examine and immunize the infant for a thousand dollars in cash, no questions asked. Miles was headed to his second checkup today. Once again, his parents couldn't go with him.

"There he is," Simone said as Ricky walked into the kitchen. "I told Mary you were getting him ready."

"Oh, look at him! He's getting so chunky," Mary gushed with a smile as Ricky handed him to her. "I love it!"

"Everything should be in the diaper bag." Simone pointed to the gray polka-dot bag that now dangled on Mary's shoulder. "Change of diapers. Some breast milk that I pumped a couple of hours ago. Baby wipes. He'll probably sleep most of the car ride."

"I don't know," Ricky said with a frown. "He's been kinda fussy today. He might not sleep."

Mary waved off their concerns as she turned toward the front door. "Don't worry, folks. He'll be fine! We'll be back before noon—less than two hours. I'll let you know what the doctor says."

"Thanks, Mary," they replied in unison as they walked her to the door.

He and Simone stood on the porch, watching as she loaded their son into his car seat. They waved a minute later when she pulled off.

"I know it's only two hours, but I hate being away from him," Simone whispered, watching as Mary's sedan kicked up dirt as she drove off the four-acre property. "I wish I could go with her. I wish I could take him myself."

"I know," he said, rubbing her shoulders. "I do, too, baby."

"How long do we keep doing this?" She turned to him. "How long do we hide?"

He exhaled. "As long as it takes, until we know it's safe."

And he couldn't say for sure when that would be. He knew Dolla Dolla might still be looking for Simone, since she'd been the only surviving witness to two murders. The idea of the drug kingpin or his goons finding her weighed heavily on him. Two to three times a day, Ricky would stand on the front porch and stare warily in the distance when he thought he heard a car approaching. Each time, it proved to be his imagination, but he didn't know if a day would come when it wasn't.

He watched now as Simone's shoulders slumped at his answer. She turned away from the dirt road and headed back inside with her head bowed. He lingered on the porch a minute longer before joining her inside the house. Ricky looked around him. The house seemed achingly quiet without Miles—his cries, his gurgles, and the tinkling of his mobile over his baby swing. He had become their nucleus; they orbited around him.

Miles dictated their schedule from when he napped, needed a feeding, or needed to be changed. He still wasn't sleeping through the night, so they would take turns waking up every three hours to feed him or just walk him around their bedroom and rock him back to sleep. When he was asleep they talked, watched television together, or made love.

Ricky had been nervous the first time they had sex after Miles's birth. He worried whether they should wait longer, but by the third week, they both couldn't resist the urge anymore. Now they made love regularly, languishing in the comfort and delight of one another's bodies. Though they had been rowdy in the past, they'd learned how to keep silent with a slumbering infant in the bassinet beside them or in the next room. The best moments for Ricky nowadays weren't slamming her against the wall or the rush when he came. It was after they made love, with Simone naked and asleep in his arms and Miles asleep in his bassinet.

Ricky would stare at the ceiling and think, "I wish it could stay this way forever." But he would always feel that annoying, unseen clock ticking, telling him this tranquil time would be coming to an end soon.

He felt it even more when he heard his cell phone buzz. His heart rate kicked into overdrive when he got calls from Dolla Dolla, asking him what was up.

"Where you been, bruh?" Dolla Dolla had asked him two weeks ago. "I haven't seen you at the spot lately."

"I've just been busy. Been hustlin'. That's all," Ricky had lied.

"You know what they say about all work and no play, nigga. Stop by tonight. Let me hook you up with some bitches that'll set your mind right."

"I want to, but I can't tonight," Ricky had said. "I got some shit lined up. I'll try to stop by next week though, if I can."

Ricky had held his breath when he heard silence on the other end. He didn't usually tell Dolla Dolla no, and he knew his business partner didn't like hearing the word.

"All right, nigga," Dolla Dolla had said. "Your ass better stop by or I'm gonna start to get offended. And you don't want to offend me."

"No, I don't, Dolla," he said, feeling like he was eating shit even as he'd said it.

At least Dolla could be held off though. Detectives Ramsey and Dominguez, who Ricky had been working with as an informant since the end of last year, still expected him to do regular check-ins with them in the city and he hadn't done one in a month.

"Where the fuck are you, Ricky?" Dominguez had barked into his phone only a week ago. "You're supposed to report back to us! We stopped by your apartment and you weren't there. You understand what you agreed to, don't you? We can still throw your ass in jail for a very long time. Call us back!"

And Simone had officially been listed as a missing person. Every now and then her smiling face would flash on the television screen during a news broadcast asking for information on her whereabouts. It was surreal. If it was up to Ricky, she would remain missing. He didn't want Dolla Dolla to know she was still alive.

He walked down the hall into their bedroom and saw her sitting on the edge of the bed, staring at nothing in particular.

"It won't be like this forever," he said, leaning against the door frame.

She glanced up at him. "No, it won't. But it's not gonna end until Dolla's gone—or I am."

"Don't say that," he replied tightly.

He didn't want to even contemplate the possibility of her ending up like Skylar and her mother.

She lowered her eyes to her clasped hands. "Sometimes I think about leaving the country. It might be better for you . . . for me. It would probably be better for Miles, too.

Just hopping on a plane with him and disappearing to the Caribbean or Canada or Europe. Change my name. Start all over again."

At those words, a knot formed in the pit of his stomach. He had thought about it, too. About sending them away, but the idea made him feel the same sense of loss as when his sister and grandmother died.

She shook her head. "But I can't do it, Ricky. I can't! I can't do this all alone. On the run *with a one-month-old*?"

"You don't have to." He walked toward her and sat down on the bed beside her. He wrapped an arm around her shoulder and squeezed. "I'm here. I'm always here, baby."

"You don't know that." When she looked up at him, he could see her eyes were filled to the brim with tears. "Anything can happen. We've been separated before. It could easily happen again."

"And I'll track you down. I did it before." He leaned in and kissed her brow. "I'm not gonna let anything happen to you two. You hear me? I swear it on my life."

She raised a hand to his bearded cheek and the tears finally spilled over. He tried to kiss them away as she clung to him. The kisses shifted to her mouth and they deepened. Within minutes, he'd peeled off her clothes and they were making love. Her tears were replaced with whimpers and moans. Two hours later, Ricky disentangled his limbs from hers and rose from the bed. Simone rolled onto her stomach, still lost in slumber. He glanced at the clock on their night table and saw it was 12:19. He frowned.

Mary should've been back by now, he thought. She'd said the trip would take less than two hours.

He tugged on a pair of boxers and jeans and walked in bare feet to the front door. He opened it and leaned against the railing of the front porch, peering at the acres and acres of open land surrounded by trees. No car was in sight. His frown deepened and he turned around and headed back inside the house.

One hour went by and then the next. Still no Mary. They called the cell phone number she'd given them to reach her in case of emergencies, but there was no response. By five p.m. they'd left a half dozen messages.

"Something's wrong," Simone said after she hung up the eighth time. She started pacing the living room. "Something happened. That has to be it!"

He stubbornly shook his head. "You don't know that."

"What else could it be?" she cried. "She hasn't called us back! She hasn't shown up! Something must have happened to her!" Simone slapped a hand over her mouth. "Oh, God, Ricky. What happened to her? What's happened to our baby?"

Ricky closed his eyes and gritted his teeth. He took a deep breath, then shot up from the sofa. He walked to their bedroom and opened the night-table drawer. Inside were two of his guns: a Glock and a Magnum. He tucked one in the back of his waistband, grabbed his car keys, and walked back into the living room. He held the Magnum out to her.

"It's loaded," he said. "I'm not going to ask if you know how to shoot it. I know you do."

Her brows furrowed. "Why are you giving me this?"

"Because I'm gonna look for Mary, and if something happens, I want you to protect yourself."

She continued to stare at the gun but didn't reach for it.

"*Take it*, Simone!"

She hesitated for a second longer before taking the gun out of his hand.

"Ricky!" Simone shouted after him when he shoved the door open, making him pause. "Bring back our baby, but please don't get killed. Please?"

He nodded and gave a half smile. "I'll try not to."

*   *   *

While on the road, Ricky tried desperately to remember the name of the pediatrician Mary said she was taking Miles to see. He tried to remember the town, but drew a blank on both. He suspected he didn't remember because Mary had never told them; she had purposely kept the details vague because the doctor was doing this illegally and could lose his license. So Ricky drove straight to Mary's house. He banged on the front door and rung the bell but Mary didn't answer. He drove around her neighborhood, then around town, searching parking lots and side streets for her tan Toyota Corolla. Simone checked in with him periodically via text. She said Mary still hadn't returned to the house.

It was almost midnight and Ricky still hadn't spotted the car, Mary, or Miles. He knew he had no choice but to make the drive back home, but his mind raced with all the possibilities of what could've happened. Had Mary had a car accident? Had she gotten arrested? Had Dolla Dolla found out about them, and was holding Mary and the baby hostage somewhere?

When he rounded the trees and pulled onto the dirt road leading to their house, he saw the swirling lights of cop cars and a lone search helicopter overhead. His mouth fell open in shock. Almost ten squad cars were parked around the house's perimeter.

So they had finally found him. Did this have anything to do with Mary? Had she snitched on them to the cops after all?

Ricky saw Simone step onto the front porch with her hands behind her back and her head bowed. A female officer was holding her arm, leading her down the porch stairs. Simone was in handcuffs.

He slammed on the brakes and the car lurched to a

stop. He threw open the door and several police officers ran across the field toward him with their guns drawn.

"What are you doing to her?" he shouted. "Why the fuck are y'all arresting her? She didn't do anything!"

"Get on the ground!" one of the officers shouted. "Get on the fucking ground or we will shoot you!"

"Do it now!" another yelled.

Ricky watched helplessly as Simone was led to one of the cop cars. The female officer placed her hand on the back of Simone's head before shoving her inside.

"This is your last warning!" one of the cops in front of him yelled. "Get on the ground!"

Ricky complied. He dropped to his knees and placed his hands behind his head. The officers raced the remaining distance between them, shoving him down hard onto the packed dirt, wrenching his arms behind his back to put him in handcuffs.

Chapter 11

Ricky

Ricky had been here before—trapped alone in a white room with a table and chairs at a police precinct. But this time, he didn't sit docilely waiting for the door to open. He paced back and forth, glaring at the door and mirror along the wall. He was a caged tiger ready to pounce on the first motherfucka stupid enough to drift into his holding pen.

"Somebody better come in here!" he yelled at the glass, knowing that police officers were probably watching him on the other side. He stared up at the camera perched near the ceiling in the corner of the room. "Where the fuck is my girl? Where's my son? I will rip this fuckin' place apart if somebody doesn't come in here right goddamn now and answer me! Y'all hear me?" he bellowed, kicking over one of the chairs, sending it flying into the cinderblock wall. "Y'all hear me?"

"Big talk for a guy in handcuffs," a voice said behind him.

Ricky whipped around and saw Detectives Dominguez and Ramsey standing in the doorway. Dominguez had his usual Cheshire-cat grin. Ramsey wasn't smiling.

"Where is Simone? Did y'all really arrest her? What the fuck did y'all do with our baby?" he asked, charging toward them. "Where the hell is he?"

Ramsey raised his hand. "Back up and calm down. We'll answer your questions after you answer ours. But we can't do that until you sit down."

"I'm not fuckin' sittin' down. Fuck you! You tell me where they are right goddamn now!"

"You violated the terms of our agreement, pretty boy," Dominguez said with a sneer. "We don't have to tell you shit. We can just send your ass to jail."

"Then do it!" Ricky spat. "Do it! You've taken everything else away from me. You think I care if I go to jail now?"

Ramsey slowly shook his head. "You don't mean that. You don't want to go to prison."

"Don't tell me what I mean! I said what I fuckin' said." He looked between the two men. "Where are they? Tell me!"

Ramsey pursed his lips and took a deep breath, making his graying mustache flutter. "They're safe. They're fine."

Ricky's jaw tightened. "Don't just tell me what I wanna hear. Tell me the truth!"

"It *is* the truth, Ricky!" Ramsey insisted. "The baby is with a social worker right now, and Simone isn't in prison. She's in another room just like yours, down the hall. She's being questioned."

At those words, Ricky felt a wave of relief rush over him. It almost made his knees buckle. He'd thought he'd lost them. He thought that he'd broken the promise he'd made to Simone to always protect them. But they were okay.

Thank you, God, he thought.

His blood pressure went down. His thundering heartbeat decelerated.

"So now you know mama and kiddy are fine," Dominguez deadpanned. "Now, will you finally sit your ass down?"

Ricky reluctantly took the chair on his side of the table. Dominguez sat in a chair on the opposite side. Ramsey closed the door behind him and took the chair that Ricky had kicked against the wall.

"You've been MIA for almost a month," Ramsey began. "That's not acceptable."

"I was with Simone and our son in Virginia," he answered. "I was there for the birth and I stayed to make sure they were safe. I didn't have a choice."

"Yeah, we heard from your baby's wet nurse or whatever the hell she is," Dominguez said. "She was picked up at the doctor's office. The doc got a guilty conscience and confessed that she'd been paying him to examine your son. He thought she might've kidnapped the baby or something, and turned her in. The sheriff's office arrested her. During questioning, she finally caved and told them everything that happened. She told them where you were."

So that was how the cops had found them. He figured that if Mary had taken Miles and sent the cops over to their house, it had to be for a good reason. The woman had been loyal to them for so long.

"So were you connected to the murders of Nadine and Skylar Fuller? Did you take them out?" Dominguez asked.

Ricky vehemently shook his head. "I would never hurt them! I came there to protect them. I told you Dolla was putting a hit out on all the witnesses. I found out that he knew where Skylar was hiding. He was sending someone over there that night. I tried to warn them but I didn't make it there in enough time. He'd already killed Skylar and Simone's mother. I thought he'd killed Simone, too, but she held him off."

"You mean she killed him," Dominguez persisted. "She

told the investigators she did. She said she was defending herself when she shot him."

Ricky stared at Dominguez, now stunned. Simone had taken the rap for Melvin even though Ricky had been the one to shoot Melvin in the head and chest. He guessed she thought she stood a better chance of not facing jail time if she was charged with murder as self-defense, but he wasn't happy with her putting her freedom on the line like this.

"So what I don't understand," Ramsey said, "is if you went there to rescue her, why didn't you bring her to us? Why didn't either of you call the police? Instead, you chose to go on the run for weeks!"

Ricky squinted. "Why the fuck would I bring her to you guys? Because you did such a good job in protecting all the other witnesses?"

Ramsey looked grim while Dominguez looked pissed at his words.

"Are *any* of them still alive? Any of the girls Dolla used to pimp out?" Ricky asked.

Ramsey and Dominguez exchanged a look and Ricky already knew the answer to his question. He shook his head again in disgust.

He had warned the detectives early on what Dolla Dolla had planned. He'd even witnessed one of the girls being murdered, and the detectives and Metro police, in general, seemed to have no interest in what he had to say. Instead, they were more concerned with Dolla Dolla's contacts. They wanted to know who else was in the drug and pimp game he was working with.

"So let me guess," Ricky said, slumping back in his chair. "The whole case could fall apart now—unless I testify?"

"You really think you're the only witness we got left?" Dominguez sniffed. "You're not special, Ricky. Even if you were, we could flip someone else. Just like that." The detective snapped his fingers.

Ricky laughed. "No, you couldn't. They're all too scared now. He has his circle, and anyone who might've thought about flipping, knows what Dolla did. They know what he's capable of. Nobody's snitchin' on him now. It's me—or nobody. That's the only reason why you're bothering with my ass, right? That's the only reason why I'm sitting here and not in jail."

Ramsey sighed and for once, Dominguez went silent.

"But don't worry," Ricky assured them. "I'll help you. The shit is personal for me now. He tried to kill my girl. He killed her family. I'll do what I gotta do to take him down."

"We're glad to hear that, Ricky," Ramsey began, "because we need you to—"

"But the deal's different this time," Ricky interrupted. "I got conditions that I need to be met, or I'm not doing it."

Dominguez chuckled as he gestured to Ricky. "Is this asshole serious? He really thinks that he gets to dictate the rules?"

"Ricky," Ramsey tiredly began again, "we don't cut the deals. That's between your lawyer and the prosecutor. We just—"

"I don't care who does what. I don't care who speaks to who. I told you I have conditions and—"

"And we don't give a shit!" Dominguez snarled, making Ramsey roll his eyes. "You're gonna do what we fuckin' tell you to do, or your girl goes to prison for twenty years and that little brat of yours goes into foster care. How's that sound?"

Ricky stared right back at him. "It sounds like we still don't have a deal." He then leaned over the table. "And if you ever threaten her or my kid again, I will fuckin' kill you. Handcuffed or not, I'm comin' for your ass and I rip you to fuckin' pieces with my bare hands. Understand me?"

"Okay! All right," Ramsey said, holding up his hands. "Everybody just calm down. We can work out a deal—if its reasonable. Just tell us what you need, Ricky."

A few hours later, the sheriff's deputy opened the door and Ricky stepped inside another room. He saw Simone sitting at a table with reddened eyes and disheveled clothes, staring off into space. When she turned and her eyes landed on him, she leapt up from her chair and ran across the room. She threw herself at him, making him stumble back. He wrapped his arms around her, holding her close.

"Oh, baby! Ricky, I didn't know if I would see you again," she wept, throwing her arms around his neck. She kissed him once, twice, three times. "They came outta nowhere! I didn't have time to react!"

"I know," he whispered, kissing her, too. "It's okay now. We're okay."

She leaned back to gaze up at him. "They still won't tell me about Miles. I don't know if he's still with Mary. I don't know what—"

"They're bringing him. They're giving him back. They promised me they would."

She shook her head. "But how do you know they'll keep their promise? I'm not gonna leave here without him!"

He took a deep breath and loosened his hold around her. "Because that was one of the conditions of our deal."

She frowned and looked at him searchingly. "*What deal?* What are you talking about?"

"Mary goes free. She tried her best to help us. She deserves to go free. You get Miles back. You're going away, but you'll be under twenty-four-hour police protection wherever they you take you this time. I don't know where that is."

Simone's frown deepened. "But what about you? Where are you going? Why aren't you coming with us?"

"I can't go with you. When all this is over, in exchange for my testimony, I can be with you—maybe."

"*Maybe?* What do you mean, *maybe?*"

"But for now," he continued, unable to answer her questions, trying to find the strength to press onward, "I have to go back to the city. I have to finish what I started."

She lowered her eyes. "So we're gonna be separated again?"

"That's the way it has to be for now."

"How long this time?"

"I don't know."

She nodded. One tear trickled over her cheek, then another. She sniffed and wiped her nose with the back of her hand. "I knew this time would come eventually, but it still feels too soon."

She dropped her head to his shoulder. He held her close, closed his eyes, and kissed her crown.

They waited for another hour before the door opened again. A woman walked in cradling Miles in a blanket. A deputy trailed in behind her. This time both Ricky and Simone stood up and rushed across the room. She greedily took the infant.

"Is he okay?" Ricky asked, cradling Miles's head.

Simone unwound the blanket and placed Miles on the table. Miles squirmed and began to whimper in the cold air as she unfastened his onesie and raised it, examining his legs, torso, and arms. She snapped the garment closed and nodded. She brought Miles back to her shoulder and rubbed his back. "Looks like it."

Ricky reached for him. "Let me hold him. Let me say goodbye."

Simone's bottom lip began to tremble as she handed their son to him. He held the boy in his arms. Miles was crying now, letting out long wails. Ricky stared down at him, unsure of what to say, diminished because he wasn't sure if he'd ever see his son again.

"I'll see you soon, okay, little man," he whispered, hoping it was the truth. "Daddy will see you soon." He then kissed his forehead.

"All right, family man," he heard Dominguez call out.

He looked up to find the two detectives standing in the doorway, waiting for him.

"We did all the shit you asked for. Come on!" Dominguez yelled. "We gotta go!"

Ricky felt like a piece of him was being ripped away when he handed a wailing Miles back to Simone. He felt another piece rip when he leaned down and kissed Simone goodbye, savoring the taste and feel of her. "This is only temporary. Okay?"

She started to cry again, but nodded.

"I love you."

"I love you, too," she whispered.

"Stay strong," he said as he backed toward the door.

"I will. You too!" she sobbed back, holding Miles against her chest, rocking him gently.

"Well, ain't that sweet?" Dominguez murmured dryly before Ramsey elbowed him the ribs. "*What?*" he cried. "It is!"

Ricky then turned around and headed to the door and into the hall, letting the door close behind him, ready to walk back into the lion's den.

Chapter 12

Derrick

The room resembled a converted cafeteria with its bare white cinder-block walls, and windows covered with metal grates so that the sun created crisscross patterns on the puke-green linoleum-tile floors. To Derrick's right and left were a series of video screens enclosed in black boxes. Hanging along each box was an old-fashioned phone receiver connected by a steel cord.

"Take the one on the end over there," the corrections officer said, pointing Derrick to an empty chair on the far side of the echoing room, near the window. It was next to a woman in a bright red wig who was currently speaking to an inmate on screen while she held a slumbering toddler on her lap. "You got fifteen minutes."

Derrick walked up to the boxes and sat down in a rickety plastic chair that looked like it'd probably been in use since the late '80s.

He watched as the blank, black screen flooded with color. Cole appeared in a gray jumpsuit with his head and shoulders bowed. Behind him was a room that looked like it was the mirror image of the room in which Derrick sat, except it was filled with inmates, not visitors. Seeing Cole onscreen in his inmate uniform was like a punch to the gut. His heart ached. He hadn't wanted the boy to end up here. He had wanted *anything* but this, but now that Cole was facing an attempted-murder charge, this is where he would have to stay until his trial.

Derrick felt like he'd failed him. Each boy at the Institute was his responsibility, and he had let this one slip through the cracks.

"What's up, Mr. Derrick?" Cole asked, still not raising his eyes.

"What's up, Cole?" Derrick whispered. "How you doin'?"

Cole let out a dry laugh. It sounded as brittle as lead, nothing like the full booming laughter the boy had had back at the Institute.

"Not doin' too good, Mr. Derrick." He finally darted a glance up at him through the video screen. "Thanks for comin' down here though."

"No problem. I wanted to check on you. Let you know that all of us are thinking about you—the staff and the students."

"Miss Owens, too?" Cole asked hopefully.

Derrick chuckled and nodded. Cole had always had a soft spot for and maybe even a crush on Morgan. "Yes, even Miss Owens."

"Why ain't she come to visit me then?"

Derrick hesitated. He didn't want to tell Cole that Morgan and he had broken up, that they were no longer on speaking terms so he couldn't answer that question for him. Instead, he shrugged.

"She took the news about you getting arrested pretty hard. I bet she's not too eager to see you in here."

Cole grimaced. "I thought she might be mad at me for what I did."

"Less mad than disappointed. We *both* were disappointed, Cole. I wish you would've told me what you were about to do. I could've stepped in. It didn't have to go down this way."

"It's nothing you could've done, Mr. Derrick." Cole wasn't glancing at him now. He was staring at him openly. "I had to do what I had to do. I didn't have a choice. I told dude that, even before I shot him. It is what it is."

"Ten minutes left!" the guard barked on the other side of the room.

"We could've told the cops Dolla was threatening your family though. We could've—"

Cole loudly shushed him and raised a finger to his lips. The young man looked over his shoulder before turning back to the screen. He slowly shook his head. "Don't do that, Mr. Derrick. Don't talk about that shit. Not in here."

"What do you mean?" Derrick looked at the receiver he held. "I'm not new to this. I know they're monitoring and recording our conversation, Cole, but everything I'm saying now, the cops already know. Even your mama said—"

"My mama ain't say nothin'! All right?" Cole argued, leaning toward the screen. "The cops know what I did. I followed dude to his apartment. I thought I could get his wallet but I couldn't. So I shot him. That's it. I needed the money. I had no choice."

Derrick squinted at Cole in confusion. Why was he lying?

Cole's mom had told Derrick that they'd told the police that Dolla Dolla had put him up to Jamal's attempted murder. They'd told investigators about the meeting in Prince George's County the night before the shooting and how one of Dolla Dolla's men had given Cole the gun and Jamal's home address. The cops knew the details of what had happened, even if they may not have believed Cole's account.

For the first time, Derrick saw desperation in the young man's eyes. He noticed that Cole stole another glance over his shoulder, like he was looking at someone on the other side of the room.

Derrick started to realize what was going on. Cole wasn't scared of the cops overhearing their conversation. He was worried more about his fellow inmates. Did Dolla Dolla have soldiers inside the prison, too? Derrick wouldn't put it past the drug kingpin. And they would probably report back to Dolla Dolla that Cole was a snitch, that he had talked to the cops about him. That could put the boy's life in danger.

"Are you good in there?" Derrick asked loudly, hoping that the boy would get his double meaning. "Do you need anything? Anything at all? Do I need to tell your mom to send you something special in your care package?"

"Five minutes left!" the guard yelled, interrupting their conversation.

Cole shook his head. "Nah, I'm good. I got what I need for now." He shifted in his chair. "I just gotta be careful, you know? It's easy to get crazy up in here."

Derrick nodded grimly.

"I'm okay, Mr. Derrick. You and my mama don't have to worry. I just keep my head down and follow the rules. It's just like the Institute, but with nasty food."

Cole laughed. Derrick wanted to join him in his laughter, but couldn't.

"You take care of yourself," he whispered.

"I will. And . . . and can I ask you something? Can you do something for me?"

"Anything. Name it!"

"Can you ask Miss Owens to come and visit me?"

Derrick pursed his lips. "I'll ask her. I definitely will."

"I know I disappointed her, but I hope she can forgive me. I didn't want to do it. You just get caught up in stuff, you know?"

Oh, yeah. I know. Trust me, Derrick thought. He, of all people, knew what it meant to disappoint Morgan, to get so caught up in his own mess that he didn't even think of how it would affect her.

"Okay. Time's up!" the guard yelled.

Damn! Already, Derrick thought, now at a loss. How had the minutes flown by so quickly? They had barely had a conversation.

Cole winced. "I know my apology won't mean much to her, but I want to apologize anyway," Cole hurried to say. "Can you tell her that, Mr. Derrick?"

Derrick nodded. "I will. Don't—"

He didn't get to finish his assurances. The screen went blank.

Chapter 13

Jamal

Jamal lingered near the revolving glass doors, watching as a line of people filed through—a man in a suit, a woman blabbing on her cell phone, a couple who seemed to be having a quiet but intense argument. He finally stepped through the doors, too, and stood in the lobby. He walked to the wall directory and frowned.

"Can I help you, sir?" the uniformed security guard asked, strolling toward him. "You lookin' for somethin'?"

Jamal nodded. "I'm looking for the Conference of Public Officials meeting," Jamal said. "I heard it was here today. I think it may have already started."

The security guard nodded. "Fifth floor. Room 508."

"Thanks," Jamal murmured before walking to the elevators.

"Sir!" the guard called out, holding up his hand, making Jamal halt in his steps. "You have to sign in."

"Oh, yeah. Sorry." Jamal painted on a smile and walked back to the desk. He grabbed a pen that sat on the granite countertop. He wrote his name and glanced at the digital clock nearby to check the time, and wrote that, too. The guard took the pen and clipboard and nodded.

"Enjoy your meeting, Mr. Houghton," he said, glancing at the false name Jamal had provided.

"Thanks," Jamal said before heading back to the elevators and pressing the up button. He boarded one a minute later and pressed number five, letting the doors close behind him.

Jamal closed his eyes. He had done breathing exercises to make it this far, but he already felt the pesky tightening in his chest as he ascended floors; the rumblings of another panic attack was coming on.

"Not now," he whispered hoarsely.

He wasn't sure if it was anxiety related to what he was about to do or who he was about to see face-to-face. He knew the mayor would likely be here today. Jamal had been slated to attend the Conference of Public Officials meeting with Mayor Johnson before he quit, so he knew it was on the older man's schedule. Johnson was one of the featured guest speakers, and he loved any opportunity to grandstand.

When the elevator dinged, Jamal opened his eyes. The doors opened and he stepped out into the corridor. He walked down the hall, drawing closer and closer to room 508. When he finally reached the room, he grabbed the chrome door handle.

No turning back now, he told himself, despite his heart racing and beads of sweat forming on his brow. He pushed the door open.

He wouldn't even need to be here today doing this if the detective had believed him, if he'd believed his claims about Mayor Johnson. Jamal had followed Melissa's suggestion to go back to the detective, to try harder to convince him of the truth.

"Did you follow up on what I told you?" Jamal had

asked the detective over the phone. "Did you question Johnson?"

The detective had loudly sighed. "Yeah, about that, Mr. Lightly . . . I spoke to the mayor's assistant and she provided the mayor's schedule for the time the shooting occurred. He was out of town. He was on a flight to Los Angeles when you were—"

"Of course, he was out of town! He wouldn't want to be anywhere near here when it happened. That's why you need to question *him*, not his assistant, Gladys. I told you that he's connected to Dolla Dolla, and Dolla Dolla has plenty of shooters working for him. I bet they set it up together."

"Mr. Lighty, we arrested the punk that shot you. He hasn't breathed a word about the mayor. The mayor was nowhere in the vicinity when the shooting took place. I have nothing . . . not a damn thing connecting Mayor Johnson to this crime! I just can't go barging into city hall accusing the mayor of D.C. of conspiracy to murder someone without any credible evidence supporting it!"

"What if I give you credible evidence?" Jamal had asked. "Then will you question him?"

"What are you talking about?"

"If I give you something that proves without a doubt that he was behind this, will you bring him in for questioning?"

The detective had laughed. "Sure. Fine. If you can give me credible—and I mean *strong*—evidence that Mayor Johnson is connected to your attempted murder, I'll see what I can do."

"You'll see what you can do?" Jamal had repeated back, incredulous. "What the hell does that mean?"

"That means that I need something to prove that this isn't a waste of time and police resources to take this further. As far as I'm concerned, we have our perp. But if you choose to hire a private detective to do your own investigation, I can't stop you. It's your money."

Jamal had fumed as he'd listened to the detective, angered by his patronizing attitude.

He would prove the detective wrong with the evidence he needed and he wouldn't need to hire a private detective to do it.

Now Jamal stepped into the large conference room and looked around him. Almost every chair was filled. He spotted one toward the back and walked to it, using a moment when the crowd clapped as one of the speakers ended his speech, to quickly make his way to the empty seat. When he sat down, he stared at the front of the room, wondering if Mayor Johnson had spotted him. It looked like he hadn't. The mayor was leaning toward another man, whispering. Jamal noticed a few other familiar faces toward the front: an assistant and a department head from city hall. But they hadn't spotted Jamal either. Both were gazing down at their cell phones.

He listened patiently to two other speakers, doing his deep breathing the entire time. The woman beside him glanced at him, squinting on occasion at his loud inhaling and exhaling, but he didn't care. He had to stay in here long enough for the mayor to finish his speech and corner him after. He had tried to go to city hall to confront him, but he had been told by one of the guards that he was no longer allowed into the building.

"I'm sorry, Mr. Lighty. I don't make the rules," one of the guards who used to say hi to him every morning had told him when he tried to walk inside earlier that week.

But he figured Mayor Johnson wouldn't be able to avoid him here.

He glanced down at his cell phone to check his recording app again. He had tested it last night, slipping it inside his sling and seeing if he could inconspicuously press the button to record. He worried now that the motion would be too obvious, or maybe he'd press the wrong button. Either way, he had to try. This was his only hope to get the detective to take his claims about Mayor Johnson seriously.

The crowd clapped again. Several more people had entered since Jamal had arrived and now lined the walls. He watched as Mayor Johnson rose to his feet, buttoning his jacket. The older man walked to the podium, smiling and waving at the crowd as he went.

Despite his deep breathing, Jamal could feel his chest tightening again as the mayor leaned toward the mike. He was starting to feel light-headed, too.

He flashed back to the conversation he'd had with the mayor about Phillip's murder and the one after that, when he quit his job. He remembered the moment when he stood in front of his apartment door and noticed the gun in the boy's hoodie. He remembered the sound of gunfire. He vividly recalled sitting slumped on his bedroom floor, filled with terror and clutching his bloody shoulder, wondering if he was about to die alone.

"Not now. Not now. Not now!" he whispered to himself, trying to push those memories out of his head.

Jamal wanted to escape. His eyes kept darting toward the door on the other side of the meeting room, but he knew if he stood now, the mayor would see him.

The woman beside him gave him another nervous glance and eased a few inches away.

Jamal closed his eyes. He counted to ten, then fifty, then hundred, willing himself to keep his ass in his chair. Finally, he heard applause. Jamal opened his eyes and saw the mayor walk away from the podium. The tightness around Jamal's chest finally loosened. He could breathe again.

A few minutes later, the audience began to stand from

their chairs. The speakers began to make their way around the room, shaking hands and having conversations with attendees.

Jamal watched as the mayor whispered something to one of the department heads before walking off. He headed to the side door with one of the assistants trailing behind him.

Jamal quickly made his way through the crowd, excusing himself and shoving someone aside when they didn't move fast enough. A few muttered at him angrily, chastising him for his rudeness, but he didn't care. He couldn't let Johnson get away.

He reached the back door, pressed the button on his phone to record, and shoved the door open in just enough time to see the mayor reach the end of the corridor.

His anxiety and fear finally subsided. He felt fury more than anything else at that moment.

"Johnson!" he shouted.

The older man whipped around and stared at him in surprise. When Jamal drew closer, Mayor Johnson broke into a grin. "Why, Jamal, I haven't seen you in a while. How have you been?"

"You know how the fuck I've been." Jamal narrowed his eyes. "And you haven't seen me because you banned me from city hall."

"Well, you have to admit that you didn't leave under the best circumstances. I'm not a fan of confrontations with disgruntled former employees."

"So much so that you tried to get rid of me? I would've expected some big goon to come after me, not a teenager. You're sending kids to do your dirty work now?"

Mayor Johnson's grin abruptly disappeared. "Uh, Brian," he said to the assistant who was now squinting in confusion, "why don't you wait for me downstairs? I need to talk to Mr. Lighty for a bit."

The young man nodded before making a hasty retreat into the stairwell. They listened to his heavy footfalls as he walked down the stairs. Mayor Johnson then took a step toward Jamal.

"I heard about your mishap," he said, glancing at Jamal's sling. "That was very unfortunate. But I'm happy they caught the young man who did it—*and* you survived. Problem solved. You should be happy."

"I'm not happy. They didn't catch everybody involved. Before he did it, he told me had no choice. You *and* Dolla put him up to that shit."

The mayor shook his head. "I don't know what you're talking about, Jamal. Obviously, the shooting has made you paranoid. You really believe I was involved in some conspiracy with a seventeen-year-old to shoot you?" He tutted. "You should see a psychiatrist for that."

"You know what you did. You did the same thing to me that you did to Phillip Seymour, but I lived. Phil didn't. You had him killed, like you tried to have me killed."

The mayor's nostrils flared. "I'd be very careful with slanderous allegations like that, Jamal."

"It's not slander. It's the truth."

"Even if it was true, you'd be just as guilty as I am if you knew who killed him and all this time, you didn't tell the police."

"What makes you think I haven't?" Jamal said, inclining his head.

"Because if you had and the cops believed you, I'd be arrested by now." Johnson took another step toward him so that they were almost chest to chest. "And because you'd know that the first bullet may not have killed you, but the second one will if you cross me again," he said through gritted teeth, poking Jamal in the shoulder not far from his bullet wound.

Jamal winced in pain.

The mayor stepped back and smiled again. "Glad to see you again. You take care of yourself!"

He slapped his shoulder, making Jamal wince once more.

Jamal watched him as he walked down the hall and opened the door. When he slammed the door shut, Jamal pulled out his cell phone and pressed the button to end the recording. He hoped this time, it would be enough.

Chapter 14

Ricky

Ricky strode down the carpeted corridor, keeping his eyes locked on the door at the end of the hall that led to the penthouse suite. He'd made this trek dozens of times in the past year, but for the first time he wasn't tense or nervous. He was completely relaxed, with a laser-like focus on the task at hand.

He was headed for his first meeting with Dolla Dolla since he'd arrived back in D.C. Detectives Ramsey and Dominguez had given him his marching orders only an hour before.

"We want names. The names of his contacts. The names of the folks he's in business with," Ramsey had said to him. "That's the deal."

"We held up our end of the bargain by getting your girl and your kid outta here," Dominguez had argued. "It's about fuckin' time you held up yours. It's been damn near a year. Get the job done!"

But Ricky was less concerned with getting the job done than doing whatever he had to do to get back to Simone and Miles, to get back to his family—a word he'd never thought he'd be able to use again after his grandmother's and his sister Desiree's deaths.

He thought about Simone and Miles all day and every night. He wondered if Miles was still cross-eyed. The doctor had said it was normal and Miles's eye muscles would eventually get stronger, but Ricky had been eagerly anticipating when his son could finally focus on his face when he spoke to him. Ricky wondered how Simone was making it through the late-night feedings alone. He still woke up at two a.m. like clockwork, a habit he'd developed so he could sit up with her and rock Miles back to sleep after she finished breastfeeding. Now when he woke up at that time, he was in bed alone. He'd stare at the ceiling until he fell back to sleep.

He missed them. He missed them so much it hurt, but he knew he was here to protect them. He was here to finally make all of this come to an end.

He adjusted his leather jacket and knocked on the door. When it swung open, he painted on a broad smile. "Hey, what's up?" he said to the hulking bodyguard who eyed him warily.

"What's up?" the guard murmured, gesturing for him to step inside.

Ricky took off his jacket and removed his phone. He faced the foyer wall and spread his legs, accepting the pat-down.

"Who dat?" he heard Dolla Dolla boom from the living room. He sounded irritated.

For the first time since arriving, Ricky's pulse quickened. A bead of sweat formed on his brow. He had to put on a performance—a good one.

"It's me—Ricky," Ricky called back, forcing levity into his voice.

The bodyguard gave him a nod and Ricky turned away from the wall. He strolled into the sunken living room where Dolla Dolla sat on the leather sofa. He had a glass in one hand and a cigar in the other. A plume of smoke snaked from his dark mouth like a serpent's tongue. Even sitting, he seemed more massive than his bodyguard.

Seeing him in person again, Ricky felt no fear or anxiety, only pure hatred. Ricky wanted vengeance. He wanted Dolla Dolla to pay for what he'd done to Simone's little sister and her mother, for all the other women he'd killed. If it meant putting on a front and Ricky lying through his teeth, so be it.

"I heard you been lookin' for me," Ricky joked.

"Yeah, I've been lookin' for your ass! Where the fuck you been?" Dolla Dolla snarled. "I been callin' and textin' your ass for weeks! You know I don't like havin' to chase a nigga down."

Ricky waited a beat. He had come prepared with a lie, but he had to make it believable.

"Yeah, I was out of town. I couldn't tell anybody because I'd be in violation of my release." He shrugged and lowered himself into one of the armchairs facing the sofa. "You know how it is."

"Out of town doin' what though?" Dolla Dolla persisted. "It's too much shit goin' on for niggas to be just disappearin'! You rush outta here one night like your damn feet are on fire, you ghost me for days, and then don't show up for weeks even when I tell you to bring your ass here. Where the fuck you been?"

Dolla Dolla was suspicious of him, of everyone around him. Ricky wasn't surprised. The man was working overtime to silence all of his "enemies," but he still suspected more of them were out there. Fortunately for Ricky, his suspicions were right; he did still have people in his inner circle conspiring against him. Unfortunately, Dolla Dolla didn't realize one of those people was sitting right across from him.

"I was in Miami," Ricky said. "I was helping a friend set up his strip club down there."

Dolla Dolla's scowl didn't soften. "A *strip club*? This is the first time I'm hearin' about this shit. What strip club?"

"I told you I couldn't tell anybody or I'd be thrown back in jail if the cops found out."

"Nigga, do it look like I be talking to cops? What the fuck would I have to say to them?"

"Dolla, come on! I was just trying to make some money. I was down there helpin' him set up operations, auditioning girls . . . you know how it is. It was an easy twenty stacks." He casually waved his hand. "Sorry I disappeared like that, but I needed the cash. I told you that months ago. I still got bills to pay . . . my car note . . . my rent. That don't stop now that Club Majesty and my restaurant are gone."

Dolla Dolla began to roll his cigar between his thumb and forefinger, studying Ricky as he did it. "So why you ain't tell me where you went? Why didn't you say you were back in town?"

"Because I knew I'd be comin' straight here. I knew you'd be lookin' for me." Ricky leaned forward and rested his elbows on his knees. He gazed into Dolla Dolla's heavy-lidded eyes. "Look, you ain't gotta worry about me. It's me—Pretty Ricky! I'm your nigga! *Remember?* I've had your back since I was fourteen years old. I got you."

Dolla Dolla studied him for a few seconds longer. Finally, he lowered his cigar back into the ashtray on his coffee table. His glower disappeared and his face relaxed.

"Yeah, I know you got me," Dolla Dolla muttered. "Shit's just been crazy around here. And you ain't the only one cash-strapped. I've been payin' lawyers out the ass since I got these charges." He cocked his head. "You know, I got a line on some easy cash, if you're interested."

Ricky nodded eagerly. "I'm always ready for some easy cash. You know that. What you got?"

Dolla Dolla gradually smiled. "I got a dude. He wants to start his own business too . . . an operation around here. He wants me to be his partner because I know how to do it, but it's too hot for me right now. The cops are watchin' me. I know they are. If I'm gonna do this, I gotta keep it on the low—and I'll need your help. You can get good money from it. No doubt."

"I'm down. What you need me to do?"

Dolla Dolla took a sip from his glass. "You keep in touch with the girls from Club Majesty?"

Ricky nodded. "Yeah, a few. Why? You thinkin' about opening another club?"

"Nah, I ain't doing that shit again." Dolla Dolla sucked his teeth and waved off the idea with a flick of his fat hand. "I'd have to find a new space. Get a liquor license, and the city would never approve that shit. I was thinking of a different type of operation this time. It'd be a way for the girls to make a little cash on the side and we could all collect a percentage. You used to have some bad bitches at Club Majesty. They used to make good money, too. I bet some of them are hurtin' right now. They probably wouldn't say no to makin' a couple stacks for two or three hours of work, if you get what I mean."

Ricky's stomach plummeted. So Dolla Dolla was getting back into the sex trade. He was going to start pimping out girls again. He had already mowed down his first crop

and now he wanted to grow another. And for some reason, Dolla Dolla believed Ricky would offer up the young
women who had worked for him, who had trusted him for
five years at Club Majesty, even though he was aware that
Ricky knew what had happened to all the previous girls.

He thinks I'm as fucked up as he is, Ricky thought.
Jokes on you, you fat motherfucka!

He could make up an excuse not to participate in Dolla
Dolla's new "enterprise," but this offered the chance that
Ricky had been waiting for—a chance to finally meet one
of Dolla Dolla's contacts.

Ricky pretended to contemplate Dolla Dolla's question,
pursing his lips. "I can think of a couple girls who might
be up for it. They might know a few more. I gotta talk to
them though."

"You do that." Dolla Dolla took another drink from
his glass. "Let me know if they're down. I'll let my partner
know. We'll set somethin' up."

Ricky eased back in his chair. "So do I get to meet this
partner?"

Dolla Dolla eyed him again. "Why do you need to
meet him?"

"Well, I'm very protective of my girls, Dolla. I mean I
trust you," Ricky rushed to say, "but I don't know this
dude. How do I know if he's gonna treat 'em right?"

"He'll treat them fine. You ain't gotta worry about it.
Just be happy you gettin' a cut of the money and leave it at
that. You feel me?"

"Still," Ricky persisted, "I'd feel better if I was there
when the girls met him. I bet they're more likely to trust
him if I give him the okay. I know how they are."

Ricky watched as irritation rippled across Dolla Dolla's
dark face, but the kingpin sucked his teeth again. "Shit

then! Damn! You can meet him. But these bitches better look they best when they come up in here. I mean it! Don't have them lookin' busted and raggedy, Ricky! Don't fuck up my reputation."

Ricky laughed and shook his head. "I wouldn't do that to you, Dolla. I got it covered. Don't worry."

"You better, nigga," Dolla Dolla grumbled. "You better!"

Chapter 15

Derrick

"Hey! Am I interrupting anything?" Morgan asked.

Derrick looked up from his laptop and found her gazing at him from his office doorway. She shoved her hands into the pockets of her sawdust-stained overalls and cocked her head.

"Can we talk?" she asked.

He closed the lid of his laptop. "Uh, yeah, we can talk. I was about to shut down for the day anyway. Come in. Have a seat."

Derrick watched as she stepped into his office and shut the door behind her. His ex, Morgan, sat down in one of the chairs facing his desk and looked down at her hands, which were clasped in her lap. She refused to meet his gaze.

He guessed from her facial expression and body language that she wasn't interested in discussing them making up and finally putting everything he'd said and done that painful night more than a month ago behind them. She wasn't going to do it today or tomorrow or the day after that. He grudgingly realized that now. Morgan probably wanted to finalize when she would pick up the last of her things. He knew how this worked. He'd made similar arrangements with Melissa when she moved out.

I'm an old pro at it by now, he thought sarcastically.

"So," she whispered.

"So," he echoed.

"I don't know how to say this," she began. "It's hard to find the right words."

"Sometimes it's better to just . . . you know . . . say whatever you have to say."

Just pull off the Band-Aid, he thought resignedly. *Do it quick.*

"I wanted . . . I wanted to put in my notice." She finally looked up from her hands. "I wanted to tell you that I'm leaving."

"*You're leaving?* You mean the Institute? So you're quitting?"

She hesitated, then nodded.

"Oh, come on! Baby, why would you—"

"Don't call me baby," she said tightly. Her gaze hardened. "Don't you *ever* call me baby again. Understand?"

"Okay, I'm sorry." He held up his hands and loudly exhaled. "I didn't mean to call you that. It's just a . . . a force of habit. I didn't mean anything by it."

She didn't respond.

"Is that the reason why you're quitting? Because of us? Because of *me?*"

She glared at him. "It's not always about you, Derrick."

In less than five minutes, he had already tripped over two verbal landmines and pissed her off.

Man, this is not going well.

"I never said it was always about me. I just said—"

"You never said it, but you never had to. *Your* needs

and *your* wants and *your* emotions are always what's most important to you. Everything else could be damned—including me."

Derrick closed his eyes and gritted his teeth. He guessed he deserved this. She had forgiven him once and taken him back and he had broken her heart all over again. But still, the way she was characterizing things didn't seem fair. He had tried. He had been willing to become a better man, a better partner this this time around. Did one night negate all of that?

But he wasn't going to argue with her. He'd done enough arguing. This time, he would listen and keep his mouth shut.

"You're selfish," she continued. "I thought you were ready to try to make this work, but I know now that you're not ready and I'm not gonna wait around anymore to see if you'll ever be."

He opened his eyes again. "Well," he began calmly, fighting down his frustration, "if what happened with us isn't the reason why you're quitting, then what's the reason?"

Her face softened. She unlocked her hands. "I just don't feel like I'm making a difference here. I'm not accomplishing anything."

"Of course, you're making a difference! The kids love you. You're one of our highest-rated instructors."

"So I win a popularity contest. So what?" She shrugged. "So a few boys think it's fun that I can show them how to build a shelf, or they get to make jokes while they stare at my ass all day. That doesn't mean I'm helping them, Derrick. It doesn't mean I'm accomplishing anything for them in the long term."

He pursed his lips. "Is this about Cole? Is that what all this soul searching and questioning is about?"

He had noticed that she still hadn't gone to visit the boy, even though he'd told her that Cole had asked for her. When Derrick had asked her why she refused to go to the jail, she'd been elusive. She said she would go eventually, but he wondered if that was true. He wondered if she was avoiding seeing Cole because of what he'd suspected all along: She couldn't stand to see the boy in handcuffs and his dull gray jumpsuit. She couldn't stand to see a boy who held so much promise now behind bars.

"Bae . . . I mean, Morgan," he said, quickly correcting himself. "I'll be real with you. There's nothing else you could've done to save Cole from his situation. You tried your best. I tried my best. We couldn't—"

"No, we didn't." She shook her head. "We didn't try our best. We didn't do all we could. We said we would work to get him out of there. We said we would do everything in our power to help him and his mom relocate so that he could get away from that guy, and we didn't."

"So you're blaming yourself? You're blaming us?"

She didn't respond, making him loudly sigh.

"Morgan, Cole had to finish out his sentence here at the Institute either way. He couldn't just pick up stakes and leave. And if he was having problems again, he should've told us. Instead, he chose to sneak out of the school and handle it himself. And look where that got him!"

"I get what you're saying, but I still feel like I've let him down. And I can't watch another boy go down that path. I can't do it."

"But not all of them will! I could've ended up just like Cole, but I came here when I was twelve and this place changed me from the inside out. For plenty of boys, it'll change them, too."

"Maybe. Maybe not." She looked away from him again. "Call me selfish. Call me a coward. I don't care. But I can't do this shit anymore, Dee."

Derrick was gripped with panic. Not only was he losing her romantically, but if she left the Institute, she would disappear from his life completely. He didn't know if he could handle that.

"I understand that you're upset. I get it! But maybe you should think about this a little longer. You don't want to—"

"I've made my decision," she said, cutting him off and rising to her feet. "I'm telling you that I'm done."

"So you're just gonna up and leave? Just like that? You told me how hard it was to find a job after you left that co-operative," he argued, trying not to sound desperate. "How are you going to find another job in less than a month?"

"I'm moving back to Atlanta. One of my girls said I can stay with her until I get back on my feet. I'll try to find a job down there."

His shoulders sank.

So she was leaving him, leaving the Institute, and moving six hundred miles away. This was getting dismal.

"I don't want to leave you high and dry, so I suggest you post a job ad for my replacement now," Morgan said. "I'll give you about a month to find someone else."

He watched helplessly as she walked to his office door, opened it, and stepped back into the hall, not giving him a chance to say anything else.

Thirty minutes later, Derrick stepped out the front door of the Institute. Once again, he was headed home to his lonely apartment. Tonight, he would likely eat dinner and drink a beer on the sofa, staring up at his flat-screen television, contemplating his life and his mistakes. That seemed to be his routine now. It was his own fault, a fate he'd condemned himself to. Though Morgan had assured him that he'd find someone new, that the loneliness would end eventually, he didn't know if it would. He didn't want anyone else. He didn't want to fall in love with another woman. He wanted Morgan, but he didn't know how he could convince her of that—not after everything that had happened. And it seemed that she was willing to travel hundreds of miles just to get away from him.

He dug into his back pocket to get his car keys and rounded the corner to head to the Institute's parking lot, but paused when he noticed a black SUV illegally parked along the curb. A skinny young man in a sweat-stained tank top and sagging jeans was leaning against the side of the SUV. A toothpick hung limply from his mouth. At his side stood two large men in white T-shirts. The fabric of their shirts seemed to strain to contain their bulging biceps and pecs.

When Derrick saw the trio, a chill ran over him. The chill didn't disappear even when the shortest one smiled at him.

"Wassup, man?" the young man said, pushing himself away from the SUV's hood, rolling the toothpick between his fingers. He strolled toward Derrick. "Your name Derrick Miller, right? You the head of this place?"

Derrick stared down at the young man and then glanced warily at his silent companions. They were both glowering at him. "Yeah. Can I help you?"

"Nah, you can't help me." The young man shook his head. His smile widened. "But I can help *you*, bruh. You just gotta do me a favor right quick."

"*A favor?*" Derrick frowned. "I don't do favors for people I don't know. Who are you?"

"Who I am don't matter." The young man flicked his toothpick onto the sidewalk. "The dude I work for is somebody you need to be careful of pissin' off though. You don't want to do that. Believe me!"

"And just who do you work for?" Derrick asked, though a small part of him already knew the answer to his question.

The young man inclined his head. "If Cole's been yappin' to you as much as we hear he's been doin', I bet you already know who I work for."

Shit, Derrick thought. So Cole had been right about his suspicions that he was being spied on by Dolla Dolla's men at the prison. But what had they heard? What did they know?

"So this is about Cole?"

"Nah, we got that handled. It's about your school. My boss likes what you got goin' on up here. He likes what you're doin' for the community and shit. He wanna help you out."

Derrick hadn't been expecting that answer. But it made him even more troubled. "Help me out how?"

"By donating to your establishment. In exchange, he wanna rent your facilities every now and then. He wouldn't need it all the time. Just to move stuff through once in a while. You'd get a monthly fee."

Now that his middle man was in jail, Dolla Dolla was going straight to the source; he was asking Derrick to take Cole's place and help him ferry his "product" through the Institute.

Goddamn, he's bold, Derrick thought. But he guessed Dolla Dolla didn't become a powerhouse in these streets from being timid.

"So what you think?" the young man persisted. "Sounds like a good deal to me."

A good deal?

The idea was unthinkable. Derrick wanted nothing to do with Dolla Dolla's criminal empire. It had already put Ricky in a tight spot, got Jamal shot, and dragged down Cole, but still, Derrick knew the risks that came with rejecting Dolla Dolla outright. He would not only put his life, but the lives of his students, at risk.

Derrick cleared his throat. "I gotta think about this. I can't . . . I can't say yes or no right away."

The young man's face changed. His smile disappeared. "Don't play games, nigga. It wastes time and my boss don't like to have his time wasted."

"I'm not playing games. I just . . . I just need time to think about this."

He really did. He didn't want to say yes because it would compromise everything he believed and professed to be, but he wasn't sure of the price he would pay if he said no.

The young man eyed Derrick a few seconds longer, then slowly nodded. "Fine. You think about that shit. But don't keep him waitin' too long." He then turned to the two large men who had been waiting patiently the whole time they were talking. "Come on. Let's go."

The trio swung open the SUV's doors and hopped inside. The young man climbed into the front passenger seat and lowered the tinted window to stare at Derrick.

"We'll come back! Make sure you have your answer when we do," he called to Derrick.

As soon as he did, the SUV pulled off with screeching tires.

Chapter 16

Jamal

Jamal heard the knock at his front door and paused from stirring the pan of Bolognese sauce. He felt a slight tightening in his chest at the noise, at the arrival of an unexpected visitor. It happened less and less nowadays—the panic attacks. But like his issues with Mayor Johnson, they still hadn't disappeared completely. He told himself the person at the door could be anybody. He reminded himself not to spiral. He took a few quick deep breaths to calm himself.

Jamal heard another knock. It was louder this time. He turned off the burner, lowered his spatula to the counter, and walked to the front door. When he stared through the peephole, he was shocked to see who was waiting for him on his welcome mat. Jamal whipped the door open and stared in disbelief.

"*Ricky?* What're you doing here, man?" he asked, smiling. He held out his hand for a dap.

He hadn't seen his boy in months, not since last year, in fact. They used to talk regularly and meet up once a week.

Seeing Ricky standing in front of him now reminded him how much he missed their friendship, the bond he, Ricky, and Derrick used to have. It made him once again regret that he had tossed it away so casually.

Ricky didn't answer him. He only glanced down at Jamal's extended hand, stepped around him, and stalked into his living room.

Jamal's smile disappeared. He frowned and closed his front door, now confused by Ricky's attitude.

"What's up? You pissed about somethin'?" Jamal asked him.

Rather than answer his question, Ricky asked his own. "You know you dead-ass wrong, right?"

"Dead-ass wrong about what?"

"You know what! Why would you start fuckin' Melissa, nigga? How could you do something like that to Dee? I knew you had changed, but I didn't know you changed *that* much."

Jamal loudly grumbled and rolled his eyes. "*Really?* We haven't spoken to each other in damn near a year and you came all the way here just to tell me that? You could've done it over the phone, or did you come here to punch me in the face like Dee did?"

"Answer the question!"

"*Why?*" Jamal yelled back before walking into his living room. "I don't have to justify myself to you, and I *damn sure* don't have to justify myself to Dee. He cheated on her! What he did broke her heart and humiliated her!"

"And that makes what you're doin' right? We were tight, Jay. We were like brothers!"

"Yeah, we were," Jamal said with a nod, "and that's why I kept my mouth shut and I didn't try anything with her for twenty goddamn years. Even though it ate me up inside every time he'd kiss her in front of me, or he'd complain about how fucking annoying she could be when he should've been happy just to have her! He got twenty years with Lissa, and he *still* fucked it up. That's on him, not me, Ricky."

"You're lyin' to yourself, bruh."

"No, I'm not! He's a selfish asshole. He did her wrong. You know he did!"

Ricky slowly shook his head. "He ain't the only selfish one."

"Oh, this is good." Jamal sucked his teeth in annoyance. "The self-proclaimed fuckboy is gonna give me a lecture on relationships and selfless behavior. Thanks but no thanks! I think I'll skip this one."

"Hey! Watch your mouth," Ricky said menacingly, pointing a finger at him. "I didn't come here to whup your ass, but I can still do it."

"Then whup my ass! Threaten me all you want. I'm not gonna apologize for hooking up with Lissa. So if that's what you came for, you might as well leave now."

Ricky let out a cold laugh. "You don't feel bad at all, do you? You're just standing there like you're the good guy . . . like you haven't done some really shady shit! You got some big-ass balls, man!"

"You don't know what really happened. You just know *his* side," Jamal insisted. "When Lissa told me she wasn't interested in me, I pulled back. We were just friends, just cool with each other. But you didn't see how bad off she was after they broke up, Ricky. She wasn't the same Lissa. She could burst into tears at the drop of a hat. She needed love and affection and she came *to me* for it. I didn't force myself on her. She said she needed me. I'm just giving her what she needs!"

"*What she needs?*" Ricky snorted and crossed his arms over his chest. "Yeah, okay, Jay. So that's what you're telling yourself. You trying to heal her with your dick?"

"Did you hear anything I said?" Jamal exploded, now beyond frustrated. "It's not just about giving her dick! I told you I love her. I'm *in* love with her, Ricky!"

Ricky went silent.

Jamal took a calming breath. "Look, I'm sorry that you feel I betrayed our clique. I guess I did." He shook his head. "No, *I know* I did. But I can't lie and tell you that I'm sorry for going after her, 'cuz I'm not. I love her, Ricky. I wanna . . . wanna make her happy."

Ricky was eyeing him now. "So you're not just tryin' to smash? This isn't just some petty shit to get back at Dee?"

"For the hundredth time—*no!* This has nothing to do with him!"

"So y'all are serious? Melissa's your girl now?"

"I didn't . . . didn't say that."

Ricky took a step toward him. He cocked an eyebrow. "Then what's all this talk about love and shit? If you two are together then—"

"We're not together," Jamal said tersely. "I feel that way about her but . . . but I don't know if she feels the same about . . . about me."

To his surprise, Ricky began to laugh again. Hearty and loud. It sounded like booming thunder in his quiet living room, making his frown deepen.

"What the fuck is so funny?"

Ricky finally stopped laughing. "I'm sorry but . . . let me get this straight . . . it's not just about ass for you because you love her, but you don't know if she's using you just for dick?"

"I didn't say she was using me for dick," he argued,

feeling his insecurities flare up. "We have a . . . a bond now. We're friends—*close* friends. I confide in her; she confides in me."

"Yeah, close friends who fuck." Ricky uncrossed his arms. "Does she come to you, or you go to her?"

"What difference does it make?"

"Just answer the question, Jay! Who usually initiates? You or her?"

"She does, I guess. I can't always feel her mood, so I usually wait for her to . . . to make the first move."

Ricky winced. "Bruh, from all that you're saying . . . it sounds like you're just her side piece."

Jamal gritted his teeth.

He hated that Ricky was saying out loud the thought that had been lingering in the back of his mind for weeks now. It had been there a week ago when Melissa came to his place. He'd thought they'd have a romantic dinner, make love, and she'd spend the night. Instead, they had a quickie, she put on her clothes, promised she'd check in on him later, kissed him goodbye, and just left, leaving him thinking, *So that's it?*

He hated this feeling like he was in limbo, but whenever he was with her that was what he felt.

"Fuck you, Ricky," he said sullenly.

Ricky held up his hands. "Hey, I'm not saying that to mess with you! I'm just tryin' to keep it one hundred. I know how you get with women, Jay. You never take shit casually. But if you're all in with Melissa, just make sure you ain't all in by yourself. I hate to see you get your feelings hurt."

Jamal inwardly winced but took a deep breath, plastering on a casual façade.

"Well, I'm sure Dee will be happy to hear that last bit.

Maybe it'll make him feel better about all of this." He then gestured toward his front door. "It was nice seeing you, but now that you chewed my ass out, I guess you wanna—"

"I didn't just come here to talk about that, nigga. I came to talk to you about other shit, too, but I wanted to get that out the way first."

"What other shit?"

"I've been out of town for a while. Got back a few weeks ago. I heard a lot of mess went down while I was gone. I heard you went full 50 Cent and got shot."

"Of course, you would make a joke about me getting shot." Jamal pursed his lips in exasperation. "How'd you find out?"

"Dee told me. He knows the kid who did it. He said the kid used to work for Dolla."

"Yeah, Dolla did it as a favor for the mayor, I bet. That son of a bitch wanted me dead. I bet he still does. I told the cops as much, but they didn't believe me."

"Why not?"

"Because the kid is an easy person to blame, and dragging in Mayor Johnson makes it too messy. I even gave them proof, a recorded conversation where he threatened me *again*, but the cops said it wasn't enough. They need something more concrete. Whatever the fuck that means," Jamal grumbled. "Short of Johnson putting another bullet in my ass, I don't know what else to give them as proof that he's involved in this."

Ricky inclined his head. "Maybe I can help you with that."

"What do you mean?"

"Get him in a convo with Dolla. Get the proof you need. Proof so good the cops couldn't deny it."

Jamal was touched by Ricky's offer. It reminded him of

how Ricky had always had his back in the old days. Whether they were mad at each other was irrelevant; his boys would always hold him down when things went bad. But he couldn't let Ricky do it this time. Ricky would be risking too much.

Jamal shook his head. "I can't do that to you, man. If I got shot, I can only imagine what could happen to you if you got involved in this. I just have to—"

"Nigga, I'm already involved in it. I'm knee-deep in this shit. Me sinking in another few inches ain't gonna make much of a damn difference, especially if it can help you."

"But you'd be working with cops. You'd be handing over info to them and—"

"Yeah, I'm on a first-name basis with some of those motherfuckas." Ricky shoved his hands into his jacket pockets. "Trust me. The Metro PD knows me well. I'm practically on their payroll."

Jamal stared at him in shock. "Since when?"

"Since last year when I got arrested during the raids."

"So what are you saying? You work for the cops now?"

"I'm saying I could help you. It's not that complicated. Just tell me what you need."

Jamal stared at Ricky for a long time, not saying anything. "You said I've changed, but you've changed, too. There's something different about you."

"What do you mean?"

"I don't know." Jamal looked him up and down, taking in his stance and facial expression. Ricky looked the same on the surface—same clothes, same beard, same devil-may-care attitude, but a new subtext was there.

"I can't figure it out," Jamal muttered. "But it's like . . . it's like your bullshit shield is gone."

"*Bullshit shield?*" Ricky barked out a laugh.

"You carry yourself differently. It's like . . . It's like . . .

the Pretty Ricky persona isn't there anymore." He shook his head again. "What the hell's been going on with you? What did I miss this past year?"

Ricky smiled. "A lot. I'll fill you in after you go in that fridge of yours," he said, pointing to the kitchen, "and get me a beer. I know you got one."

Jamal laughed and nodded. "Beer coming up."

Chapter 17

Ricky

"So why'd you call us?" Ramsey asked as he pressed the accelerator and the unmarked Ford sedan lurched forward into busy afternoon traffic.

"That's all I get?" Ricky snapped, slumping into the back seat. "*Why'd you call us?* No 'Hello, Ricky!'? No 'How you been?'"

"Stop fuckin' around and just answer the question! Did you finally get us what we need or not?" Dominguez said over his shoulder from the front passenger seat. "We don't got all day!"

Ricky was accustomed to Detective Dominguez's rudeness now. It no longer annoyed or infuriated him. He could dismiss Dominguez like a guard dog that snapped and growled from behind a chain-link fence, because he knew Dominguez was all bark and snarl, but as long as that fence was up, he was no bite. The detective could do nothing to him—at least, for now. So Ricky laughed again and took his sweet time in answering their questions.

He'd called them after his meeting with Dolla Dolla two days ago and told them he had news. This time *he* was the one summoning *them* to some random street corner to meet up to talk. This time they were the ones who had no clue what was going on.

"I met up with Dolla. He was talking about getting into the pimp game again. He has a partner he wants to start up with. He asked me for my help," Ricky said.

"Why the hell would he want your help with that?" Dominguez asked. "He knows something about you that we don't know? When were you pimping out girls?"

"Don't even joke about that shit," Ricky said with a curl in his lip. "What he did to those girls, I would never, *ever* do. I don't care what the fuck he thinks."

"So why does he want your help, Ricky?" Ramsey persisted.

"Because I used to manage Club Majesty. He knows the girls there who used to work for me still trust me, and I might be able to talk them into doing some shady shit."

"And he wants you to meet his partner?" Ramsey repeated. "The guy who'll actually handle this escort service?"

"Yeah, I was waiting for y'all to catch on to that part."

"Shit! Finally! It took you long enough to net one of his contacts." Dominguez turned completely around in the passenger seat, looking more eager than a kid on Christmas morning. "So who is he? What's his name?"

"Don't know yet. I'm supposed to meet him in about a week when I dig up some girls."

"So get to crackin'! Bring him some of your hoes so we can find out who the hell his partner is!" Dominguez ordered.

Ricky told himself not to let his anger flare up at Dominguez. The man's default was to be as irritating as jock itch, but he couldn't let a comment like that slide. He had to set him straight.

"First of all," he began through clenched teeth, "the

women who worked for me were dancers, not hoes. I ran
a strip club, not a goddamn brothel. I told you more than
once—I'm not a fuckin' pimp, so stop acting like I am!"

"Okay. Okay, calm down, Ricky," Ramsey said, holding up a hand from the steering wheel. "He didn't mean
anything by that."

"And secondly," Ricky continued, "I'm not handing over
another woman I know to that motherfucka, even if I'm just
faking it. I've seen what he does to women. I couldn't look
myself in the mirror again if I did."

"Well, if you aren't gonna bring him girls from your
club, then how are you supposed to meet his partner? I
thought that's what you told him you'd do. I thought that
was the deal," Ramsey said, leaning over to glance at him
in the rearview mirror as he drove. "I'm confused."

"Oh, I'll bring him girls—just not the ones he thinks
I'm bringin' him." He adjusted his seat belt. "That's where
you two come in."

Now both Ramsey and Dominguez were squinting in
confusion. They exchanged a look.

"We don't look too convincing in wigs, Ricky," Ramsey
deadpanned.

"Funny. No, I need cops . . . two *female* cops who
could pass for dancers. And they gotta look good. I mean
nice faces . . . bomb bodies . . . At Club Majesty, we were
very particular about our dancers. These can't be average
chicks. I mean some bad bitches, you understand? They
can pretend to be my girls, but they can't wear any recording devices. Dolla's men will find whatever mikes they're
wearing if they do."

"Wait, even if we can get two undercover cops to do it,
won't Dolla know that these women didn't work at your
club?" Ramsey asked.

"Yeah, wouldn't he realize he's never seen these chicks
before?" Dominguez chimed in.

Ricky shook his head. "No, because I was responsible for hiring all the girls at Club Majesty. He didn't know who the fuck they were. He didn't care! And the few times he showed up at the club in person, he was either high or drunk. He wouldn't remember them either way. Don't worry. As long as they look good, he won't ask too many questions."

Both men fell silent in the front seat and Ricky started to wonder if they were going to tell him no. If they did, he didn't know how he was going to pull this off, but to his relief Ramsey eventually nodded.

"All right. All right," Ramsey said. "We'll set it up. We'll talk to the lieutenant and see what we can do . . . who we can get, but we may need a little more time than a week."

"Just make sure it ain't much longer than that," Ricky said, "or his partner may not want to wait that long."

"We won't," Ramsey assured him. "This moves to the top of our list. Don't worry."

"Good," Ricky said. "And while y'all are working on that, I've got something else I need from you."

"I'm sorry. Did you mistake us for Santa Claus and his reindeer?" Dominguez asked sarcastically. "Or maybe you thought we were a genie in a lamp that grants wishes." Dominguez rolled his eyes. "Can you believe this guy?" he asked Ramsey, who seemed to be pointedly ignoring him.

"What do you need, Ricky?" Ramsey asked.

"A mike that I can use with my phone to record. It has to be one that I can hide though."

"I thought you said you can't bring any mikes around Dolla," Dominguez said. "You told us his bodyguards might find them."

"This ain't for Dolla. It's for something else . . . *some-one* else."

"For what? For who?" Dominguez pestered, maddening Ricky even more.

"Don't worry about it. Just get it!"

"Ricky," Ramsey began. "We can't just lend out recording equipment. If we're going to collect surveillance, we need a warrant. We need—"

"No, you don't," Ricky interrupted. "Y'all find a way around that shit when you need to. This time is no different. Besides, the info I'm gonna collect, you'll be able to use later against Dolla. Just give me what I need to get it done."

"Great! Well, is there anything else you need, Mr. Reynaud? Anything else we can get you?" Dominguez asked dryly. "Would you like us to take you to lunch? Do you need us to pick up your laundry, too?"

"Nah, I'm good." Ricky gave an icy smile. "But you can drop me off on the corner over there. I'll walk back to my car."

When the Ford Taurus pulled to a stop, Ricky threw open the door and hopped out.

"Well, stay in touch and we'll get you what you need," Ramsey said as Ricky slammed the door closed.

"I bet you will," Ricky muttered as he watched the car pull off. He took a quick glance around him and then walked down the block in the other direction.

Chapter 18

Derrick

Derrick hesitated before knocking on the screen door. He glanced over his shoulder at the pristine lawn and cluttered screened-in porch and contemplated heading back to his car. He knew he shouldn't be here. He'd be lucky if the door wasn't slammed in his face as soon as the person inside realized who had been knocking. Or maybe they wouldn't open the door at all. But he had no other option; he desperately needed advice, and this was the only place he could get it. This was the only person whose advice he trusted without question.

He knocked and shoved his hands into his jeans pockets. He soon heard the sound of a dog barking. He then heard the click of claws against hardwood and the rhythmic thump of heavy footsteps approaching.

"Otis! Otis! Stop makin' all that damn noise! It's just the door," Mr. Theo, Melissa's father, said to his Labrador as he swung the front door open. He peered through the metal screen and saw Derrick standing on his welcome mat. When he did, a scowl settled onto his dark, wrinkled face.

"Uh, hey, Mr. Theo," Derrick said awkwardly. "How are you doin', sir?"

He hadn't called him *sir* in years, probably not since the early days when he'd arrived at the Institute for his assault charge. Mr. Theo, the then director of the Institute, had seemed like yet another authority figure who was there to boss him around, to knock him down with his hands or his words if he got out of line. It would take them months to build trust and a relationship that wasn't so tentative or formal back then. But now, after his nasty breakup with Melissa, his relationship with her father felt stilted and formal again.

"What you doin' here, Dee?" Mr. Theo asked, shoving his barking dog aside.

"I just came here to talk to you. I had something I wanted to—"

"I'm sorry, but I ain't got nothin' to say to you. You broke my baby girl's heart. That's not somethin' I take lightly."

Derrick lowered his gaze to his feet. "I know. I didn't want to break her heart. That wasn't my intention."

"But it's what you did." He pointed at him. "I warned you. I warned you about having your cake and eatin' it, too. But you didn't listen. You stood in my house . . . in my own damn kitchen and lied to me. You told me I had nothin' to worry about. You said *whatever* you had goin' on with that girl at the Institute you had ended it. You said you had it covered."

"And I really thought I did. I thought I had it all covered. I thought I had it all fixed, but I didn't. That's obvious now. I still don't have it covered and *nothing* is fixed. That's . . . that's why I'm here."

Mr. Theo eyed him warily, but he didn't slam the door in his face. That was a small relief.

"What are you talking about, Dee?" the older man

said. "You're not comin' here to try to convince me to help you to get Lissa back, are you? I hope that ain't it, because I don't think—"

"No, Mr. Theo." Derrick shook his head. "She and I are done. I've accepted that."

"So why are you here?"

"Everything is falling apart, and it's not just my personal life. It's at the Institute, too. One of my boys . . . one of my boys was arrested for attempted murder. He tried to kill Jay."

"*What?*" Mr. Theo cried. "Lucas and I sent Jay flowers and a card when he was in the hospital, but I didn't know the boy that shot him went to the Institute."

"Yeah, well, believe it or not, that boy is mixed up in bigger things than just the shooting—and now he's gotten me and the Institute tangled up in it, too. I don't know what to do. All the choices I have seem like bad ones and I . . . I just . . ."

Derrick stopped talking and slowly raised his eyes when he heard the screen door creak open. Mr. Theo waved him inside.

"Come on. Ain't no point having a conversation like this on my front porch. Not something this big." He glanced down at his Labrador. "Go on and have a seat in the dining room while I put the dog in the backyard where he can run around and make all the damn noise he wants."

"It's probably a little early for a drink," Mr. Theo said a few minutes later as he walked into the dining room with two cold beers, "but we'll just tell ourselves it's nighttime somewhere. Maybe in London. Here you go."

Derrick smiled and took the beer Mr. Theo offered to him. "Thanks."

Mr. Theo pulled out a chair on the opposite side of the oak table and sat down.

"I'm out of Michelob," he said as he twisted off the beer bottle's lid. "All we got is this orange-flavored shit that Lucas likes. I think it tastes too much like soda, but it'll work in a pinch."

Derrick twisted off his lid, too, and took a drink. Mr. Theo was right. It did taste a lot like soda.

"Where is Lucas?" Derrick asked.

Lucas was Mr. Theo's boyfriend. They had become a couple not too long after Mr. Theo came out of the closet and he and his wife separated.

Mr. Theo lowered the bottle from his mouth. "Lucas is with his mama. They go shopping about once a week."

"You didn't want to go with them?"

"Oh, hell no!" Mr. Theo said with a chuckle before taking another drink. "I wouldn't want them dragging me around shopping malls all day, while I carried their bags like some bellhop. Besides"—he inclined his head—"his mama is still a little uncomfortable around me. It's been an adjustment for her like it was for Melissa. I don't want to push it by being all up in her face. It'll just . . . you know . . . take some time. That's what I tell Lucas. If my baby eventually got comfortable with the idea of me being with a man, his mama will have to get used to him being with one, too. Especially since he's been out a lot longer than me."

Derrick stared at his bottle label, at the smiling orange in sunglasses. "So Melissa is around more now?"

Mr. Theo nodded. "She stops by to have dinner with us twice a month. Sometimes she and Lucas cook dinner together. She hasn't brought anybody new with her, though I've been asking when she plans to get back out there. *You* moved on. She may as well, too."

Derrick looked up from the bottle label. He wondered why Melissa hadn't told her father about Jamal. From what he had witnessed at the hospital more than a month ago, the two seemed pretty hot and heavy. But maybe their relationship wasn't as serious as he'd thought. Maybe it had already fizzled out. But he guessed it wasn't his place to say anything to Mr. Theo about them. If Melissa had decided not to discuss her romantic life with her father, that was up to her.

"But you didn't come here to talk about Melissa," Mr. Theo said. "You said things at the Institute have gotten worse. How bad we talkin'?"

"*Real* bad," Derrick said.

He started from the beginning and told the story of when he discovered the two suitcases in the dormitory: one filled with cocaine, the other filled with money. He talked about how Cole had been working for Dolla Dolla and how he and Morgan had finally convinced him to stop doing it— or at least, they thought they had. But now that the boy was in prison and Dolla Dolla was sniffing around the Institute again, Derrick was pretty sure his assumptions had been all wrong.

"I don't know what to do," Derrick said when he finished his story. "I can't let him bring more of those suitcases in there. I don't want to have a damn thing to do with any of that shady shit. But if I tell him no, if I tell him I won't do it, I know there's a price to pay."

"So it sounds like you know what you gotta do, but you're scared to do it. You know what it will mean," Mr. Theo said. "You already know the price you'll have to pay, Dee."

"But I'm not just scared of what will happen to *me*. It's what will happen to the boys at the Institute and the teachers there if I don't go along with this. That has me really worried. If it was just me, I would take that stand and deal with the consequences." Derrick lowered his eyes. "But it's not just me. I've hurt a lot of people lately thinking about myself, thinking selfishly. I don't want to do that shit again."

Mr. Theo nodded. "But when you hurt other people in the past, it wasn't because you made a hard decision to keep them first in mind. You told yourself that, but the truth was, it was all about you, Dee. It was all about what *you* wanted and what you were trying to keep secret to protect yourself. Ain't that right?"

Derrick winced. Mr. Theo may be giving him a dose of the truth, but it was a bitter dose. It was also one he badly needed.

"This is different though, son. You really are trying to do right by everybody. I know that ain't an easy choice but I bet, deep down, you already know the choice you have to make."

Derrick hesitated, then nodded.

"And I support you in whatever you decide. You know that."

Derrick nodded solemnly. "Thank you, Mr. Theo. Thank you."

It was the little relief he could take, knowing what he would have to do in the near future.

Chapter 19

Jamal

"I feel like a failure," Melissa announced.

Jamal paused, stopping them mid-step on the sidewalk. He frowned at her.

They had just left the Cuban restaurant where they'd had dinner. She'd invited him out to eat after the disastrous job interview he'd had earlier that day. But even during the meal he couldn't stop replaying the interview in his mind: how he'd stumbled over answers to the simplest questions, how he'd fidgeted nervously in his chair. He could tell from the expression on the face of the interviewer at the law firm that he wasn't getting a callback.

It hadn't been a panic attack, just nerves, but he wondered if anxiety would always plague him now.

It had been well over a month since the shooting. The sling was finally gone and the scars would start to fade. Physically, he was getting closer to being back to his old self, but psychologically he still wasn't. Something told him that as long as things were unsettled with Mayor Johnson, his life would probably stay that way, too. Ricky said he would help him take care of it, but who knew how long that would take? Who knew if his friend would be able to follow through.

"Why do you feel like a failure?" he asked Melissa now.

"Because I've been trying all night to cheer you up and it's not working!" She linked her arm through his as they started walking again. "I'm out of ideas."

"Just hanging out with you cheers me up, Lissa. It always does."

She grinned and kissed his cheek, and suddenly, he did feel a bit better.

Jamal always did around her, no matter how dark his mood. Even before they started hooking up, even before they started hanging out all the time, he'd found it hard to be depressed when Melissa was around. No matter what seemed to be going haywire in his life, she was the one thing that always seemed right.

"You're sweet," she whispered, wiping her smudged lipstick off his cheek. "So what's next? Do you want to head to a movie? Maybe play some pool? It's not really my thing, but I'll try."

"Why would you play pool if it's not your thing?"

"Because I thought you liked to play pool! It's not that big of a deal. Plus, it might distract you . . . you know, cheer you up!"

He stopped again and faced her. "You're amazing, you know that?"

"Oh, here we go!" She laughed in exasperation. "Because I'm willing to play pool?"

"No! Because you . . . well, because you . . ."

"Because I what?"

He wanted to say so much, to confess everything he was feeling right now. It was hard to believe emotions he had harbored for years hadn't waned but had grown and gained even more depth. He wanted her. He loved her. But did she feel the same way? Could she?

"What?" she repeated.

Instead of responding, he brought his mouth to hers and kissed her, long and hard. When he pulled back a minute later, they were both gasping for air.

She laughed again. "Well, if you wanted to skip all that, you should've just said so." She cocked an eyebrow and gave him a quick peck. "Back to my place, it is."

Melissa gripped the headboard and threw back her head, shouting out his name. He loosened his hold on her bottom and fell back hard against the mattress when she collapsed on top of him. They both landed on the sheets in a big sweaty heap.

"Oh, damn!" she cried. "I'd say we should do that again, but it might kill me."

She gave him a sultry kiss.

He knew she was joking, but he was too high on euphoria to joke.

"I love you," Jamal whispered as soon as Melissa pulled her mouth away from his. He gazed up at her adoringly and ran his thumb along the plump bottom lip he'd been sucking on only seconds ago.

He couldn't keep his feelings inside anymore. He had to say the words. "I love you, Melissa, with every part of me."

She nipped his thumb playfully and laughed. "You get so sappy after sex."

He flinched, not because of the nip, but because of what she'd said. "*Sappy?* You think I'm . . . I'm sappy?"

"Not all the time! Just after we . . . you know." She rolled off of him, resting her head on the pillow beside his. Her smile disappeared as her eyes scanned over his face. "*What?* What's wrong?"

"Why do you think it's sappy for me to tell you I love you?"

She shrugged. "You're just in a mushy mood. It's the sex high. I get it!"

When he didn't reply, she leaned over and licked his shoulder. "Oh, come on. Lighten up, Jay!"

"Lighten up?" he repeated, narrowing his eyes. "Lighten up?"

He couldn't keep the hard edge out of his voice. Frankly, he didn't want to.

"I'm sorry. I know you're having a rough day. That sounded callous and I hadn't meant it to be. I was just saying I wasn't trying to make you feel bad. I noticed you always say I love you after we have sex, that's all. We'll forget about it though. We can move on."

"But I don't wanna move on, Lissa."

She frowned.

So they were finally going to have "the conversation."

Guess it's about time, he thought. *I've been avoiding it long enough.*

"Look, I don't . . . I don't tell you that I love you because of a 'sex high.' I really do love you." He turned onto his side, rested on his elbow, and gazed at her. "I got shot. *Remember?* I lost two pints of blood. I didn't think I was going to make it. When something like that happens, it makes you see the world differently. You see things clearer. When you almost *die,* you realize that you have to put aside all the bullshit. So I'm not gonna pretend that I don't feel what I feel—not anymore. Or that I'm only saying it because I'm drunk or hyped up from good sex. I *love* you, Melissa Stone. I have since I was twelve years old, and I hid it way longer than I should've." He pursed his lips and took a deep breath. "And I wanna know if you love me, too, or is this just a passing thing for you? Am I wasting my time?"

She loudly groaned and covered her eyes with her hands.

That was not the response he was hoping for.

"Shit! Bina warned me this might happen," she whispered.

"*What?*"

"My friend Bina. She said we shouldn't blur the lines, that it would only get confusing. But I told her we were okay. That we could handle it. Damn it, I thought we'd be okay!"

"Melissa, what are you talking about?"

"Don't do this to me. Don't corner me like this by telling me you love me! Don't ruin it, Jay. *Please?*"

"How is me professing my love to you 'ruining it'? What the hell does that mean?"

She removed her hands from her face and sat upright. He watched as she raised the bedsheets to cover her breasts. "I mean what we have is good. What we just did was *really* good! I enjoyed it. You did, too, right? I get that after you were shot, you decided to live life to the fullest. And I think you should! I do. Embrace it. But why complicate what we have? Why not just . . . enjoy life? Let's just be what we are, Jay. No more, no less. Let's just . . . you know . . . enjoy each other."

Enjoy each other?

Jamal was no longer offended; he was hurt. Ricky was right: Jamal was her side piece—no more, no less. Jamal had worried all along that Melissa didn't love him like he loved her, that she would never feel anything for him that was remotely close to what she'd felt for Derrick, her ex, but it was eviscerating to hear it out loud. He slowly rose from the mattress, pushed aside the sheets, threw his legs over the side of the bed, and climbed to his feet.

"Oh, come on, Jay!" she called after him as he stalked

across her bedroom to the en suite bath. "So now you're pissed at me? Now you're leaving?"

"Yeah, I'm leavin'," he muttered as he stepped onto the bathroom tile and removed the condom, tossing it into the wastebasket. He could barely hold up his head. He thought he'd felt like crap after the interview, but now he felt ten times worse. He was so ashamed and heartbroken. He felt like a cheap one-night stand. Like his condom, he had been used and discarded.

"But why?" she asked.

"You wanted some dick, and you got it. Now it's time for me to go!"

"Oh, stop it! Stop acting like this! You know you're more to me than just 'some dick'!" She climbed off the bed, wrapping the bedsheet around her. "You're my—"

"*Your homie?*" he shouted over his shoulder before lifting the toilet lid and seat, using the word she'd often jokingly called him. He started to pee. "Your friend? Your *side piece?*"

She furiously shook her head. "You're not gonna do this. Damnit, you are *not* gonna do this to me!" She stomped her foot. "You're not gonna make me feel bad for being honest with you. I never lied to you! Not once."

He finished and flushed. "No, you didn't. I will admit that," he said, turning to the sink to wash his hands.

"Jay, I was in a relationship for damn near two decades. We were engaged. I thought Dee and I were going to spend our lives together—and he cheated on me!"

"I'm not Dee, Lissa."

"I know. I know you're not! I'm just not ready to start another relationship. I'm gun-shy, okay? I'm not ready to tell someone that I love them or open up like that again. Not yet. The ache finally started to ease up. I don't wanna go back to the highs and the lows, and that hurt. That hurt sucked *so* much! I don't wanna go on that roller coaster ride again. It's nothing personal against you! It's just . . . I'm just . . ." Her words drifted off as he finished washing his hands. He turned to her.

He could tell from the desperation on her face that she wasn't trying to be cruel, that she really was trying to explain herself to him, maybe even to spare his feelings. It was one of the many traits that he loved about Melissa: how compassionate and thoughtful she was. But no matter what she said, she couldn't spare his feelings tonight. Her rejection still stung. She didn't understand that he was already on the very roller coaster ride she didn't want to be on. He was experiencing the highs and the lows of falling in love. She said she wasn't ready to try a relationship with someone else, but when would she be, and would that person ever be him?

Probably not, he realized.

"I get it," he said, now resigned to the truth. "I don't like it, but I get it."

She took a step toward him, then another. She took his wet hand, laced her fingers through his. "Then please let's just be friends."

"Friends who have sex," he said cynically.

"We can do that—or not. We can go back to the way things were before, if that's what you want. But I need a friend, Jay, not another man to fight with, cry over, or keep me up at night. I've been a good friend to you, right? I held you down, and I'll continue to. I'll support you in whatever you need, but . . . I'm just not here for a love thing. I'm sorry. That doesn't mean you're not important to me though, because you are! I care about you. I always will. That won't change!" She gazed into his eyes. "Trust me," she whispered.

She was saying all the right words, doing all the right things. Despite his misgivings and disappointment, desire flared up again. He wanted to kiss her. He wanted to tug her into his arms and make love to her again right against the bathroom wall. If she couldn't love him, at least he could fulfill his need for her. She was willing to grant him that. And she cared for him. He believed her when she said that.

But "care" wasn't the same as "love." Jamal wasn't lovesick enough to not realize how pitiful it all sounded, how sad it was that he was willing to take every little handout she gave him because he was so eager for a piece of her. But the truth was he wanted more from Melissa—much, *much* more. He wanted all she had to give because he was willing to give the same. Any less wouldn't do. She hadn't lied to him, but he had been lying to himself all this time. This unrequited love for Melissa Stone wasn't healthy. It was bordering on masochistic.

I can't do this anymore, he thought.

"And I'm sorry, but I have to go," he said, making her expression change. She looked disappointed as he tugged his hand out of her grasp and walked around her. "I have to get out of here."

She stood in the bathroom doorway as he gathered his clothes and put them back on. Five minutes later, he walked out of her apartment, unsure of when or if he would ever speak to Melissa again.

Chapter 20

Ricky

Ricky cocked an eyebrow as he watched the two under-cover cops in the elevator compartment. The blonde, whom he was supposed to call Vanessa, finger-combed her hair into place as the elevator ascended, checking her reflection in the gold-plated double doors. The buxom black one, who called herself Candy, leaned forward and shoved her hand into the lace cups of her bra. She lifted one breast then the other. She jiggled them around, making her caramel-hued skin quiver. When she was finished adjusting, she stood upright, smoothed down the front of her low-cut blouse, and met Ricky's assessing gaze.

"Can I help you?" Candy asked, glaring at him when she realized he'd been staring at her the whole time.

Ricky shook his head and stifled a laugh. "Nothin'. Don't worry about me, sis."

"I'm not your *sis*," Candy hissed. "And you look like you had somethin' to say. Go ahead and say it!"

This time he did laugh. "You're so worried about your tits, but you might wanna focus on that wig on your head instead. It's on crooked."

She frowned and glanced at her reflection. Her short auburn wig was off; it sat too far back from her brow by about a quarter of an inch, showing her real hairline. She shifted it forward and glanced at him again. "Good attention to detail," Candy mumbled. "Thanks."

"No prob," Ricky said. "Happy to help."

The elevator dinged and came to a halt. A few seconds later, the gold doors opened, revealing the cream-colored hallway leading to Dolla Dolla's apartment.

"It's showtime," Ricky whispered and then gestured toward the open doors. "Ladies first."

At those words, the undercover cops' demeanors changed. They pushed back their shoulders, painted on smiles, and strolled out of the elevator in front of him. He took a deep breath and followed them into the hall, letting the elevator doors close behind them.

When he'd met the two women a few hours ago, he hadn't been convinced that they were right for the job. One of them had come in wearing sweats and a baseball cap. The other looked like she'd just rolled out of bed and wore no makeup. Her hair had been in a sloppy bun. Seeing how they looked, he had pulled Detective Ramsey aside.

"You motherfuckas are tryin' to get me killed," he had whispered shrilly into the detective's ear. "If that was the case, you could've just shot me back in that field in Virginia. You didn't have to make me come back here!"

"What are you talking about?" Ramsey had asked.

"I mean what is this shit? I told you that they had to be some bad bitches, or Dolla would never believe they used to work for me. This ain't it, bruh!"

Ramsey had closed his eyes and held up his hand. "Don't worry. They clean up nice. They both have worked undercover vice as escorts. Just let them get dressed and put their faces on. You'll see."

Ricky had paced the room for a good hour, waiting for the magical transformation Ramsey had promised. When the women stepped out of the adjoining room in their full regalia, he had braced himself for disappointment. But he was pleasantly surprised.

"What I tell you?" Ramsey had whispered to him with a smile. "They clean up nice, don't they?"

Ricky now watched the women as they walked down the hall. The blonde stood at about six feet in her stilettos. She was all bust and no hips, but he could easily see himself hiring her to dance at Club Majesty. She would've gotten a decent share of tips. The black cop though was the real killer. She was all curves but with toned arms and legs. She also projected a saucy attitude that the male patrons would've loved at his old strip club. Her body and demeanor reminded him a lot of Simone when he'd first met her.

Simone . . .

At the thought of her, his heart tugged. It felt like a sharp stab to the chest. He wondered what Simone was doing right now. He wondered if she was eagerly waiting for him like he was waiting for her, counting down the days until their family would be together again. Or was she doing the opposite? Was she pushing him to the back of her mind and trying not to think about him because there was the possibility they might never see each other again? He didn't know how long this would take or if they would even be reunited in the end. Would she get tired of waiting for them to be reunited and just . . . move on?

Don't forget me, baby. I'm trying to get back to you, he thought desperately, hoping his words and devotion carried to her—wherever she was. *I'm trying my damnedest.*

When he and the undercover cops reached Dolla Dolla's door, the cops stepped aside to let Ricky ring the bell. He heard the chime, and a second later the door opened, revealing one of Dolla Dolla's bodyguards. The guard slowly looked both women up and down, leering at them openly.

"Pick your chin up off the floor," Ricky joked, leaning against the door frame. "Dolla in?"

The bodyguard nodded. "Yeah, he waiting for y'all in the living room."

"Cool," Ricky said, gesturing for the women to step through the doorway.

They began to stroll toward the foyer but paused when the bodyguard called out, "Hold up, y'all! I gotta pat you down."

The two women exchanged a look and laughed.

"Pat us down?" Vanessa asked. Her voice was light and playful. "I can't fit a gun underneath this dress, sweetheart."

"Me neither," Candy said with a giggle, gesturing to her low-cut blouse, obviously trying to distract him with the breasts she had so carefully put on display.

The bodyguard shook his head. "Sorry. I don't make the rules, girls. Face the wall."

Ricky noticed that both of them hesitated before walking to the textured wallpaper and placing their hands on it while spreading their legs. His heart rate started to kick up.

He had expressly asked them not to bring weapons or listening devices, no matter how small. They had pushed back on that one.

"If we're there to collect info to give to the D.A., how the hell do we document this if we can't record anything?" Vanessa had asked back at the deserted office building where they had gotten ready.

"We'll figure it out," Ramsey had assured her, "but what he says goes with this one. You can't bring a mike or a camera. It's too risky."

Vanessa had seemed annoyed at that answer. Ricky wondered now if she had ignored Ramsey and stashed something under her dress anyway. If she or Candy had, and the bodyguard found it, all hell would break loose. He was sure of it. And all the blame would fall on Ricky's shoulders.

Ricky now watched nervously as the bodyguard began to pat down Vanessa. He didn't do it as efficiently as he usually did Ricky's pat-downs. He lingered on the obvious spots— her breasts, inner thighs, and ass—making Vanessa roll her eyes. When he finished, he stood upright and nodded.

"You're good, baby," he said before heading to Candy. "You next."

Ricky watched as Vanessa stepped away and Candy spread her legs a few inches wider. She stuck out her butt and stared up at the guard, meeting his gaze with a sultry one of her own.

"Face forward," he said firmly.

"Anything you say, big guy," she murmured and locked her gaze on the wall.

He started to pat her down, sliding his hands along her hips and torso. When he got to her breasts, the bodyguard paused and frowned. He narrowed his eyes and Ricky's heart rate went from a gallop to a mad dash.

Shit, Ricky thought. *This chick wore a wire.*

Despite his warnings, she had done it anyway. That must have been what she was shifting around in her bra back in the elevator. Ricky held his breath, bracing himself for what the bodyguard was about to pull from her breasts.

Candy looked up at the guard, licked her full lips, and grinned.

"Feel somethin', honey?" she asked.

The guard ran his large hands over her breasts again. "You got somethin' in here? What am I'm feelin'?" he asked.

"My nipples," she said, making Vanessa laugh. "They're hard right now, that's all." She cocked an eyebrow. "Do you need me to pull down my top? You can check yourself, if you don't believe me."

Finally, the bodyguard's frown disappeared. Her deflection worked. He laughed, too, and his hands shifted to her arms.

Ricky exhaled with relief.

The bodyguard finished her pat-down a minute later and then did Ricky's. He gave them all the okay.

"You can head in now," the bodyguard said.

Ricky and the girls walked into Dolla Dolla's sunken living room. When they did, Ricky saw that Dolla Dolla wasn't alone. He had a few more of his guards standing behind the sofa, but on the other side of the sectional sat a short Latino guy with a handlebar mustache, wearing a gray suit. Behind him were two more guards—bald Latinos with broad shoulders and arms as thick as tree limbs. All their heads swiveled in Ricky's and the women's direction when they entered the room.

"Pretty Ricky!" Dolla Dolla boomed. "There your ass is! We've been waiting on you, nigga!"

"So these are the girls, huh?" the short guy asked. He shoved himself up from the sofa, buttoned his suit jacket, and staggered toward them with a glass in his hand. He stopped about a foot in front of Candy and Vanessa and began to circle them like a vulture, looking them up and down drunkenly with heavy-lidded eyes.

To the women's credit, they weren't intimidated by his outright inspection. They stood tall and stared right back at him.

"Yeah, this is Vanessa and Candy. They used to work for me at the strip club. And I'm Ricky." Ricky inclined his head at the man. "And you are?"

"It don't matter who I am," the man slurred, reaching

out to grab Vanessa's chin and run a hand down her neck. "Just know that I can make you *a lot* of money."

"Hey!" Vanessa said, angrily swatting his hand away. "Don't touch me like that."

The man chuckled, then sneered at her. "You better get used to being touched by strangers, *puta*, if you're plannin' on sellin' pussy. What the fuck you think you're about to do? Give out handshakes?" He glanced at Ricky. "What kind of stuck-up bitches did you bring in here?"

Ricky's jaw tightened. He watched as Vanessa's and Candy's faces changed, as their ready smiles disappeared.

The man turned to Dolla Dolla, taking another drink from his glass. "Do we get to try them out tonight, or what? Or do we have to take their word that they know how to fuck?"

Candy's mouth fell open before she caught herself. She turned and glowered at Ricky, who shrugged at her, silently conveying, "I don't know what he's talking about!"

Dolla Dolla hadn't mentioned anything about having sex with the girls tonight.

"Dolla," he began cautiously, "you didn't tell me that was part of the deal. I thought I was just introducing them."

"And that's all we doin' right now," Dolla Dolla said, then held up a hand when it looked like his partner was about to voice his displeasure. "Yo, José, chill, man! They just got here. Let them sit down and relax. Shit! Have another drink."

José stared at the women a beat longer before staggering back to the sofa. Ricky gestured them toward the sunken living room and they walked ahead of him.

"Come on, ladies. Take a load off," Dolla Dolla said. "Ricky, let me introduce you to José Palacios. José, this my nigga Ricky Reynaud. He used to run a strip club for me."

José nodded. Ricky did the same.

"We here to talk business, right?" Dolla Dolla glanced between the two men. "So let's talk some business."

As it turned out, José was less interested in talking than he was in getting a piece of ass. While Dolla Dolla went over the finer points of their future escort services and talked about operations José already had in New York and Houston, José kept trying to grope the women. More than once, Vanessa and Candy had to shove him away or ease off of him. When Candy looked only five seconds away from kicking José in the balls, Ricky finally called it. He'd had enough.

"All right, Dolla, I think me and the girls better go," he said, rising to his feet.

"Already?" José asked. His head lolled to the side as he laughed. "But we were just starting to get to know each other!"

"You wanted to meet the girls, I let you meet the girls. Now I'm taking them back home."

"But we didn't even get to test the merchandise," José lamented. "I came all the way here for nothing?"

"Next time. Next time, bruh," Dolla Dolla said. "I'll walk y'all to the door, Ricky."

The two women practically leapt up from the couch and ran to the front door. Ricky trailed after them, keeping pace with Dolla Dolla as he walked.

"Look, I'm sorry it went down that way, man," Dolla Dolla whispered. "I didn't know he was gonna get drunk off his ass and get out of pocket like that."

"It's okay, Dolla," Ricky muttered.

"Nah, it ain't okay. But he's real about doing this. If your girls are interested or if you got some others to bring on board, let me know. We can set this up."

"I will, Dolla."

"I appreciate that shit, Ricky," he said, slapping his shoulder. He began to turn away.

"Hey, Dolla, can you do me a favor?" Ricky called after him.

Dolla Dolla paused and turned back. "Go ahead. What you need?"

"I need you to set up a meeting with somebody. Somebody important. I need to ask them somethin'."

"Who?"

"Mayor Johnson," Ricky said.

He hadn't forgotten Jamal's dilemma. He hadn't forgotten his promise to help his old friend either.

Dolla Dolla narrowed his eyes. "What you need to talk to him for?"

"It's somethin' with the restaurant. Some D.C. tax stuff they've been bothering me about. It's hard to explain. But I need someone at city hall on my side. Who better than the mayor, right? I figured if I talk to him and explain my situation, he might help—as a favor to you."

Dolla Dolla gradually nodded. "All right. I'll set somethin' up for you."

"Thanks, Dolla," Ricky said, giving him a fist bump.

A few minutes later, Ricky and the undercover cops emerged from the revolving doors of the condo complex onto the sidewalk. The sound of the city night filled the air with blaring horns, the chug of a passing bus, and jazz music playing in the distance.

"Sorry about that, ladies. I didn't know it was gonna go down that way," Ricky said to them.

Candy shrugged as they walked. "Hey, criminals and assholes are unpredictable. And he's both. So we know how that goes."

"I hope it wasn't a waste though," he said. "I hope y'all got what you needed."

"Oh, don't worry about us, sweetheart," Vanessa said with a wink. "We got everything."

Ricky squinted. "Huh?"

He watched as Candy reached up to her wig, like she was scratching her head. She pulled out a quarter-sized mike. He gaped. So she *had* worn a wire.

"Everything's recorded," Candy said.

The women linked arms and strolled away, leaving him in shock.

"Well, I'll be damned," Ricky mumbled.

Chapter 21

Derrick

"Hey! Hey! Hey!" Derrick said as he strolled through the Institute's foyer. He had to leap aside to keep from getting hit in the head by a sailing football that was being tossed among five boys. "We don't do that inside! Y'all know that."

"Yes, Mr. Derrick. Sorry, Mr. Derrick," the boys murmured in reply as they jogged down the hall.

Derrick shook his head in exasperation, but chuckled to himself. If the worst offense he had to deal with today was boys playing football in the hallways, he was grateful.

His days had been pretty trying as of late. This was the first in weeks that had been humdrum, almost uneventful. He'd had his meetings. He'd even conducted a few job interviews, one of which was for Morgan's replacement. The candidate had looked very promising, but Derrick was holding off on making a final decision. In his heart, he was still hoping against hope that Morgan would change her mind about leaving the Institute. He wished she would stay.

Now the day was over and he could head home to his quiet apartment that was still filled with boxes he hadn't unpacked, though he had moved in weeks ago. He just couldn't find the energy to do it. He wondered why but realized once again that Morgan was the answer. Now that he knew for sure that he'd never be sharing his new apartment with her, he still didn't have the will to try to make it a real home.

"Y'all have a good night. See you in the morning," he now said to the boys over his shoulder.

"See you, Mr. Derrick!" a few called back.

Derrick then pushed open the glass door and stepped onto the sidewalk. He reached into his pocket but halted in his steps as soon as he saw them.

Dolla Dolla's men stood around his parked car like they had been waiting there the whole damn day. One of them, the chicken-chested thug who had been the big talker last time, was even reclining on the Nissan's hood.

Damn, Derrick thought.

He had spoken too soon. It turned out his day wasn't going to be uneventful after all.

"There he is! The man himself," the chicken-chested thug said, smiling and pushing himself away from Derrick's hood. "We been waitin' on you, nigga."

Of course they had. Derrick knew Dolla Dolla wouldn't wait long. He'd want his answer eventually. Unfortunately, Derrick still wasn't certain what his answer would be even after the counsel he'd received from Mr. Theo, but it looked like his time to contemplate had already run out.

"So you ready to do business?" Chicken-chested asked. "Dolla's given you plenty of time to think this shit over. He wanna know your answer. He wanna know *now*."

Derrick stared back at him. He then glanced at the faces of the men who stood around him. They were all glaring at Derrick. They looked like junkyard dogs, dark and hulking, trying to sniff out the fear in him, ready to pounce at the slightest sign of weakness.

"Yeah, I've thought about it."

"*And?*" Chicken-chested asked.

"If I say yes," Derrick began, trying his best to buy a few precious minutes as he contemplated his answer, "what does that mean for me?"

Chicken-chested cocked an eyebrow. "So we *are* talking business then?"

"That's what it sounds like, right?"

"I think I like you, nigga." Chicken-chested laughed. "Well, if you wanna know how much you get out of this, Dolla said he's willing to give you a cut of everything that comes through your school. That can mean a lot of money for a dude like you who drives a ride like this," he said, jabbing his thumb at Derrick's car and sneering at it derisively. "For what Dolla can give you, you at least can get a better whip for starters, bruh."

"And by stuff coming through . . . you mean like the suitcases Cole brought in here?"

"Sometimes," Dolla Dolla's emissary said. "And sometimes other things."

"What 'other things'?" Derrick asked, squinting at him.

"Shit, I don't know, man! What's with all the damn questions? Either you gonna do this or you're not."

"I just wanna know what this all means. If I'm putting myself and my kids at risk, I wanna know all the terms."

"*Your kids?* All them little niggas yours? You they daddy?" Chicken-chested asked, laughing again.

Derrick shrugged. "I may as well be. For a lot of them, I'm the closest thing they have to a father. I don't take that shit lightly."

The emissary eyed him. "Well, if that's the case, you know what your answer is then, right? If you so worried about your kids, you don't wanna bring no smoke here.

You make sure you ain't gonna have any problems. Because if you say no to what Dolla is asking you to do, you gonna have a lot of problems, my nigga. You feel me?"

Derrick considered his warning. He also considered the numerous mistakes he had made in the past and his selfish decisions. He had disappointed so many people—Melissa, Morgan, and even Mr. Theo—all because he had put his needs, wants, and desires above theirs.

He didn't want to run amiss of someone like Dolla Dolla or "bring smoke" to the Institute's campus, but the boys inside the facility thought of the Institute as a refuge. Their entire lives they'd dealt with dealers, hustlers, pimps, boosters, and bullies who had brought nothing but chaos to their lives. But within those walls, they were free of all that strife and pain. At the Institute they were offered a path to change their lives. They were shown a different way.

He had already let Dolla Dolla weasel his way in once, with the two suitcases, and he'd ended up sacrificing Cole in the end because he didn't stop it as soon as he knew what was going on. If he gave Dolla Dolla a permanent foothold at the Institute, what would it mean for the rest of the boys? Would Dolla Dolla think *he* ran the place? Would he start recruiting them to work for him, to be his soldiers?

No, Derrick thought. He couldn't let that happen.

"Yeah, I feel you," he said with a slow nod, "but I can't do it. I'm *not* gonna do it. Tell Dolla I appreciate the offer, but the Institute ain't up for sale. I ain't either."

Chicken-chested didn't immediately respond. He simply glowered at Derrick. He then glanced over his shoulder at the other men who stood around his car. He flicked his hand at Derrick, like he was flicking dust aside. He sucked his teeth.

"Handle this nigga," he said.

Four of the goons stepped forward. Derrick tossed his satchel to the ground and took a stance with his hands up, ready to go down fighting if he had to. But he was stopped short by the sound of several feet hitting the pavement behind him.

"Yo, you okay, Mr. Derrick?" he heard a voice call out.

Derrick turned to find almost a dozen boys running out of the lobby door toward him. Among them were the boys who had been in the lobby tossing around the football. Unbeknownst to him, they must have been watching the conversation the entire time through the foyer's windows. They must have seen when it had gone left and alerted the other boys to what was happening.

"We got a problem?" one of the taller boys barked at Dolla Dolla's men.

Derrick had seen the boy around the Institute. The other boys called him Snoop because of how much he resembled the rapper. Derrick noticed that the boy's hands were curled into fists at his sides. He wasn't the only one. Several of them looked like they were willing to fight for him at that moment. Derrick was touched, even honored that the boys were willing to defend him, but he didn't want to put them in harm's way. He knew what Dolla Dolla's men were capable of.

"Nah, we good," Derrick said. "They were just about to leave."

For a few seconds, there was a silent standoff. Dolla Dolla's men didn't budge, and neither did the Branch Avenue Boys who were huddled behind Derrick. Finally, Dolla Dolla's emissary sucked his teeth again, realizing they were outnumbered.

"Man, fuck this," he said to his men. "If we don't get

this nigga today, we got other chances." He eyed Derrick. "We won't forget this, nigga."

Derrick watched as they all turned and walked away, feeling a sinking sensation in the pit of his stomach.

He would pay a price for what he'd done today; he just didn't know what that full price would be.

Chapter 22

Jamal

"Good morning," Jamal murmured as he stepped out of his apartment building's elevator with his head bowed.

"Good morning, young man!" his elderly neighbor sang.

She wasn't wearing a pink tracksuit today like she had months ago when he'd last spoken to her. She'd switched it out for a green one with silver piping. She looked like an elderly inhabitant of the Emerald City in the Land of Oz. As he passed her and walked toward the lobby doors, she held up a wrinkled hand.

"I heard what happened to you a couple of months ago. The shooting, I mean," she said, making him pause and turn to face her again. "This is a nice neighborhood. I was surprised it happened, but I'm glad to hear they arrested that boy. I'm happy to see you're okay, that you're doing better."

He nodded and forced a smile. "Thank you, ma'am." He turned to face the door again.

"You *are* doing better, aren't you?" she asked, halting him once more.

Jamal stifled a sigh and nodded again.

He hadn't planned to get dragged into a conversation this early on a Saturday morning, before he'd even had his coffee, but he wouldn't disrespect one of his well-meaning elders. He could hear his mother's admonishment of "I taught you better, Jay," even in his head.

"Yeah, my shoulder's healed. I'm not wearing a sling anymore," he said, pointing to his arm.

"Not all wounds are on the outside, sweetheart. Have you healed on the inside, too?" she asked, squinting at him.

Jamal raised his brows, surprised at her question. He began to nod a third time but stopped himself. Instead, he pursed his lips. He shook his head. "Not yet," he finally whispered.

"Aww, baby." She reached out and placed a hand on his shoulder where the scar from the bullet wound still lingered and would probably never go away. "Give it some time. I'll pray for you."

"Thank you," he said before turning and finally crossing the lobby and heading out the glass door. He continued down the sidewalk to his neighborhood coffee shop a few blocks away.

The truth was that Jamal felt slightly worse now than he had right after the shooting. Everything still had yet to be reconciled as long as Mayor Johnson remained free, and Jamal had lost his solace, his emotional rock when he lost Melissa. Well, he hadn't *lost* her, exactly—he had voluntarily walked away from her. He hadn't seen or spoken to Melissa in almost a week, and he planned to keep it that way. He would have to go cold turkey—a full Melissa Stone cleanse. He knew he had to, in order to protect himself. He had bared himself emotionally to that woman too many times for her to continue to shove him away, to tell him that the love he wanted from her, she could never give. Why continue to be Sisyphus, pushing a boulder up a hill over and over again, only to see it roll back down to the bottom? He'd just have to let the boulder stay where the hell it sat. Melissa would go her way. He would go his.

Five minutes later, Jamal stepped through the door of the coffee shop and walked straight to the end of the counter to pick up his drink. He had preordered that morning. He just wanted to grab his coffee and head back to the solace and quiet of his own apartment.

"Grande espresso, no foam with a double shot of mocha," the barista called out before placing the paper cup on the counter.

Right on time, Jamal thought as he reached for the cup. But rather than his fingers gripping paper, they grasped onto thin air. He stared in surprise as a petite blonde swiped the cup and raised it to her lips to take a sip. She tossed her hair over her shoulder and turned to walk away.

"Uh," he said, "I think that was my order."

She stopped and turned to face him again. She blinked and lowered the cup from her mouth. He watched as she raised the cup and stared at the label. They both saw his name clearly printed on the side.

"Oh, my God! I'm so sorry!" she cried. Her pale cheeks flushed pink with embarrassment. "I ordered the same drink. I thought it was mine!"

Jamal grimaced, smothering his annoyance. "That's . . . that's all right. I'll just . . . uh . . . order another one, I guess."

"Or you can have mine," she offered, pointing at the counter where several other cups sat waiting, none of which were a grande espresso, no foam, with a double shot of mocha. "It's not there now, but they should have it up soon."

"Yeah. Sure," he muttered.

"Again, I'm so sorry! Next time I'll be sure to check the label."

"Yeah, next time," he said, turning away.

"Wait. Wait!" she said, making him pause. "You seem really familiar to me for some reason. Have I seen you somewhere?"

He shrugged. "I used to be deputy mayor."

"Deputy mayor! Yes, I remember you now. You were one of my patients. You're Jamal. Jamal Lighty! Your mother was a hoot. I'm Sam!" She pointed at her chest. "Samantha! I was your nurse at the Washington Hospital Center."

His eyes widened. "Oh! I didn't recognize you."

She laughed. "Most patients don't when I'm out of my scrubs." She pointed to her crown. "And my hair isn't in a ponytail. I usually wear it down outside of the hospital. It makes my face look a little different."

"It kinda does." He nodded appreciatively. "It flatters you though."

Her cheeks flushed pink again. She lowered her eyes and ran her fingers through her hair. "Thanks."

She really did look cute with her hair down. He didn't remember her being quite so cute at the hospital, but his focus hadn't been on her at the time.

I'd been more focused on being grateful that I was still alive—and on seeing Melissa again, he thought.

"Grande espresso, no foam with a double shot of mocha!" the barista shouted, setting another cup on the counter.

"Guess that's me," he muttered, reaching for the cup. He glanced at the label and saw the name "SAM" written on it. "It was nice seeing you again," he said to her before turning away from the counter.

"Hey, Jamal!" she called out to him. "I still feel kind of bad for taking your coffee."

"It's no problem." He held his cup aloft. "I've got this one."

"But I feel like l still owe you something. Can I buy you a muffin or a scone? *Please?* It'll make me feel less guilty."

He chuckled. "I'm not really a muffin or scone kinda guy."

"Then a cookie or a pound cake," she said. "Come on! I'll get us both one. While we wait in line, you can tell me how you're doing now. I love catching up with my former patients."

Jamal hesitated.

"Unless you have to rush off. I don't know. Maybe . . . well, your girlfriend is waiting for you?"

Jamal cocked an eyebrow. *His girlfriend?* He watched as Sam gnawed her bottom lip, as she pivoted from one foot to the other. Was she flirting?

"No," he said, now smiling. "No girlfriend. I don't have one, actually."

"I don't have one either! I mean . . ." She laughed anxiously. "I don't have a girlfriend *or* a boyfriend. I don't . . ." She closed her eyes and winced. "I should stop talking, shouldn't I?"

He joined her in her laughter. She really was cute. "You're fine. But I'll take you up on that slice of pound cake if you're still offering."

She opened her eyes and grinned. "Absolutely!"

They were out of pound cake so she bought them both a slice of coffee cake. They sat at the counter near the window facing the busy sidewalk on the two remaining free stools, and talked for a solid two hours. He found out that Sam had become a nurse only five years ago and before that had been an unemployed grad student in Chicago. She had two sisters and a dog. She lived with a roommate in Logan Circle but was looking for a new place. She'd just come back from vacation in Santorini with her sorority sisters. She showed him a few of the pictures on her Instagram account.

"Oh, my God! What time is it?" she said, glaring down at her phone. "Crap! I'm supposed to be across town right now. I'm meeting my friend in ten minutes. I'm never gonna make it there in enough time though. I better text her." She furiously began to type on her phone screen after hopping off her stool.

Jamal frowned. "Sorry I took up your time and made you late."

"No! No, I had a great time talking to you, Jamal. I stayed because I wanted to." She grabbed her purse off the back of her stool and threw the strap over her shoulder. "It was nice. I had fun. Maybe we can . . . I don't know . . . do it again sometime?"

He could see the opening she was leaving him to ask her out on a date, likely to do something more than sip espressos and eat coffee cake. The truth was, he would like to ask her out. He'd take her to dinner and a movie or they'd try one of the jazz clubs in Northeast. He thought Sam was funny and smart and he loved the way her cheeks went pink when she admitted something embarrassing. But his life was such a mess right now. He had no job and no prospects of one. He was still plagued by the rare panic attack, and he still didn't know if another hitman was waiting around the corner to take him out. Was he really in a good place to start something with someone new? And he had walked out of Melissa's bedroom only a week ago, feeling rejected and brokenhearted. Would he be trying to move on too soon?

"Maybe," he said as Sam stared at him eagerly. "I'm . . . uh . . . gonna be out of town for the next few weeks though. Maybe when I get back, I can slide in your Instagram DMs and set something up."

"I'll make it even easier for you," she said. "Can I have your phone?"

"For what?"

"Just give it to me!" she said with a laugh.

He frowned but handed his cell to her. He watched, amused, as she quickly typed a number with her name beside it into his text message app. She handed him his cell phone back.

"Here's my number. Let me know how you're doing. I like to keep up with my patients. Or you can call me for . . . whatever else." She waved. "Look. I gotta go. It was nice seeing you again, Jamal."

"Same," he said as he watched her walk out of the coffee shop. He glanced at his cell phone screen and her number, wondering if he would ever call her.

Chapter 23

Ricky

Ricky strolled into the waiting area, zeroing in on the white-haired black woman who sat primly at her desk, typing away at her keyboard. When he entered, she glanced up at him and did a double take.

"Good afternoon," he said, smiling. "I'm here to see Mayor Johnson."

"Do you have an appointment?" She shifted in her chair while slowly looking him up and down.

You can side-eye me all you want, honey, Ricky thought. *I know I'm one of the best-dressed niggas up in here.*

For his meeting with the mayor, he had worn a gray pinstriped three-piece suit and periwinkle-blue silk tie, both of which he had purchased two years ago while in New York and had set him back about three stacks. He'd even worn gold cufflinks and a tie clip. Attached to that tie clip, on the back, was a small Bluetooth mike that Detective Ramsey had given him on loan from the Metro Police that had exceedingly good sound quality. It was recording him and the woman now.

"No, I don't have an appointment," he told the mayor's

secretary. "But Mayor Johnson and I have a mutual acquaintance and he told the mayor I would stop by sometime today."

Her expression went from apprehensive to downright patronizing, like she'd seen this song-and-dance routine many times. "Well, the mayor happens to be on a call right now, Mr.—"

"Reynaud. Ricky Reynaud."

"Yes, the mayor happens to be on a call right now, Mr. Reynaud, and he has a meeting scheduled immediately after. He has a very packed schedule today. I would suggest you call and schedule a meeting next time if you wish to speak with him. I'll let you know the soonest date he has available." She then turned back around to face her computer screen, turning her back to him.

Ricky stifled the urge to roll his eyes.

Okay, the old biddy wasn't going to make this easy. He guessed he would either have to turn on the heat or the charm. He would go for charm first.

"Gladys, is it?" he said, glancing down at the plaque on her desk. His smile widened. "Can I call you Gladys?"

"No, you may not. You can call me Mrs. Sumpter," she answered succinctly as she continued to type.

"Well, Mrs. Sumpter, I understand the mayor is busy but I would greatly appreciate it if you would at least let him know that I'm waiting out here for him."

"I would do that, but I was given explicit instructions not to interrupt his call," she said, clicking her computer mouse.

All right, charm ain't workin', he thought, cocking an eyebrow. *I tried to be nice. But if she wanna play this game, I can play.*

"Now if you'll excuse me, Mr. Reynaud," she continued, "I have—"

"Gladys, tell the mayor I'm out here. Do it now."

She whipped around in her chair and laughed. "Excuse me?"

"You heard what I said. And tell him don't leave me waitin'."

She sputtered. "I don't know who you think you're talking to like that, but I will call security if you don't—"

"No, I don't think you know who *you're* talkin' to. I represent one of Johnson's most important constituents, Stanley Hughes. Are you familiar with him?" Ricky asked, still smiling.

Stanley Hughes was Dolla Dolla's government name and had obviously wrung a bell with the old woman. Her face immediately went ashen and slack when Ricky said it.

"I'd hate to have to go back to Mr. Hughes and tell him the mayor's secretary turned me away, that she wouldn't even let Mayor Johnson know I was here. I wonder what he would say."

Gladys's brown nostrils flared. Her wrinkled lips pinched. "I'll . . . I'll let the mayor know you're here," she whispered.

"You do that," he said before strolling to the leather sofa on the other side of the waiting room and sitting down. He then watched as she raised the headset to her ear and dialed a number, making him wonder if the mayor had even been on a call like she'd said or she'd been lying the whole damn time.

"Mr. Johnson," she said into the phone, "you have someone waiting for you, sir."

"Fifteen minutes," Mayor Johnson said to Ricky as he ushered him into his office and shut the door behind him. "You have fifteen minutes and no more. I have a busy schedule today."

"Yeah," Ricky said dryly, unbuttoning his suit jacket and sitting down in one of the armchairs facing the mayor's desk. "Your secretary already told me that."

"I recognize you," Mayor Johnson said, pulling out the padded leather chair behind his desk. "Haven't we met before?"

Ricky placed an ankle on his knee and leaned back in his chair. He adjusted his tie, hoping that the mike was catching all this. "Yeah, but not under the best circumstances. I believe Dolla Dolla was busting your balls for not getting the prosecutor to drop the charges against us."

Johnson flopped back into his seat. "Ah yes, now I remember. So is that what you're here for? To pester me again about getting those damn charges dropped?" he loudly groused. "As I told your boss, something like that is beyond my control."

"He ain't my boss. He's my business partner. And actually, no, that wasn't what I wanted to talk to you about. You see, Mayor Johnson, it's my restaurant. The cops shut it down and now I—"

"Anything related to police matters is out of my hands," Johnson said, throwing up his empty hands as if they were evidence of what he couldn't do, of how they were tied. "I'm sorry."

"But you didn't let me finish what I was gonna say. After the raids, the city not only shut down my restaurant but put a lien against it for unpaid—"

"And by the way," the mayor continued, ignoring him, "I don't appreciate Dolla sending his people here to ask favors of me, especially considering the last half-assed favor he did when I needed it. Sending a child to do a man's job . . . what kinda garbage was that?"

Ricky paused. He hadn't expected their conversation to head in this direction this soon, but he was more than willing to pursue it. That's what he was here for, after all.

"Yeah, I heard about that shit with the deputy mayor . . . how you asked Dolla to have him killed."

"And he sent a seventeen-year-old boy to do it! Like it

was some low-level errand. Like he was delivering a package, as opposed to taking out someone who has been a nuisance for me since the beginning. It's just ridiculous to—" He paused and eyed Ricky. "Never mind."

No, keep talking, Ricky thought. All of it was now being transmitted through the mike and recorded on his cell phone.

"I should stop. You'll probably go running back to your boss, telling him everything that I said," the mayor mumbled.

"I don't go running to nobody. I told you, I work *with* Dolla, not for him. I'm my own man, Mayor Johnson. We're in business together, but no business arrangement is perfect. Sure as hell sounds like the one you had with Dolla wasn't."

"Only because he didn't complete the job like I asked! The little son of a bitch is still on my ass, threatening to go to the cops with information about me! Dolla is pissed that he could serve thirty years to life, and now he's trying to drag me down too! I wouldn't be surprised if he sent that kid on purpose, knowing he would fuck it up!"

"Nah, that doesn't sound like Dolla."

The mayor stilled and eyed Ricky. "Then why didn't he ask someone like you to do it? I'm sure you do this type of thing all the time, right?"

"You mean why didn't he ask me to kill Deputy Mayor Lighty?"

"*Former* deputy mayor," Johnson corrected.

"Guess I was busy that day, so Dolla ain't ask." Ricky tilted his head. "You still interested in having it done? You still want him taken out?"

The mayor studied him silently. Ricky wondered if he had overplayed his hand. If the mayor was now starting to get suspicious. Maybe he wondered if this random person claiming to be one of Dolla Dolla's emissaries was trying to entrap him by soliciting a murder. Luckily, Johnson was one of those types who always thought he was the smartest guy in the room—which made him easier to con.

"Are you offering?" the mayor finally whispered.

"It depends." Ricky shrugged. "What are *you* offering?"

"That little problem you're having with your restaurant . . . the lien . . . I can make it go away if you take care of Lighty for me. But I need it done quickly. This can't drag on for weeks and weeks."

"How do you want it done?" Ricky asked.

"I don't care. I assume you have the expertise in that department."

The mayor was acting so blasé, like he was talking about what he would have for dinner that night, not having Jamal murdered.

"Do you want it quick—or do you want it slow and painful?"

The mayor grinned. "I'd like it to be something to remember. If you could get a recording of that son of a bitch screaming for mercy, even better."

"Gotcha," Ricky said with a wink, having heard more than enough.

Thank *God* he had done this. Jamal's fears had been right. He was still in danger and the mayor wouldn't stop until Jamal was dead or someone else stopped him.

Ricky rose from his chair. "Well, I thank you for taking the time to talk to me, Mayor Johnson. And I'll work on that little thing for you. You'll know as soon as it's done."

"Good. I look forward to it," the mayor said as Ricky walked to his office door and strolled back into the waiting area.

Chapter 24

Derrick

He heard the sound of his ringing phone even before he shoved his office door open. Derrick juggled the binders and multiple folders from the earlier meeting in his hands as he jogged to his desk. He hoped whoever was calling wouldn't keep him long. The Institute's staff meeting was starting in less than ten minutes. He didn't want to be late or the instructors would start grumbling.

He set down his stack and raised the receiver to his ear. "Hello, Derrick Miller speaking."

Derrick frowned when he heard weeping and sniffing on the other end. "Hello?" he repeated.

"Mr. Miller," a woman answered between hiccups, "I'm so sorry. I didn't mean to . . . b-but I had to call you. I h-h-had to tell you."

Derrick's frown deepened when he recognized the voice on the other end of the line. It was Cole's mother. "Ms. Humphries? Is that you? Is everything okay?"

As soon as he asked the question, she started weeping again. She mumbled something but her words were unintelligible.

"I'm sorry, ma'am, but I . . . I can't understand what you're saying. What's wrong?" he asked, now overwhelmed by a sense of unease. "What happened?"

"Cole!" she screamed into the phone, almost making him pull the receiver from his ear. "Cole is gone! They killed my baby!"

Derrick walked into the meeting room fifteen minutes later, feeling numb all over. He looked at the faces of those seated around the rectangular table in the center of the room. Many of the instructors were laughing and talking. A few were glancing down at their watches or scrolling through their cell phones, waiting for the meeting to start. Though Derrick tried hard to avoid her gaze, his eyes locked with Morgan's as soon as he shut the door behind him. She had been giggling and whispering with one of the other instructors when he entered, but at the sight of him, her ready smile disappeared. She stared at him quizzically. He knew she could sense something was wrong. Of course, she could.

"Hey, everybody! Everybody, can I have your . . . um . . . can I have your attention?" he shouted, forcing his lips to move, to utter words even though he wasn't sure if he was making any sense.

Besides the sound of chairs being shifted, the room instantly fell quiet. He had their full attention.

Derrick anxiously licked his lips and closed his eyes, still remembering his conversation with Cole's mother and the details she had shared with him about Cole's death. No, make that Cole's *murder*.

Derrick wondered if his recent rejection of Dolla Dolla's offer had been the reason behind it—and the thought paralyzed him with guilt. Maybe the drug kingpin was trying to send a message that this was what happened when you didn't cater to his wishes. But why had he been so cruel as to take the life of a scared teenage boy to make that point?

Because he knew how it would rip you apart, Derrick thought dismally.

Derrick opened his eyes and glanced around the table. Again, his eyes landed on Morgan. She wasn't going to take this well. He was sure of that.

"Sorry that I was . . . that I'm late," Derrick said. "I had to take an important phone call."

"You can make it up to us by keeping the meeting short, Derrick!" someone called out.

A few laughed awkwardly at the joke.

"Well," he began, "you're gonna get your wish because I am gonna keep this short. I had an agenda lined up today, but it doesn't feel right to talk about budgets and curriculum right now." He cleared his throat, trying to work up the courage to say what he had to say next. "The phone call I got before the meeting was from Cole Humphries's mom. I know some of you have had him in your classes and have asked me for updates on him since his arrest. You wanted to know how he was doing. Well, I'm sad to say that . . . that Cole's mom told me . . ." He took a steadying breath. "She told me today that Cole is dead. He died this morning."

"*Dead?*" a math instructor echoed. His chubby face had gone pale. "What do you mean *dead*, Derrick? What happened to him?"

"He was murdered in jail."

One of the instructors let out an audible gasp. A soft murmur of voices filled the meeting room.

He noted that Morgan didn't say or do anything. She just stared at him blankly.

"I'm going to ask that you guys keep this information in here, among yourselves for now. Please don't tell the students yet what's happened to Cole, especially his classmates. Sometime this afternoon, we're going to hold an assembly where we will let them know, but I don't want this in the gossip grapevine, okay? I don't want any crazy rumors."

"Crazy rumors about what?" an English instructor asked.

"About how he died," Derrick said. *And why he died*, Derrick thought, but didn't say the words aloud.

Many of Cole's classmates who knew he had a connection to Dolla Dolla would come to their own conclusions.

"How did he die though?" Morgan asked. Her green eyes were big and wet with tears that were threatening to spill over. "Do they know who did it?"

Derrick pursed his lips again and shook his head. "They're still investigating it. They don't know much, and what little they do know . . . well . . . I'd rather not go into detail right now if that's okay with everybody. But I'll share more info when its available."

Several people nodded. A few more whispered or mumbled "okay" or "sure."

"I know this is a lot to take in. Losing one of our own is . . . is not something that's easy to accept," Derrick said, lowering his eyes. "But we'll get through this. I know we will."

He was trying to sound encouraging, but the words felt hollow. Everyone in the room knew that the Branch Avenue Boys' Youth Institute was a place where boys went to get a second lease on life. Instead, one of those boys had not only lost his second chance—but he'd also lost his life entirely at the young age of seventeen. His murder wasn't just a gross injustice. There was something profoundly wrong about it, something uneven. Yes, children died every day all over the world from starvation, neglect, war, and any number of atrocities, but to know one of them personally, to have tried to save him and failed was a pain that was indescribable.

"I'll send out an email to reschedule the meeting we had slated for today. In the meantime, say a prayer for Cole and his family. Thanks, everybody," he said.

Unlike in the past when Derrick would adjourn the meeting, everyone didn't rise to their feet and run for the door. They lingered in their seats and glanced at one another. Gradually, they stood and shuffled to the door in silence, like they were leaving a funeral. Only Morgan lingered behind.

Derrick watched the door and waited until everyone else had left before he slowly walked toward where she was sitting. He took the seat beside her and saw that she was crying. He reached out and placed a hand on her shoulder. It was the first time he'd touched her since that night at the education banquet.

"How did it happened?" she asked between hiccups. "Tell me how it happened, Derrick. And I don't wanna hear any bullshit about how the investigation is ongoing. You know something. I *know* you do!"

Derrick closed his eyes and loudly exhaled. "His mother said it happened this morning in the showers. They don't know who did it. But one of the corrections officers found him in there on the floor. He was already dead. He'd been stabbed more than a dozen times."

Morgan bit down hard on her bottom lip as the tears swam over her cheeks. She wiped them away with her hands. "That asshole he was working for is behind this. You and I know that."

"Probably," he said. He didn't mean to sound so cool and detached, but with all the emotion Morgan was pouring out, it seemed better to contain his. "Cole told me in his own way that he was worried about his safety. I was hoping he was wrong."

"Well, he wasn't wrong—and now he's dead! And the people who killed him will probably go unpunished and the son of a bitch behind it is still walking around and still capable of hurting or killing whoever the hell he wants," she said before shoving Derrick's hand off her shoulder and shooting to her feet.

"Morgan," he began, but she quickly shook her head, silencing him.

"Don't. Don't, Derrick. I don't want to hear any more!"

He then watched as she stalked toward the open doorway and out into the hall.

He didn't run after her. He thought better of it. Besides, how could he make her feel better when he felt so bleak himself?

Chapter 25

Jamal

Jamal screamed as he awoke, swinging and batting wildly at the hundreds of bees that had been attacking him in his dream. He opened his eyes and realized he wasn't running in a forest, trying to elude an angry swarm that he had haplessly stumbled upon. Instead, he was in his darkened bedroom. He sat up, tiredly rubbed his eyes with the heels of his hands, and frowned. So if he wasn't dreaming anymore, why did he still hear buzzing? He glanced at his night table. That wasn't bees he was hearing, but the insistent buzz of his cell phone. The sound had somehow made it into his dreams. Someone had just sent him a text and for some reason they had sent it before six a.m. The sun wasn't even up yet.

"Who the hell is texting me this early?" he mumbled.

He reached for his phone, removed it from his night table, and put on his glasses since his contacts were now floating in a solution in his bathroom. He stared down at the text message on the screen.

I sent you something last night. You still ain't opened it. Check your email, nigga!

Jamal's frown deepened. The text was from Ricky. What did Ricky email him that was so damn important?

Jamal pulled back the cotton sheets and threw his legs over the side of the bed. He yawned as he pulled up the email app on his phone and scrolled through the list, finding Ricky's email within seconds. When he did, he saw an MP3 file. He clicked on it and heard Ricky's voice. Less than a minute after that, he heard Mayor Johnson's, too—and he almost dropped his phone.

"Yeah, I heard about that shit with the deputy mayor . . . how you asked Dolla to have him killed," Ricky said on the recording.

"And he sent a seventeen-year-old boy to do it! Like it was some low-level errand," the mayor replied. *"Like he was delivering a package, as opposed to taking out someone who has been a nuisance for me since the beginning."*

Jamal sat stupefied as he continued to listen. His mouth fell open in shock.

"Goddamn," Jamal whispered, shaking his head in awe. "Ricky did it!"

Jamal sat in the police station, looking anxiously at the door as one police officer filed out, then another. He was searching for a familiar face.

Jamal had already left three voicemail messages today with the detective who he'd told about Mayor Johnson's involvement in his attempted murder, and, so far, he hadn't received a response. He didn't want to wait any longer. If the man wouldn't return his damn phone calls, then he would come to him directly.

He leaned forward in his chair, resting his elbows on his knees, staring at the linoleum beneath his feet until his vision began to blur. Finally, he spotted the detective strolling in with another man. Both were wearing cheap suits and paisley ties. When Jamal saw him, he shot to his feet.

"Detective Wingate," he called out.

The detective stopped talking mid-conversation and turned away from his companion. He stared at Jamal quizzically.

"Mr. Lighty?" he said, strolling toward him. "What are you doing here?"

"Did you get my voicemails? Did you get any of them?" Jamal asked, unable to keep the urgency out of his voice.

The detective slowly shook his head and shrugged. "No, I've been in the field all day. Why?"

The son of a bitch told me to call his cell phone at any time if I needed anything and he doesn't even answer or check his messages. That's just great, Jamal thought in exasperation.

"I got that additional evidence you said you needed," Jamal said, holding up his cell phone. "You have to listen to it. It could put Johnson away for good."

The detective exchanged a look with his companion that Jamal couldn't help but interpret as "Do you see the shit I have to deal with?" His thin lips quirked into a patronizing smile. He murmured something to his companion, who nodded before heading toward the door leading to the station's inner offices. The companion opened the door, stepped inside, and let it shut behind him just as Detective Wingate strolled toward Jamal.

"Mr. Lighty," the detective began, dropping his voice to a whisper, "look, you've already expressed to me your worries about the mayor and his threats. But I told you that you—"

"These aren't just threats. Someone made a recording of him trying to put a hit on me. He offered them a favor if they would agree to kill me. It's all on here." He pointed to his phone.

Wingate squinted. "*They?* Who's they?"

"A friend of mine."

"I see." Wingate was giving him that look again. "You should know that we prefer to do our own police work with this sort of thing. Your 'friend' could be prosecuted for conducting secret recordings of—"

"But he works for you guys," Jamal interrupted.

"Huh?"

Jamal glanced over his shoulder to see if anyone was listening to their conversation. Luckily, everyone else standing around the crowded police station lobby seemed oblivious to what they were talking about.

"He's an informant," Jamal whispered. "He's been working for you guys for a while now. He's been working with two detectives with the Metro Police. I swear it to you! You can call them and check him out if you don't believe me."

Wingate's expression remained impassive but Jamal could tell he was listening to him now. He wasn't being dismissive like before.

"What detectives?" Wingate asked. "What are their names?"

"Ramsey and Dominguez, I think."

"*You think?*" Wingate repeated, scanning him with those cynical blue eyes again. "Well, what's the informant's name? If he's your friend, you should know that for sure, right?"

Jamal hesitated.

Ricky was putting his life on the line every day as an undercover informant. Even in the recording, in the portion Jamal could hear, Ricky had left out his name. If you didn't know him personally or recognize his voice, you wouldn't know who Johnson was speaking to. Ricky hadn't trusted many people with that secret, and though Wingate was with the police department, Jamal didn't know for sure if he could trust him with Ricky's identity either.

Jamal had betrayed his friends enough in the past; he didn't want to do it again.

He shook his head. "I'm not telling you anything else until you listen to this. Listen to the whole thing. Then you can talk to the detectives. They can vouch for this guy without revealing his identity."

Wingate studied him for a long time, not saying anything. Eventually, he nodded.

"Fine," he said as he walked to the closed door that other officers were disappearing inside. "You can come with me and I'll listen, but this informant of yours better check out or none of this stuff is admissible."

Jamal pursed his lips. "I understand."

Wingate paused with his hand hovering mere inches from the door handle. "But if you've got what you've claimed you've got—"

"It's no claim. It's *exactly* what I said it is."

Wingate cocked an eyebrow, gripped the handle, and tugged the door open. He gestured for Jamal to step in front of him. "Well then, let's have a listen, shall we?"

Detective Wingate listened to the recording. He did it three times, and each time he blinked at the end like he wasn't sure if he'd heard exactly what he thought he'd heard.

"This really happened?" he asked. "I mean . . . Mayor Johnson really said all this?"

Jamal nodded as they sat alone in an office with a lone cabinet and computer.

"Well, I can't make any promises on how far we can go with it, but there's no way we can ignore a threat like this one. This is . . . this is something. Jesus!" the detective said, slumping back in his chair in shock.

Wingate didn't make Jamal any assurances, but Jamal knew in his heart that this time Johnson wasn't getting away with it.

Jamal emerged from the police station an hour later, smiling ear to ear. He strode down the stairs and walked toward his car, feeling more optimistic than he had in months, maybe in more than a year. Suddenly, a thought dawned in his head—one that had nothing to do with Johnson or his fight to stay alive. It seemed to come out of nowhere, but he suspected it was a product of the new-found buoyancy he was experiencing. He felt willing to take a chance and to let go of past burdens. What better way of doing that than to try something new?

Jamal reached into his pocket and pulled out his cell phone. He scanned through old texts until he found it. When he saw her name and number, his smile became a full on grin. He dialed the number as he walked down the sidewalk and used the remote to unlock his car door.

"Hello?" a female voice answered hesitantly.

"Hi, is this Samantha?"

"Yes, this is she."

"Uh, this is Jamal. You gave me your number a couple of weeks ago."

There was a pause on the other end.

For a split second, he wondered if maybe she had forgotten him. Maybe she gave her number to random dudes all the time. Maybe after she had given him hers, she had pushed him to the back of her mind when he didn't call her right away.

"We met at a coffee shop," he elaborated, now feeling slightly embarrassed. "I used to be one of your—"

"I know who you are, Jamal!" she said, laughing. "I was just surprised to hear from you. I was hoping you would finally call. How are you?"

He sighed with relief. "I'm better. Definitely better than when you last saw me," he said as he opened the car door. "Look, I won't beat around the bush with this. I was calling you because I'd love to take you out this week. I mean out to dinner if . . . if that's okay."

"Hmm, straight to the point, huh? Well, lucky for you,

I like a guy who doesn't beat around the bush," she said, laughing again. "I'd love to go out with you. Unfortunately, I can't do it this week though. I'm on the late shift at the hospital, but I'm free most of next week. How about Tuesday night?"

He climbed behind the wheel and shut the door behind him. "That would be perfect. Send me your address and I'll pick you up at seven on Tuesday."

"Seven, it is."

He hung up and stared down at his phone screen. *Are things finally starting to get better?* he wondered. *Shit! I hope so.*

He inserted his key, threw his car into drive, and pulled off.

Chapter 26

Ricky

Ricky removed his hands from the wall and turned away from the textured wallpaper when he felt a pat on his shoulder.

"Okay, you're good," Dolla Dolla's bodyguard said over the sound of thumping music. He winked at Ricky. "Have a good time, man."

Ricky nodded, forcing a smile, but as he headed into the living room, his smile disappeared. Though he could see several men and women sitting on the leather sectional and armchairs in Dolla Dolla's living room—laughing and talking, drinking glasses of champagne, and snorting lines of blow—he was in no partying mood. Once again, he had a mission to accomplish and not a lot of time to do it.

Derrick had finally confided in him yesterday the "issue" he had been having with Dolla Dolla. Derrick had only told him after one of his students had turned up dead in jail. Now Derrick was worried that Dolla Dolla's inability to strong-arm him into using the Institute as another front business for his dirty dealings would lead to more deaths.

"I knew he would come after me," Derrick had told Ricky. "But I can't let him come after any more of these boys. I was willing to go down . . . to make the sacrifice, but I can't stand to watch him pick them off one by one, if that's his plan."

"You should've told me this sooner, Dee," Ricky had argued. "You should've told me what he was tryin' to do."

Derrick had shaken his head. "You had enough on your plate. I don't even like bringing up this shit now, but he took one of my boys. This has to stop, Ricky. If you can get him to back off, I'd appreciate it."

Ricky now walked into the sunken living room and glanced up at the stripper who was dancing topless on the glass coffee table. He then scanned the rest of the room in search of Dolla Dolla.

The drug kingpin was a hard man to miss thanks to his gargantuan size. And if you didn't see him, you could certainly hear his voice booming louder than a sonic jet.

Nah, he ain't out here, Ricky realized when he still didn't hear or see Dolla Dolla. But the man was somewhere in the apartment though. It was his party, and Dolla Dolla loved a good party.

"Hey, you're Ricky, right?" someone shouted to him.

Ricky turned around to find José Palacios sitting on one of the armchairs, sandwiched between two half-naked, buxom women. One, who he gripped by the bottom, held a fingertip covered with white powder up to his left nostril. José leaned down, took a hit, and grinned.

"Yeah, it's you!" José pointed up at him, wiping his nose. "I thought so. So where are your stuck-up bitches?" He laughed. "They decided they weren't interested in doing business with us, huh?"

Ricky nodded. "Yeah, they passed."

José laughed again. "Ah, well!" He reached up to massage one of the women's breasts and then leaned forward to lick her nipple through the paper-thin fabric of her shirt, making her giggle. "We still got plenty of bitches to go around. Grab one if you like. We're giving everybody a taste tonight. Let them try out the merchandise."

"Maybe later," Ricky muttered dryly. "I'm lookin' for Dolla Dolla. Do you know where he is?"

"In the bedroom in the back, maybe," José said, no longer looking at Ricky. Instead, his heavy-lidded eyes were locked on one of the young women and his hand was snaking its way up her short leather skirt. Just as she spread her legs in invitation, Ricky turned away. He'd had enough of José and his little peep show. He was here to find Dolla Dolla and plead Derrick's case.

He walked out of the living room and made his way down the hall to Dolla Dolla's bedroom at the end of the corridor. The door was cracked open. As Ricky neared it, he heard muffled whimpering. It sounded like someone was crying in there, definitely not what he'd expected to hear considering all the partying that was going on in the rest of the apartment.

He eased the door open farther and saw the entire bedroom—the grand four-poster bed in onyx black, the two night tables, wardrobe, and behemoth-sized flat-screen TV on the far wall.

Dolla Dolla was standing at the edge of his bed in a navy-blue satin robe while a girl who looked no more than seventeen lay on the bed in her lace underwear, biting down on her lower lip, holding in her sobs as tears ran down her face.

"Stop that crying shit!" Dolla Dolla bellowed at her. "I ain't bring you back in here for this."

Watching them, Ricky's stomach turned. It was like he was getting a replay of Skylar, of how Dolla Dolla had seduced her with his lies and charm and eventually forced her into prostitution. And Skylar and her mother had paid a deadly price in the end. Simone and Ricky had suffered gravely, too—hell, their little family was *still* suffering because of what had happened to the young woman and how it had affected all of them.

But it looked like Dolla Dolla was back to his old ways. This was a sign that the fat son of a bitch hadn't learned from all the havoc he'd unleashed the first time around. He seemed well on his way to doing the same shit all over again, Ricky realized. Unless someone stopped him, that is. It looked like that task still rested on Ricky's shoulders.

"Stop that shit!" Dolla Dolla ordered, slapping the girl across the face, making her scream in alarm. "I don't have time for—"

"Dolla!" Ricky called out, stepping into the room.

He wanted to intervene, to get Dolla Dolla off of her, but once again, he had to hold back. He was getting so tired of holding back.

"*What?* What the fuck y'all want? Can't y'all see I'm busy in here?" Dolla Dolla shouted, whipping around with fury. But when he saw Ricky standing in the doorway, his hardened, bulldog-like face softened. "Shit. Ricky, I ain't know it was you."

"José told me you were back here. I wanted to talk to you. But I can come back if you're busy," Ricky said, glancing at the girl who was still crying.

"Nah, I ain't busy." Dolla Dolla shook his head and sneered at her in disgust. "This bitch is just wasting my time." He grabbed her arm and dragged her to her feet, making her cry out again. "Get up. Get your ass up! Get out of here. Go cry somewhere else!"

She wrapped the bedsheets around her and staggered toward the open door with her head bowed and her shoulders slumped. Ricky stepped aside to let her past. As she neared him, she raised her head slightly to look at him. For a few seconds, he locked gazes with her. Her big brown eyes were full of pain, fear—and desolation. Just like Skylar's had been. The girl turned away and kept walking into the hall. She disappeared past the door frame, headed to God knows where.

"You believe that shit?" Dolla Dolla grumbled before strolling to his night table. He reached for a lit cigar in a crystal ashtray and popped it into his mouth. "She got my juices all going and then start whinin', actin' like she ain't never seen a dick before. I ain't got time for that shit!" He chewed the end of his cigar and glared at his empty bed, like he was glaring at the girl. "It's all right. I'll get another bitch tonight. I'm getting my dick wet one way or another. And the next bitch better not sit there cryin' the whole fuckin' time." He raised an eyebrow at Ricky. "So what you need? Why you come back here anyway?"

"I got a favor to ask you," Ricky said.

"*Another* favor?" Dolla Dolla sat down on the edge of the bed, tightening his robe belt around his waist. "You been asking for a lot of favors lately, nigga."

"But this time, it's not for me. It's for somebody else."

"Yeah? And who's that?"

"He runs the Branch Avenue Boys' Youth Institute in Southeast. His name is Derrick Miller."

Dolla Dolla stopped chewing his cigar. He stilled. "Yeah, I know him. What about him?"

"He's worried that he pissed you off. He thinks he offended you by turning down your offer to pay him to use the Institute for some of your operations. He wants to apologize, Dolla. He hopes you can let it go."

"You damn right he pissed me off!" Dolla Dolla grumbled. "And no, I ain't lettin' that shit go! The only apology I'll accept from that nigga better come right after he says he changed his mind. He better be willing to give me what the fuck I want and do it for a lesser price! If not, I don't wanna hear shit from him."

"Dolla, he runs a school. He's responsible for those kids. He wouldn't have done what he did if it was just him to be concerned about. He's worried about their safety, too."

"And he should be! I already got that little snitchin' nigga who used to go there. I'll get the other ones, too— and then come after him in the end. Your friend will just have to deal with the consequences like every other motherfucka who crosses me."

Ricky closed his eyes. "Dolla, they're *just* kids. Come on, man! You can't—"

"Don't tell me what the fuck I can or can't do!" he shouted, making Ricky's eyes flash open. The drug kingpin shot to his feet. He pointed menacingly at Ricky as he charged across the bedroom. He stopped only when they were inches apart. "I get you wanna defend your friend and all, but don't forget who the fuck you are and who the fuck *I* am! You hear me? Don't get outta pocket! I don't care how long you worked for me. You can get it just like every other nigga out there. I got two bullets for you, too. One for here and here," he said, jabbing his finger against Ricky's temple and then plucking him underneath his chin. "Understand?"

Ricky's jaw tightened. He took a slow, deep breath. "Understood."

"Now if you really wanna help your dude out, I suggest you go back to him and tell him to give me what the fuck I want. Then maybe . . . *maybe* I'll spare all those little niggas at that school. Until then, I don't wanna hear any more about this shit."

"Yes, Dolla," Ricky said.

He was now feeling a volatile mix of adrenaline and rage. It would be so easy to reach out and wrap both his hands around Dolla Dolla's throat and start squeezing. Dolla Dolla was a large man; he'd put up quite a fight, but

Ricky might be able to do it, to successfully strangle him to death. But he couldn't. He couldn't do it even though every fiber in his being screamed for him to do so because he knew what was at stake.

Dolla took a step back and casually waved him off. "If that's all you had to ask me, we done here. You can tell José to send in another girl. And this one better be ready."

"Yes, Dolla," Ricky whispered before turning around and heading out of the bedroom, bottling all his rage once again and hoping he was doing it for a win in the end.

Chapter 27

Derrick

Derrick walked into the Institute's cafeteria, caught off guard by the transformation that had taken place there in only a matter of hours. The long rectangular tables where a hundred or so boys usually sat—laughing over their meals and tossing balled-up napkins and plastic straws at each other—had been stacked against the walls. All the plastic chairs had been arranged in several rows with a center aisle where people now milled about, looking for somewhere to sit in the crowded room. Toward the back of the cafeteria, where the staff usually stood behind a stainless steel counter, dispensing trays of food and cartons of milk and juice, was now a podium and mike. Beside it was a large display board. It showed a collage of photos of Cole Humphries at different points in his short life. Cole at eleven or twelve years old, sitting on a sofa with his mom at their home. Cole at sixteen years old, posing on a street corner with his boys in his old neighborhood, grinning at the camera and throwing up hand signs. Cole as a six- or seven-year-old with missing front teeth, sitting next to a Christmas tree.

Several of the boys at the Institute had asked to hold a memorial service for him when they got word of his murder, which wasn't surprising to Derrick. He knew how popular Cole had been at the Institute when he was alive. But some of the instructors had objected to holding a memorial service for a former student who was being charged with attempted murder at the time of his death, wondering what message it would send to the rest of the boys, so Derrick had put the question of a memorial service to a faculty vote. The yeas had won in the end, and the service was scheduled.

Derrick had invited Cole's mother to attend, and she had tearfully accepted the invitation over the phone. She now sat up front with her head bowed as she wept softly, waiting for the service to begin. One arm was wrapped around Cole's seven-year-old brother, who was sobbing. Cole's mother's other arm was wrapped around his three-year-old little sister who looked confused by what was happening around her and kept looking over her shoulder, peering curiously around the cafeteria.

As Derrick walked toward the podium, he glanced down at the papers he held in his hand. The office assistant had typed them. One sheet was his speech. The other showed the agenda for today's service, along with those who had asked to speak. The list was long, but he didn't see Morgan's name on the list. He looked around him. He didn't see Morgan in the cafeteria either. He'd hoped she would come today, that maybe she could find some peace from her grief by sharing it with others, but it looked like that wouldn't be the case.

Derrick cleared his throat and stepped behind the podium. He tapped the mike, causing the speakers on the floor to emit a thumping sound.

"Uh, please take your seats," he said. "If everybody can be seated, we'll start the program."

The last few who were standing excused their way down the rows and finally took the last remaining chairs.

Derrick nodded and scanned the faces in the crowd. Eighty percent of those seated were the same age as Cole or a couple of years younger. None of them were crying. Most were stoically looking forward with their eyes focused on Derrick. These boys had schooled themselves not to show emotion or weakness, to project a toughness that wouldn't make them prey to those around them. But he could still see the pain, sadness, and strain on their young, brown faces, like they were trying their best to put up a brave front and hold back their tears but were on the verge of losing that battle.

Again, he was struck by the feeling that he had failed them—*all* of them. He hadn't protected Cole and he couldn't assure them that he could protect them either. What other boys in the crowd would he lose before all this was over? Who else would get killed?

Can't think about that, he told himself, returning his eyes to the papers in his hand. He had a job to do right now and he had to focus on it. He leaned toward the mike.

"I'd like to thank everybody for coming today to honor the memory of one of our own, Cole Humphries," he began. "Several of his teachers and friends have asked to come up here and offer kind words in his memory. As director and someone who knew Cole, I'd like to offer a few of my own. Cole was at the Branch Avenue Boys' Youth Institute for a short time . . . only about a year or so, but even then he made a big impression on a lot of you. He made a big impression on me, too. That boy made me earn my paycheck," he joked with a winsome smile, drawing a few laughs from the crowd, including from Cole's mom, who wiped at her reddened eyes.

"But I'm not here to talk about all the stuff Cole did wrong. You can check his rap sheet for that. I'm here to talk about who he was as a person . . . who he was on the inside. They say," Derrick continued, bracing his hands on the podium, glancing down at his speech notes, "what you do in life isn't as important as the memories you leave behind with those who knew you. I remember Cole as a young man who was smart, funny, and personable, with a lot . . . *a lot* of potential. And even though he made his share of mistakes, as I can attest to from how many damn times he was in my office," he said with a chuckle, earning more laughter from the audience, "I know if given enough time he would've learned from those mistakes. He would have undergone the change that many of you have . . . that even I did when I came here more than twenty years ago when I was angry at the world, mistrustful of help, and ready to give up on everything and everyone, including myself. Cole . . ." Derrick paused. He closed his eyes. He was starting to choke up. "He would've learned better. He would've grown. He would've become the man that would've made me . . . that would've made himself proud."

He opened his eyes again and found that several of the boys who had been holding back tears only minutes earlier were now crying openly or holding their T-shirts over their faces to hide their tears. Several of the faculty members were crying, too. He was about to look at his notes again when the door at the front of the cafeteria opened. Morgan strolled in, wearing dress slacks and a blue silk blouse—a definite departure from the T-shirt and overalls she usually wore at the Institute to teach her woodshop class. She was also wearing her curls down today, framing her face, making her look soft and vulnerable. She crept to one of the few remaining open chairs and sat down. When she did, Derrick returned his attention to his speech, relieved that she had come after all.

"I think the best thing we can do to honor Cole's memory," Derrick said, "is to try our best to come close to the life he could've led . . . the one I believe he was meant to lead if he was still here. Take advantage of every moment and opportunity. Treasure your family. Respect your mamas and your daddies. Stay tight with your boys—the ones that truly have your back—because some of those relationships you will carry with you throughout your life. Don't be scared to take a chance. Don't be afraid to be vulnerable. Those tears y'all are crying now," he said, pointing to the audience, "aren't anything to be ashamed of. Don't hesitate to love," Derrick said, his eyes once again drifting to Morgan.

She was too far away for him to say for sure, but he could've sworn that she held his gaze this time.

"Thank you," he said with a nod before folding up the sheets of paper and stepping away from the podium. The crowd clapped and Derrick took the seat reserved for him in the front row. He then watched as more than a dozen people went up front to offer speeches and condolences to Cole's family. A couple couldn't finish, breaking down into sobs. When they reached the end of the program, Derrick slowly stood up. He walked back to the podium and leaned toward the mike.

"This brings us to the end of our memorial service," he said. "Thank you all for your kind words and for showing your love for Cole today. I also want to thank—"

"Wait!" Morgan said, shooting up from her chair, holding up her hand. "Wait, Derrick!"

He gazed at her in surprise. All eyes in the room turned toward her.

Morgan anxiously gnawed her lower lip. "I'd . . . I'd like to say something. It'll be quick. I promise. Can I . . . can I come up?"

Derrick nodded. "Of course. And take as long as you need."

He watched as she swiftly walked up front. He stepped

aside and let her stand at the podium. He could see that she was shaking. He placed a gentle hand on her shoulder to calm her and she whipped around and looked at him, caught off guard by his touch.

"It's okay," he whispered, then dropped his hand.

She still looked nervous, but with those words, she stopped shaking.

"Hi," she said into the mike. "I'm Morgan Owens, carpentry instructor here at the Institute. Cole was in one of my classes. Not only was he very talented and creative . . . so creative . . . he was a good boy at heart. I know he was. When one of the other boys harassed me in my class, he defended me. He tried to come to my rescue. He didn't have to do that, but he put his neck out," she rambled. "And he told me about his dreams, how he wanted to go to college, how he wanted to build furniture or maybe become a carpenter. He told me . . . he told me he hoped to make enough money someday to take care of his mother and his brother and sister," she said, looking at Cole's mom. "I told him he could do it. I told him I had total faith in him, and he said he believed he could do it, too, because he trusted me. He trusted what I said." She lowered her head and sniffed. "I wish I was worthy of that trust. I wish I had been a better teacher and confidante to him. I wish I would've gone to the jail to visit him like he kept asking me to. I just . . . I just didn't know what to say." She cried as tears spilled onto her cheeks. "But I know now it wouldn't have mattered what I said. All that would've mattered was that I was there. That I showed him I still believed in him. But now it's too late and I'm . . . I'm so sorry. I'm . . ."

She couldn't finish. Derrick watched as she abruptly turned away and strode from the podium to the center aisle and then the cafeteria door. Despite all eyes being on him, Derrick went after her. He jogged across the cafeteria and burst through the double doors. He found her striding down the hall.

"Morgan! Morgan, wait up!" he called after her.

But she didn't stop. She fled into the stairwell and he caught her just before she hit the stairs. He grabbed her arm and yanked her back to him. When he did he could see her entire face was red now. She was choking on her own sobs. He pulled her into an embrace and held her close.

"It's okay," he said, rubbing her back as she cried on his broad shoulder. "It's okay."

They stood there for several minutes. Finally, her sobs eased and her tears went from streams to a trickle. She eased back from him and gazed into his eyes—and he couldn't resist. He leaned down and kissed her and God help him, she didn't shove him away but kissed him back. Her lips were as warm and soft as he remembered, and when he slipped his tongue inside her mouth, she moaned with acceptance. He shifted his mouth from her lips to her chin to her neck, kissing the skin over the collar of her silk shirt.

"I missed you, baby. I wanted you back so much," he whispered, and for the first time, he felt her tense. This time, she did shove away from him.

"No," she said, glaring at him, shaking her head. "No."

She then turned around and headed downstairs, leaving him standing alone on the floor above.

Chapter 28

Jamal

Jamal laid out two dress shirts on his bed—one periwinkle blue, the other with white and gray vertical stripes. He scrunched up his nose as he considered them for his first date with Nurse Sam, unsure of which one to wear.

He was taking Sam out to dinner at a Mexican restaurant in Arlington, Virginia, which was closer to her home. The restaurant wasn't so high-end that he felt the need to wear a tie tonight, but he didn't want to show up in just jeans and a T-shirt and come off too casual. He wanted to show her that he was making an effort, that he cared. It seemed important to do so, to go through all first-date rituals. The agonizing over what to wear . . . The double-checking dinner reservations . . . The making sure he carried a full pack of gum but not a full pack of condoms because he'd more than likely need the former rather than the latter for a first date.

Unable to make a decision on which shirt to wear, Jamal turned away from the bed and headed back to his closet to find a sweater to throw on instead, but he paused when he saw in the corner of his eye an image flash across his flat-screen TV. He turned around to stare at the television and saw an anchor sitting in front of the headline, "Late Breaking News." He reached for the remote on his bed and turned up the volume.

"You heard it here first, folks! Channel 7 has gotten word that D.C. Mayor Vernon Johnson was arrested today at his home in Southwest. Johnson's city hall offices and those of several staff members also have been raided, according to sources," the male anchor said, his pale face looking grave. *"The mayor's office has yet to release a statement confirming Johnson's arrest, but we have an eyewitness video of what happened."*

The screen then cut to footage of Johnson being led down the brick steps of his tony Capitol Hill brownstone in handcuffs. The video quality didn't look as polished as the rest of the broadcast. It looked like someone had taken it with a handheld camera or cell phone. But you could still see everything: the mayor's wife standing in the doorway looking horrified and near tears, shouting frantically to the cops to leave her husband alone, the onlookers staring in awe with their own camera phones ready as they watched the scene unfold. Vernon's balding head was bowed and his face was grim. He was whisked away to a waiting police cruiser where the door stood open. It was slammed shut behind him as soon as he was shoved inside.

Jamal stared at the TV screen in shock. Detective Wingate hadn't told him whether they had finally decided to press charges against the mayor, let alone that they would do it this soon.

The irony wasn't lost on him either that the way he had gotten word of Johnson's arrest—caught off guard while watching the television—was the same way he had learned of the reporter Phillip Seymour's murder. But while news of Phil's murder had been a traumatic, gut-wrenching shock, this was a welcome surprise. It seemed like some justice would finally be served.

The broadcast cut back to the anchor desk. *"So far, there is no word on exactly why Mayor Johnson was arrested,"* the anchor continued, *"but sources say his arrest is the product of an ongoing investigation, which means we may expect more arrests in the near future."*

Jamal pressed the button on his remote to turn off the television.

The mayor had boasted to Jamal long ago that no judge or jury would ever find him guilty of a damn thing. Now they would see if his boast was correct.

He glanced back at the shirts on his bed, feeling a sense of peace he hadn't felt in quite a long time.

"Periwinkle," he said with a confident nod. "That's what I'll wear tonight."

Jamal watched as Sam reached across the platter of nachos, guacamole, and pico de gallo at the center of the table with her fork in hand.

"Oh, wow! Your fajita looks good! Do you mind if I try some of your steak?" Sam asked as she stabbed into one of the steak strips.

"Umm, no. Be my guest," he said with a laugh as she popped the steak into her mouth.

"I'm sorry," she said through a mouthful of food, looking mildly embarrassed. Even her cheeks flushed pink, making her look even cuter, in his opinion. "I probably should've gotten a yes first before I did that."

"It's fine. You don't have to apologize."

"No, I do! I just do stuff like that. It's one of the bad habits of being a nurse. You take charge a lot. You take the lead." She reached for her glass of Bordeaux and took a sip. "It's hard to turn it off. I bet it scares off a lot of guys. It would certainly explain my dating history."

He shook his head and ate some of his fajita. "It doesn't scare me off."

"You mean you like women who take charge?"

He took another bite of his meal. "Within certain contexts. Yeah."

She inclined her head, licked sour cream from her lips, and smirked. "And what context would that be, Jamal?"

He caught the flirtatious twinkle in her eyes and he started laughing again. She joined him, chuckling softly over the lip of her wineglass.

They had been on their date for less than an hour and already he felt sparks between them. Laughter came easy with Sam. And they obviously had chemistry. Compatibility was still in question but he guessed he would find that out over time if they went on another date, but chances looked good that they would. It was a relief. This was yet another sign that he was moving in the right direction.

"So besides take-charge women, what other things do you like?" Sam asked. "Sports? Movies? *Hang gliding?*"

"Yes, yes, and no to hang gliding. How about you? What do you like?"

"The same things, I guess. I like football . . . basketball . . . movies, when I have time to watch them. I'm also a bit of a news junkie. Quick stuff I can grab online during my rounds." She sliced into her empanada. "I even did some research on you online after we had coffee that day."

"I think everybody checks out LinkedIn pages before a date nowadays though."

"I checked out a lot more than your LinkedIn page, Jamal. Articles . . . video clips on YouTube. You were a pretty big deal when you were deputy mayor."

He shook his head again. "Not really."

"Oh, come on! Don't be modest," she chided, smiling and leaning over her plate. "I saw those pictures of you on Google. You used to hang out with some really important people."

Yeah, that had been one of the stipulations he'd had in the beginning when he worked out his deal with Mayor Johnson. In order to keep the mayor's dirty secrets, he'd made the mayor take him to all the events where he could hobnob with big dogs of politics and the business world. He thought it would help him move up the ladder, to get some badly deserved recognition. But it hadn't done that; it had only flattered his ego and landed him in more trouble than it was worth.

"And you reported directly to Mayor Johnson, right?" Sam asked.

Jamal slowly nodded as he wiped his mouth with his dinner napkin, unsure of where she was going with this line of questioning.

"So were you caught off guard like everybody else by what happened today? I mean about the mayor getting arrested! Or do you know what happened?" she whispered with wide blue eyes. "That would just be so crazy if you—"

"Sam," he said, interrupting and holding up his hand, "look, I'll talk about anything else you want tonight, but I'd just rather not talk about my time working for Johnson. It wasn't a high point for me. When I left city hall, I was more than happy to move on from it. So I'd rather not go through the whole postmortem of my time there if . . . if that's okay with you."

"Oh! Of course!" She winced. "I'm so sorry, Jamal. I didn't know it was a touchy subject for you."

"Again, no need to apologize. And I wouldn't expect you to know."

She sheepishly lowered her gaze to her plate. "God, I am screwing this up so much, aren't I?"

"Screwing up what?"

"Our date!"

"No you're not! I'm having a good time."

She slowly raised her eyes from her plate. "Really?"

"Definitely. Besides," he said, "if you feel that bad, you can give me some of your empanada to make up for it."

She grinned. "I'd be happy to." She grabbed a forkful of the flaky crust and fed him a bite.

Long after they had finished their meals, they had lingered at their table, still talking and laughing. In fact, they had lingered so long that they started to get anxious glances from their waiter, who Jamal suspected was wondering when they were going to leave so that the restaurant could finally open up another table. But he and Sam ignored the waiter, not wanting to end their evening sooner than necessary.

Somewhere around ten o'clock, Jamal walked Sam back to her car, which was parked in a nearby lot. They held hands as they strolled, gazing at the first chilly night of September.

"I had a good time," he said.

"I had a good time, too," Sam replied. "Are you sure you did? You're telling me the truth?"

He chuckled. "I swear I'm not lying." He stopped in front of her Toyota Prius. "I really had a good time, hence us talking for three solid hours."

She gazed up at him. "I hope I see you again, Jamal. It would suck if I didn't. It seems like we're off to a pretty good start. Call me and set something up. Okay? I'm busy all next week but the week after . . ." Her voice trailed off.

"I will." He leaned forward to give her a hug goodbye but was caught off guard when she kissed him instead. Her lips were soft and thin, but firm. She opened her mouth slightly and darted her tongue against his lips, easing them open. The kiss deepened and the spark Jamal felt earlier started to catch flame. He wrapped his arms around her and held her close while they kissed.

When Sam breathlessly pulled back a minute later, she grinned. "Yes, we are off to a good start," she whispered before giving him another quick peck.

She unlocked her car door and climbed into the driver's seat. He stood on the sidewalk and watched as she pulled away, giving a quick wave over her shoulder at him.

When her Prius turned the corner, he turned back around and headed to his car, which was parked a few blocks away. A smile was on his face. A hop was in his step.

Yes, things were finally looking up for him.

As Jamal neared his car, his cell phone began to buzz. He slowed his gait, reached into his pocket, and squinted down at the text message on the screen. It was from Melissa.

> Hey, Jay, how u been? Just checking to see if you still wanted to go to that play with me at Shakespeare Theater Co next week. The tickets are non-refundable so I'll give them away if you're not interested. No pressure either way. (I know you said you needed space.) Let me know! Hope you're doing OK.

In true Melissa fashion, she ended her text with an innocuous smiley-face emoji that almost seemed to mock him.

And just like that the grin on Jamal's face and the hop in his step disappeared.

"Shit," he muttered, tucking his cell back into his pocket.

Chapter 29

Ricky

Ricky walked toward the parallel-parked unmarked vehicle, pausing to glance around him to make sure no one was watching as he made his way from the spot where he'd been waiting underneath the bakery awning. He was becoming even more cautious nowadays, knowing that the stakes were getting increasingly higher. One wrong move could mean the end of him and everything he held dear.

He opened the back passenger-side door and hopped inside. The instant he slammed the door shut, the car lurched forward with the rev of the engine and rattle from the exhaust, merging into Northwest D.C. traffic.

Detective Ramsey, who was driving, glanced at Ricky in the rearview mirror. "All right, you called us. We came. What did you need?"

"And make it quick," Detective Dominguez said. "I promised my wife I'd be home by seven tonight. I wasn't expecting any last-minute detours."

"Aww, I'm sorry," Ricky replied sarcastically, tilting his

head. "Did I inconvenience you? Do I need to send you home with a note?"

"Ricky," Ramsey said, sounding irritated, "just tell us why you called us. Come on! You said it was important."

He slumped back in his seat and nodded. "Because it is important."

Ricky had reached out to Detectives Ramsey and Dominguez soon after the party at Dolla Dolla's house. He hadn't been able to convince Dolla Dolla to back off of Derrick, putting his friend's safety and the safety of his many students at risk. If Ricky couldn't intervene with this one, it was about time the cops finally did. They'd been sitting on their big fat asses for months while he did all the heavy lifting.

"I saw the news. You guys arrested Mayor Johnson yesterday," he began.

"Yeah. *So?*" Dominguez challenged, glancing at him over his shoulder, being as charming as ever.

"So why the hell is the mayor behind bars but Dolla isn't?" Ricky sucked his teeth. "I helped y'all with both. I gave you Mayor Johnson. I gave you one of Dolla's contacts like asked. *Both* of them should be in jail!"

"It's not that simple, Ricky," Ramsey insisted. "One doesn't necessarily mean the same thing for the other. Those are two different investigations—one of which wasn't even ours. We weren't aiming for Mayor Johnson."

"But you guys got him anyway. And frankly, you should've been aiming for him all along," Ricky said. "I told you he was dirty. He's a lot dirtier than some of the goons Dolla has coming in and out of his place. But y'all were more concerned with—"

"And in the case of Mayor Johnson, that detective had recorded conversations to work with," Ramsey said, speaking over him. "He had definitive evidence to present to the D.A."

"What are you talking about? I thought those under-cover cops got a recording, too! She had a damn mike in her wig."

"You gave us one . . . *one* damn recording to work with!" Dominguez threw back at him. "Excuse us if we ain't shoutin' 'case closed!'"

"You know why I can't record Dolla. They pat me down and take my phone every time I walk in there!" Ricky argued.

Ramsey nodded. "Your hands are tied, so our hands are tied, Ricky."

"He's tricking out girls again. He's doing the same shit that got my girl's sister killed. That got her mother murdered," Ricky said, the bleakness coming through in his voice. "He's threatened my friend's life and the lives of the kids who he's responsible for. Dolla had a kid killed in jail. And y'all niggas are really just gonna sit here and tell me your hands are tied? What the fuck is the point? Why am I risking my life every damn day for this investigation if y'all can't do anything?" He punched the back of the seat in a fit of anger, "I swear to God you two are fuckin' useless!"

"Hey! Fuck you, you piece of shit!" Dominguez yelled, unbuckling his seat belt and turning around in his seat so that he could glower over his shoulder. His face had gone full crimson. He looked like a pock-marked tomato. "You're lucky I don't come back there and beat the crap outta you!"

"Then let's get it poppin', nigga!" Ricky held up his hand and beckoned him. "I've been wantin' to whup your ass since the moment you first opened that ugly-ass mouth of yours."

Just as Dominguez reached over the back of the seat to lunge for Ricky, Ramsey reached up to grab his arm and tugged him back. "Stop! Stop that shit, the *both* of you! Or you're gonna make me have a damn car accident! Dominguez, sit the hell down."

He pulled at the other man's suit jacket and Dominguez half-heartedly yanked it out of his grasp before slumping back into his seat. He still looked pissed, but at least he was raging in silence now.

Meanwhile, Ricky wished Ramsey had let them fight. He hadn't lied when he said he'd wanted to beat up Dominguez since the night after the raids back in December and the cocky, smart-mouthed detective had strolled into the interrogation room months ago. He might feel some emotional release if he could slap the shit out of Dominguez or punch him in the face. Instead, he still felt lost, angry, and depressed.

"Let's understand something, Ricky," Ramsey began, pulling into another lane of traffic. "I'm not gonna just sit here and let you disrespect us by telling us we're just sitting around . . . that we're fucking useless. We've been collecting evidence and doing our own investigation outside of what we do with you, okay? We've done our own footwork for almost a damn year."

"Yeah, right," Ricky murmured sullenly.

"And don't act like we haven't done shit for you. When you asked us to get your son back, we got him, didn't we?" Ramsey persisted. "When you asked for us to put your girl in protective custody, did we not arrange that as well?"

Ricky didn't answer him. He couldn't. Every time he thought about Simone and Miles, he felt like someone was yanking at his heart or dipping a bucket in the well of emotions that went so deep inside him, he wasn't sure the well had a bottom. He missed them. He yearned to be with them. He thought about them every day that he woke up and when he closed his eyes at night. He wished he could pick up the phone just to hear Simone's voice. Miles would be more than three months now, almost four. He wished he had a picture of his growing boy. Instead, all he had was memories. Memories of the month they'd spent together, and it terrified him that that month might be the only memories he'd ever have of them being together as a family.

"This is a two-way street," Ramsey continued, oblivious to his melancholy. "You help us out, we help you out. I understand that you're frustrated. But the wheels of justice can't always spin at the speed that you or I may want. If we want to send Dolla Dolla away for a long time, if you really want to end this—we gotta do it right. Okay?"

Ricky continued to stew silently in frustration, knowing that Ramsey's elaborate explanation basically meant that nothing would change. He would have to keep going back to Dolla Dolla's place, mentally taking notes of everything he observed so he could tell the cops later. Dolla Dolla would continue to do his thing, destroying lives and having a good time while he was at it. Once again, Ricky felt stuck between a rock and a hard place. Once again, he felt like the situation had been taken out of his control.

"Just pull over and let me out," Ricky said, shaking his head in exasperation as he gazed out the car window. "I'm done talking."

"Our fuckin' pleasure," Dominguez mumbled.

Less than a minute later, Ramsey pulled up to the curb in front of an office building. Ricky hopped out.

"We're working on it, Ricky," Ramsey called after him. "Trust us. We're not gonna leave you hangin'."

Ricky slammed shut the door and watched as they pulled off.

He wasn't sure if he did trust Detective Ramsey, despite his assurances. In the back of his mind, he suspected that in the end he would be left swinging in the wind.

Chapter 30

Derrick

Derrick gazed through the double-paned glass and found Morgan sitting on a stool in her workshop with her satchel thrown over her shoulder. She was laughing with a half dozen of her students.

Today was her last day at the Institute. Though she had stayed longer than the month she had promised, he suspected the kiss they'd shared in the stairwell after Cole's memorial service had pushed her too far. She'd emailed him the very next day that she would be gone by that Friday, whether he'd hired her replacement or not. Now he watched as she said her last goodbyes to the kids she had loved and respected so much. He observed from a distance as she hugged them and wished them all good luck.

He stood back as the boys strolled one by one out of the workroom, giving one last wave goodbye to her before they entered the hall. They glanced up at him as they passed. "Hey! What's up, Mr. Derrick?" one of them said.

"Hey," he murmured with a nod before stepping into the workroom's doorway when they had all left.

Morgan was opening drawers and shoving stuff from

her desk into her satchel. She was buckling it closed when she looked up and saw Derrick leaning against the door frame. When she saw him, her face changed. Her arched brows drew together.

"I wasn't expecting to see you down here," she said.

"I wasn't expecting it either. But our exit interview should've started fifteen minutes ago," he began, shoving his hands into the pockets of his slacks. "You didn't show up so I came looking for you. I figured I'd find you in your workroom."

"I didn't know you were serious about that . . . the exit interview, I mean."

He squinted at her. "Why wouldn't I be? I ask all employees to do one before they leave. It helps me to find out more about their experience . . . find out areas where we can improve."

She choked out a laugh and slowly shook her head. "Okay, fine. Go ahead and ask your questions. We can do it while I gather the last of my things."

You're really in that much of a hurry to get out of here? he thought with dismay, but he didn't ask her the question aloud. He already knew what the answer would be.

"So how would you rate your experience overall at the Institute while working here?" he asked. "On a scale of one to ten."

She shrugged as she opened a bottom drawer. "About a six . . . maybe six and a half."

"*A six and a half?*" he cried.

"You said overall! If I had to give one score for everything, I would say my experience working with the kids has been an eight or a nine. But working at an understaffed, under-funded place like this one isn't easy, so I'd rate that about a five. I was going with the average between the two. I thought I was being generous."

He rolled his eyes. "But you knew that coming in. I told

you we didn't have a lot of money or resources to work with."

"You're right. But there are some things I didn't know coming in. Some things that made the experience more challenging."

"Like what?"

"Like faculty dynamics. You've got a few divas on your staff, Derrick. They've been here so long that they act like they own the place; they boss around everyone else. Another thing is the security staff. Sometimes I felt like I had to be a buffer between them and the kids because some of those dudes can be so aggressive with how they handle situations. This is more of a school than a juvenile detention center. I don't think some of them get that," she muttered as she slammed a drawer shut. "And you know . . . other things came along in a way that I didn't expect."

The workshop fell silent as she continued to pack her things.

"Like us," he said when he couldn't take the silence anymore.

She hesitated, then gradually nodded. "It probably wasn't the best idea to get in a romantic relationship with my boss. But I'm a grown woman." She shrugged. "I did it willingly. I knew the risk I was taking. Now I've gotta deal with the price of that bad decision."

A bad decision.

So that's how she would classify their relationship? Funny, out of all the mistakes he had made in the past year and a half, falling in love and pursuing her wasn't the one he'd considered the bad decision. Yes, it had come with a lot of blowback. He'd lost Melissa. He'd lost his damn cat. He'd lost Mr. Theo's respect. But the payback had been so much more. He thought he'd finally found the woman who matched him and understood him. He thought he'd finally gotten it right.

"Well," he said, stepping into the room, "you might rate your experience here a six but—"

"Six and a half," she corrected.

"Fine. Six and a half. But I'd rate you a lot higher. I still consider you one of the best instructors we've had in a very long time. The kids will miss you. I'll miss you, too, Morgan."

And he meant it with every part of him.

This was the part of the exit interview when he usually offered the former instructor a handshake and asked them to stay in touch. But he really wanted to hug her, to pull her into his arms and hold her close. But he did neither. Instead, he watched as she closed another drawer and nodded.

"Thanks," she whispered before tugging her satchel farther up her shoulder. She looked around her. "I should get going. I was trying to leave early, before all the classes ended for today. If I had to say goodbye to everyone, I'd be here until midnight."

"I understand," he mumbled.

"Goodbye, Derrick." She then walked around him and headed to the doorway.

"Bye."

When she exited the room, he stood in the center, feeling an emptiness he couldn't describe. It wasn't supposed to go down this way. None of it. Cole should still be alive and headed to his next class. Derrick should be standing here asking Morgan what they should pick up for dinner tonight, not saying goodbye to her forever.

He started to walk out of the room, but his eyes landed on a book that sat on top of a pile of papers on her stool. He recognized it. It was a journal she sometimes scribbled some of her furniture design ideas in, ones that she considered making later. She must have missed it in all the things that she'd packed, but she would probably need it.

He grabbed the book and raced to the door. He then ran down the hall and up the stairs to the floor above, hoping he would catch her before she left.

"Morgan!" Derrick shouted after her just as he saw her push open the glass doors to head outside.

She must not have heard him because she kept walking with her head bowed.

"Morgan!" he shouted again. He jogged after her and pushed the door open. "Morgan!"

This time she did stop. She turned on the sidewalk and faced him.

"You left this," he said, holding out her design journal to her.

"Oh," she said with a sniff. "Thank you. I don't know how I forgot that."

As he drew closer, he could see there were tears in her eyes. He frowned. "Are you okay?"

She closed her eyes and one tear trickled onto her cheek. "Please . . . *please* stop asking me that! You know I'm not okay, Derrick." She roughly wiped her nose with the back of her hand. "But once I get out of here and on a plane to Atlanta, I'll feel better."

"I disappointed you. I failed you. I know I did. I wish I could go back and change everything, but I can't."

She shook her head and opened her eyes. "No, you can't. But that—"

Her words were drowned out by the sound of a gunning engine and screeching tires.

The noise drew their attention. It drew the attention of the dozen boys playing on the Institute's basketball court, too, even though they all were used to the sound of busy traffic making its way up and down Branch Avenue. You could hear it in the classrooms, the offices, and the dorms. Sometimes instructors had to shout or close their windows to be heard over it. But for some reason, it sounded different this time. Derrick wasn't sure why.

He turned in just enough time to see a black SUV racing toward them with the passenger-side window down. He couldn't see the driver or who was inside but he heard the tell-tale *pop*, then another. He had grown up and lived in the inner city long enough to know what that sound was.

"Get down!" he shouted to Morgan.

"*What?*" she yelled back just as he grabbed her hand and roughly yanked her to the cement, making her scream in alarm as she landed sprawled on the sidewalk. He shoved her down flat and lay on top of her. He didn't even think about what he was doing; he automatically used himself as a human shield for her as the popping continued.

He heard the sound of rapid firecrackers going off mixed with that of shattering glass, shouts and screams, and the ring of bullets bouncing off of metal and brick. Derrick felt one bee sting in his back, then another in his arm. He knew the whole thing probably lasted less than sixty seconds, but it felt like an eternity.

When the shooting finally stopped and the SUV pulled away, he slowly raised his head and looked around him. He saw the busted windows and doors on the Institute's exterior. He saw that a woman across the street had run for cover behind a mailbox and a man crouched behind a Ford Explorer. Derrick looked at the basketball court. Some of the boys were yelling for help, screaming that one or two of them had been shot.

He pushed himself up and looked down at Morgan. "Are you all right?" he asked frantically, terrified at the idea that she'd been hurt. "You didn't get hit, did you?"

She looked shaken but unharmed. "N-n-no," she stuttered. "I'm . . . I'm o-o-okay."

"Run inside and make sure everyone is okay in there, too. Make sure they call the police and tell them to send an ambulance." He rose to his feet. "I gotta check on the kids on the court."

He started to run toward the basketball court but grabbed on to the chain-link fence to steady himself when he suddenly felt light-headed.

"Derrick!" Morgan screamed, catching him before he collapsed to the ground. "Oh, Derrick, baby! Oh, my God! You've been shot."

He looked down and realized that his dress shirt was soaked in blood. That must have been the "bee stings" he'd felt earlier.

Well, shit, he thought almost with dismay. He tried to stagger back to his feet but felt like he was losing a battle to jelly limbs. His head lolled to the side.

"Derrick! Derrick!" she screamed again as his eyes fluttered closed.

Chapter 31

Jamal

Jamal stood in the theater lobby, looking at the people streaming by him, giving himself a pep talk. He was meeting Melissa tonight for the play she'd bought tickets for a month ago, back when they were still hooking up, back when he'd thought he'd had a chance of winning her heart. But now he knew differently, so he wondered why he was here exactly.

Because she texted me and asked me to come. Because Melissa is cool, and I still like her as a person. And it is possible for a man and a woman to be friendly with one another—even if they've had sex, he told himself while glancing at the time on his cell phone screen.

He'd done it before. He'd had relationships with other women that had fizzled out in the end and he'd still remained friends with them. He could still say a casual "hi" and keep it moving when he saw them in public. *This evening with Melissa is gonna be no different*, he told himself.

And besides, he wasn't even interested in Melissa like that anymore, he told himself. He hadn't seen her in weeks—almost a month—and he'd had his date with Sam only last week. And Sam was a sexy, funny woman whom he'd had chemistry with. She was obviously a better fit for him—much better than Melissa.

Jamal was simply seeing *Othello* tonight with an old hookup, an old friend. There was no need to make it bigger than it was.

We'll shoot the shit. Have some laughs. Maybe grab dinner and go our separate ways, he thought with a shrug as he continued to search for Melissa. *No big deal.*

"Jay?" he heard her call, and he turned in the direction of her voice. He saw her walking across the crowded lobby, excusing her way through a group of six, huddled together near the theater entrance. When she drew closer, she came at him with open arms.

"Oh, Jay!" she said, slamming into him and giving him a hug like she hadn't seen him in ten years instead of just three and a half weeks. "Oh, God!"

Fuck, he thought, feeling her arms around him and her supple body pressed against his. His stoic resolve instantly faltered.

This wasn't the same as meeting other women he once dated or had feelings for, and he couldn't believe that he'd deluded himself into believing it would be. He didn't feel bland detachment right now. He wanted to keep holding her. He wanted to kiss her. Being with Melissa again put him emotionally smack-dab where he was almost a month ago, standing in her bathroom, waiting for her to confess that she felt the same way about him as he did for her, only for her to say, "I'm just not here for a love thing."

Melissa stepped back, loosening her hold on him. "Shit! I'm freaking out right now. I'm still shaking."

Jamal frowned. "Why are you freaking out?"

"You didn't see it on the news?" she asked, now wide-eyed. "You didn't hear what happened?"

He shook his head, confused. "No. What . . . what happened?"

"There was a drive-by shooting at the Institute. It happened a few hours ago. A couple kids were killed. Derrick got shot, too."

Jamal stared at her in disbelief. "What . . . h-how . . . is he okay?"

She nodded. "He's better, but he's still recuperating in the ICU. I just got off the phone with his mama. She said he's in stable condition, but it was touch and go at first. They're all at the hospital right now waiting for him to wake up. But the doctor said his prospects look good."

"Well, that's good . . . I mean that's great! I guess that's the best-case scenario you could ask for, considering . . . well, everything." Jamal pursed his lips, still stunned but happy to hear Derrick was going to be all right. "So I guess you're off to the hospital then. You know, you could've canceled. I would've understood. You didn't have to come all the way here to tell me you're going to check on him."

Jamal knew she probably wanted to be at Derrick's side right now. He knew that despite her anger and heartache, she'd want to be there when Derrick opened his eyes. But Melissa surprised him by crossing her arms over her chest and shaking her head.

"I wasn't heading there. I told you, his mama said he's stable now." She shrugged. "Besides, *that chick* is up there with them. His mama said she's been hanging out in the waiting room waiting for news on Derrick." Melissa sighed. "She's his girl now. I'm not. I'd just be intruding. I'll give him a call when he's out of the hospital. I'll send flowers, too."

"Oh," Jamal uttered, shocked at how casual she sounded.

Maybe it really was over between them. Maybe she'd finally moved on.

"Sorry for dropping this bomb on you," Melissa said. "I really did think you knew already about the shooting. It's been all over the news."

"I didn't watch any news today, and besides checking sports scores, I haven't read anything online since this morning."

"Well, anyway . . . let's change the subject. I've been obsessing about this for hours. I want to talk about something else. How have you been? What's going on with you?"

"I'm fine. Not much has changed," he lied.

"*Really?* Because I heard about the mayor's arrest. When I did, I instantly thought about you," she whispered, raising a hand to his face. She ran a thumb along his cheek tenderly, making the knot tighten in his stomach again, making the yearning grow ten-fold. "I wanted to call you after I heard, but you said you . . . well, that you needed space. I thought it might be too soon to reach out to you. I hope it gave you some relief to know he can't bother you anymore though." She searched his face. "Did the panic attacks stop? Do you feel better now?"

"Yeah, uh . . . much better," he said distractedly as he tugged her hand away from his cheek. He glanced at the closed doors leading to the theater.

He hoped the performance would start soon. The sooner it began, the sooner it would be over—and he could leave. It was a mistake to come here today. He should've waited longer to see her again.

She eyed him. "Is everything okay, Jay?"

He turned to look at her again. "Yeah, why?"

"I don't know." She took off her jacket and looped it over her arm. "You just seem . . ." She shook her head again and smiled. "Never mind."

He pointed in the distance. "Looks like the doors are opening. We better get in line."

They arrived at their seats five minutes later. They were

close to the stage—only about four rows back. Jamal couldn't believe it, but he felt worse in such a confined space. Now their knees and elbows brushed. Now they were so close that if he turned to his right, he would be dangerously close to her neck and ear. It took all his will-power not to lean over and nip her earlobe or lick the spot on the base of her neck that made her moan.

She smiled at him again, unaware of his carnal thoughts. "So how's the job hunt going? Are you still looking, or did you find something?"

"I've gone on a few more interviews. I got an offer yesterday, but I still haven't decided if I want to take it."

"*Really?* That's good news! What offer?" she asked, sounding excited. "Tell me! Where?"

"It's hard to describe. It's with a consultancy group. But like I said, I don't know if I want it anyway."

"Oh."

They fell into another awkward silence. They both looked around them, staring at the audience and the empty stage, looking at the playbill.

"So what have you been up to?" he asked, taking his turn at making an attempt at chitchat. He figured he should. He had resolved that this would probably be the last time he would see her in person for quite a while. It was obvious that his emotions were still too strong and the hurt was too raw. But tonight, he could at least be cordial.

"Not much. Looking forward to the kids taking Thanksgiving vacation in a month so I can finally have some days off. I've kind of been in work mode. I've been stuck in my apartment . . . just me and Brownie, working on my lesson plans and grading papers. I finally went out for the first time in weeks last Tuesday to this tapas restaurant on M Street. I'd never been there before but the guy who took me there said the food was good."

"A guy?" His ears perked up at that. "So you . . . you went out on a date?"

"A *blind* date," she clarified. "One of the teachers at my school set it up. He was nice, but I just didn't feel anything." She nudged his knee. "So how about you? You getting back out there? Met anybody?"

You mean have I gotten over you? he wondered flippantly.

He didn't know why she was talking about this. Why the hell would he want to hear about her blind date, or tell her about his dating life? Did she forget what they were to each other, what he'd felt for her? But maybe this was her attempt to move on, to re-create the platonic friendship they'd once had. He'd play along for now.

"Yeah, I went on a date last week. She's a nurse that I met at the hospital center when I was shot. We ran into each other again, and I asked her out."

"*Oh?* What's this nurse's name?"

"Samantha. Samantha Connolly."

"Samantha?" She nodded thoughtfully. "Let me guess . . . a pixie-looking type, right? Cute, blond, and petite?"

He nodded and inclined his head, now surprised. "How'd you know?"

"I just know you have a type," she said with a snort. "Those are the kind of girls you're usually attracted to. You've been that way as long as I've known you. You love you some little white girls."

What the hell is that supposed to mean?

He also noticed that Melissa had conveniently forgotten that he'd been attracted to her. She didn't fit that "type."

"And I guess you have a type, too? Tall, dark-skinned dudes with dreads?" he jabbed, alluding to her ex, Derrick.

She side-eyed him. "Not really."

"Could've fooled me," he muttered bitterly before slumping back in his chair.

The house lights went down and the stage lights came up. The performance began.

They didn't talk again until intermission. It had less to do with how engrossing the Shakespearean performance was and not wanting to be rude, than feeling like unsaid words were piling up between them. He could feel the tension mounting as the night pressed on. When the house lights came up again and people stood from their chairs to head to the bathrooms in the lobby, he and Melissa stayed seated.

"So what do you think of the play so far?" she asked.

He shrugged and kept his gaze focused on the empty stage. "It's fine." He frowned when she loudly grumbled beside him. "What?"

"Jay, are you sure everything is okay?"

"Of course, I'm sure. Why do you keep asking me that?"

"Because you're acting weird. You're not even talking."

"I *am* talking! Did I not just answer your question?"

"Forget it!" She sucked her teeth in exasperation and shook her head. "Just forget it."

"Forget *what*? What is your problem?"

"You really wanna know what my problem is?" She shifted in her chair to glare at him. "I asked you out tonight because I missed you and I . . . I thought we could be cool, that we could still be friends. But if you don't want my friendship anymore, Jay, that's fine with me."

"I never said that!"

He hadn't said it, but it was the truth. That's how he felt. He'd be better off if he never had to see her again, if they never spoke to one another. He knew that now. He'd take her silence over this slow torture.

"I know how men are," she continued. "Now that we're not fucking anymore, it's deuces for you, and that's fine. It won't hurt my feelings. Just let a girl know though."

"*What?* What the hell are you talking about? You can't just throw random shit out like—"

He didn't get to finish. Someone behind him loudly shushed him as the house lights went down again and the play resumed. By then, Jamal had to fight every urge not to get up and walk out on her. He didn't need this shit. He certainly didn't need a guilt trip from Melissa, of all people. She was the one who had crushed him, not the other way around.

When the play finally ended and the cast took their bows, he and Melissa stood from their chairs and headed to the aisle. It turned out she wanted to get out of there just as much as he did. They walked into the lobby and heard the thunder outside. They gazed out the glass doors and saw the heavy downpour.

"Did you drive or take the Metro?" he asked, staring at the rain.

She blew air through her bubbled cheeks. "Metro."

The theater was about five blocks from the nearest Metro station. He couldn't let her walk in this—no matter how pissed she'd made him.

He held up his car keys. "Come on. I'm parked up the street. I'll drive you home."

She stubbornly shook her head. "Nah, that's okay. I'm good."

"Let's not argue. It's raining cats and dogs out there, Lissa."

She pulled out her cell. "It's fine. I'll just catch an Uber." She tapped a few buttons on screen. "I can have one here in . . . shit!"

"What?"

"I guess it's busy tonight with the rain. The nearest ride is about twenty-five minutes away."

"So I'm driving you home then?"

She looked like she wanted to mount another argument but instead looked again out the glass doors at the heavy downpour and dropped her phone back into her purse. "I guess so," she murmured.

Chapter 32

Jamal

They did the twenty-minute drive in strained silence, not looking at one another. When Jamal passed the entrance of her apartment building, Melissa turned to look at him. She pointed to the car window. "Aren't you . . . aren't you going to pull over so I can hop out?"

"It's still raining. Besides, I should walk you upstairs," he murmured, making her close her eyes and slump back against the leather headrest.

"You don't have to do that, Jay."

"I know I don't have to do it, but it doesn't feel right to just shove you out the door and gun the engine. *Okay?* Just let me do this," he said tightly.

He might be irritated with her, but he was still a gentleman.

"Okay, it's up to you." She opened her eyes and sighed. "Thank you."

He didn't reply. Instead, Jamal made a right, to turn into the building's parking garage. He pulled up to the yellow and black gate and lowered the car window to press the glowing button to receive a parking ticket.

A minute later they were walking to the garage elevators. They were both silent. Only the sound of their shoes thumping against cement and echoing against the cinderblock walls filled the space where their voices would usually be.

It felt wrong to be so stiff and awkward around Melissa. When they were alone, their conversation usually flowed easily, but it hadn't tonight. All they'd had were biting words for each other and he wasn't sure why.

Because you're still angry and hurt, a voice in his head said.

So what was her excuse? Why was she so hostile?

Jamal pressed the up button, shoved his hands into his coat pockets, and they both waited for the elevator to arrive.

"Thanks for coming out tonight," Melissa ventured a few seconds later.

"You're welcome," he said, keeping his eyes on the elevator's steel doors.

"You didn't seem like you had a good time though."

"You didn't seem like you *wanted* me to have a good time. You took shots at me the whole night."

"I just asked you why you were acting so weird. I didn't take shots at you."

"Yes, you did."

"No, I didn't."

"Yes, you did, Lissa!"

"No, I did not!"

He finally turned to look at her. "*You love you some little white girls, don't you?*" he said, mimicking her voice, recalling her words from earlier. "*Now that we're not fucking anymore, it's deuces for you.*" He barked out a biting laugh. "What kind of shit was that? You had your foot on my neck and you wouldn't let up."

She slowly exhaled. "Okay, you're right."

"Thank you!"

Suddenly, the elevator chimed, and the doors opened. She stepped inside the compartment and he followed. The doors closed behind them. It began to ascend to the fourteenth floor.

"I didn't mean to act like an ass all night," she whispered.

"So why did you?"

"Damnit, I don't know!" she huffed, ruffling her hair in frustration. "I know it doesn't make sense, but this is all new to me, Jay. I've never been through something like this before. I'm not sure how to act . . . how to handle . . . well . . . everything. I guess I'm just being overly sensitive."

He glanced up at the digital readout. "Yeah, well, it's hard for me, too."

She scrunched up her face, making her nose wrinkle. "It is?"

"Of course, it is! Why wouldn't it be? We were . . . close. Then we weren't anymore. I needed space to come to terms with everything that happened . . . how it played out. I realized I have to move on."

The elevator came to a halt. The doors opened and he gestured for her to step out first. She seemed to hesitate before doing so, but she finally stepped into the hall and he followed her onto her floor. He watched as Melissa crossed her arms over her chest like she was warding off a chill despite the wool pea coat she wore. They walked down the carpeted hallway to her door.

"So that's what you're doing? Moving on?"

He nodded. "I'm trying. That's why I went out on a date with Sam."

Melissa came to a stop beside him. "So you really like her?"

"I don't know." He shrugged. "I guess she seems nice.

She's cute. Funny. We had some chemistry. Seems like we have potential."

She resumed walking. "Were you going to ask her out again?"

"Yeah, I was thinking about it. I should probably do it soon though. I don't want too much time to go by and let her think I'm not interested anymore."

Melissa went quiet again. She dropped her eyes to her ankle boots as they neared her door.

"*What?*" he asked again, laughing. "What's with the face? Is me dating another white girl really that annoying to you?"

"No," she said, shaking her head. "It's not that. I just brought up the white stuff to be petty because I . . ." She didn't finish.

"Because you what?"

"Nothing. It doesn't matter." She shook her head and waved him off. "Look, take my advice. If you really like her, call her. Do it ASAP if this looks like it has potential. Don't keep fucking around and let her pass you by."

He stilled, surprised to be getting this advice from her. "Really?"

"Yes, really!" She nodded. "If it makes you happy. I *want* you to be happy, Jay. I always did."

Funny, the one thing that would've made him happy was the one thing she wasn't willing to give.

Melissa licked her lips and cleared her throat. "Thanks for bringing me home. I appreciate it. Drive home safely. Okay?"

She then turned and walked to her apartment door.

It was so abrupt. Melissa didn't even hug him or say goodbye, which wasn't like her.

He stood awkwardly in the hallway, watching her pull her keys from her purse. He heard her sniff. "Lissa?"

She didn't answer him but instead accidentally dropped her keys to the carpeted floor and cursed under her breath.

"Lissa?" he said again, walking toward her. She fell to her knees to retrieve her keys and stood. She mumbled something he couldn't hear. "Lissa, are you okay?"

"I'm fine!" she shouted. He could see now that there were tears in her eyes, that her hands were shaking. "I said, I'm fine. Please just go!"

"You're *not* fine! You're crying. What's wrong?"

Tears spilled onto her cheeks despite her attempts to wipe them away. "Shit, I didn't wanna do this. I promised myself that I wouldn't."

"Do what?"

"I wanted to be a good friend to you, Jay," she rambled. "You've been a good . . . a good friend to me. You deserve that! And you're in a good place now. You've moved on. You seem so . . . *so* much better now. I—"

"Lissa," he said, grabbing her shoulders, "*what* are you talking about?"

She closed her eyes and pursed her lips. Her nostrils flared as she took another shaky breath. She opened her eyes again. "I'm in love with you. That's why I asked to meet up tonight. So I could see you again."

He stared at her in awe.

"That month we spent apart, when I couldn't see you or talk to you. I kept wanting to call you. I promised myself that I wouldn't." She gave a sad laugh. "Finally, I couldn't take it anymore. I had to make up an excuse to do it, so I came up with the tickets for the play. I just couldn't stay away! I realized why the ache for Dee had disappeared. It wasn't because I wasn't in love anymore; I was just in love with someone else—with you."

"You're . . . you're in love with me?"

"Yes!" she shouted, sounding irritated. "And now I'm

in this crazy-ass situation where I'm telling you to go on a second date with another chick because she seems right for you and she doesn't have all my goddamn baggage. Now I'm vulnerable again and I hate it! I hate this shit, Jay! I'm—"

"Where I used to be," he finished for her. "You're exactly where I used to be when I was confessing my feelings to you. I was vulnerable, too, Lissa. Shit, I still am!"

She stilled. "I'm sorry," she whispered. "I'm sorry I made you feel this way. I never wanted to hurt you. Why would I want to hurt you? I love you, Jay."

He didn't need to hear anything else. He brought his lips to hers.

Jamal could taste the saltiness of her tears on his lips and tongue. He eased her apartment door farther open and pulled her inside, yanking out her house keys and slamming the door shut behind them. They fell back against the door as her keys tumbled to the floor with a loud clatter. They yanked off their coats and began to tear at one another's clothes. Buttons popped. One of her bra straps ripped off its plastic hinge. She hiked up her leg and wrapped it around his waist. He cupped her round bottom, squeezing it as he dragged her toward him, keeping his mouth glued against hers.

It was the same frantic intensity as the first time they'd made love, but this time, it wouldn't be a fifteen-minute tryst on a sofa arm. He'd make sure of that.

"Come on," he said, grabbing her hand. He turned and almost stumbled over Brownie, who meowed softly, flopping onto his side.

"Sorry, Brownie. I missed you, too, buddy. I swear, I'll give you all the attention you want in about an hour," he said as he walked around the cat and led Melissa down the hall to her bedroom. "Maybe two."

He dragged her into her bedroom and shut the door behind them. She tugged him toward the mattress and sat on the edge of the bed. She gazed up at him. "I missed you so much," she whispered.

He stroked her face and hair. "Show me how much you missed me."

She lowered the zipper of his jeans and tugged down his boxers. She held him in her hand and took him into her mouth and he groaned and buried his fingers in her hair.

He didn't know how long he stood there while she licked and sucked. He couldn't think. He couldn't speak. When he felt himself drawing close, he yelled for her to stop and she pulled her mouth away.

"What?" she asked licking her lips. "What's wrong? You didn't like it?"

"The opposite. I liked it a lot," he said breathlessly, with a grin. "But we're not finishing this way. Not tonight."

He eased her back onto the bed and pushed her skirt up her thighs. She raised her hips so that he could tug off her panties and toss them aside. He pulled down one of her bra cups and held one of her breasts. He massaged the nipple before lowering his hand between her legs. As their tongues danced, he felt her go wet underneath his fingertips. She whimpered against his lips. Her hips began to buck rhythmically. He couldn't hold back anymore. He pulled his hand away and plunged forward, gliding inside her with one swift stroke.

As he pounded into her, Melissa fisted the bed sheets in her hands. She whined and moaned. She begged him to go faster, not to stop. Her screams got louder and louder. They were so loud that he was sure her neighbors could hear. She turned and buried her face in a pillow, trying to stifle her yells.

"No," he said, shoving the pillow aside. "I want to see

you, baby. Yell all you need to." He spread her legs and plunged into her again, making her cry out like he was torturing her. "But I want to see your face."

He wanted to see the ecstasy and loss of control when she finally came. He didn't want her to hide anything from him.

"I love you, Lissa," he said, raising her left leg, bracing her ankle on his shoulder so he could dive even deeper.

"Shit! I . . . love . . . you, too!" she shouted between gasps, making him grin again.

And she did come about five minutes later, and it was as glorious as he'd anticipated. She screamed. She cursed. She shouted his name as she pounded her fists against the mattress and clawed at his back. He came about a minute later, seeing bursts of stars in his line of vision.

They both lay in bed holding one another. She rubbed his back. He tiredly trailed butterfly kisses along her neck.

"Tell me why we stopped having sex?" she asked when their heartbeats finally returned to a normal pace. "I forget."

He raised his head so he could gaze down at her. "You said we were better off as friends and you weren't ready to start another relationship."

"Oh!" She squinted. "That was really stupid of me."

"I agree," he said with a laugh before kissing her neck again.

"So we're officially boo'ed up now."

"I guess so."

"No backing out! No changing your mind, homie."

He laughed again. "Hey, I wanted this from the beginning! You were the one holding out."

She went somber. "I'm sorry. I had a lot of baggage. I still do, Jay."

"I know. I've been there and I've definitely got my own. We'll work through it. Just meet me halfway," he said, rubbing his thumb and forefinger along her cheek. "Okay?"

She nodded, and as if to illustrate her point, she raised her mouth to his for another kiss.

He met her before she was even halfway there.

Chapter 33

Ricky

Ricky practically ran down the linoleum corridor, dodging past a man in a hospital gown hooked up to an IV and a woman lying on a hospital bed in the hall. He drew curious glances from those he passed.

"Can I help you, sir?" one of the nurses called to him, but he ignored her. He was on a mission and he wouldn't be deterred from it; he had to find Derrick. He had to make sure his boy was okay.

Ricky glanced at the plaques along the entrance of each room he passed, looking for the right number. When he finally did, he shoved the door open and yanked back the tan curtain encircling the hospital bed. He saw a nurse bending over Derrick, taking his blood pressure, as he sat up in bed looking simultaneously bored and annoyed. Both she and Derrick looked at Ricky in surprise when he burst into the room.

"Shit!" Ricky yelled, grabbing his chest, catching his breath. "Nigga, I thought you were at death's door! What the hell are you doing sittin' up?"

"Uh, excuse me, sir?" the nurse said, looking mildly horrified. "Do you mind?" She gestured to Derrick and the pressure cuff.

Derrick grimaced. "Ricky, can you give us a couple minutes? She won't take long."

Ricky looked at Derrick, then the waiting nurse. "Oh." He nodded. "Yeah, umm . . . yeah, sure." He then closed the curtain again.

Five minutes later, the nurse exited. As she walked out of the hospital room, she looked Ricky up and down. "You can go in now."

He stepped back inside the room and found Derrick where he'd left him, sitting up in bed with monitors and an IV connected to his arms, hands, and torso. Derrick's dark skin looked a little gray, but otherwise he looked all right. Ricky's relief was indescribable.

"I didn't know what I would find when I came here, Dee," Ricky said, walking toward him. "I thought you would be hooked up to a respirator or something. I thought you'd be covered in bandages."

Derrick gave a smile. "I am covered in bandages. You just can't see most of them. They're all under my hospital gown." His smile quickly evaporated. "But at least I'm alive. Two of my boys didn't make it."

Ricky took one of the chairs near the bed. He nodded. "I heard."

He had seen the aftermath of the melee on the news. The blood on the concrete. The police officer, and the police tape encircling the basketball court. Pictures of the two boys who had been killed. They looked a lot like him and Derrick at that age.

"Twelve and fourteen years old," Derrick said, almost in a whisper. "They were even younger than Cole was when he got killed, Ricky. One of them was set to go home next month."

"Damn," Ricky muttered.

"You know he did it, right? He killed them and he tried to kill me, too."

Ricky braced his elbows on his knees and lowered his head. He scrubbed his hands over his face. "Yeah. Yeah, I know."

He had secretly hoped that Dolla Dolla wouldn't follow through with his threat, but he should've known better. Once again, he had foolishly placed his hopes in a man who proved to be more ruthless and deadly than he could anticipate.

"Which one of them is next, Ricky?" Derrick asked. "Who else will he kill?"

Ricky raised his head and vehemently shook it. "No one else will be hurt or killed. I promise you, Dee."

"How can you be so sure though? How the hell can you make that happen?"

He sat back in his chair. "I'm not. The cops are gonna do it."

"But you said you already asked them to—"

"Yeah, but this time I'm not asking them to take care of it. I'm *telling* them." He shot to his feet and pointed down at the floor. "Enough of this shit! This ends today."

Ricky looked up and down the roadway for the gray unmarked police car, praying this was the last time he'd ever have to do this. He glanced down at his cell phone screen and tucked it back into his jeans pocket. Detectives Ramsey and Dominguez should've been here ten minutes ago.

Of course, when it's important, they make my ass wait, he thought with exasperation.

Finally, he saw the car rounding the corner, following

close behind a Dodge Stratus. He jogged toward the sedan as it pulled to a stop. He opened the back door and hopped inside. As usual, as soon as Ricky slammed the passenger door shut, the detective floored the accelerator, pulling into D.C. traffic so fast that he almost got whiplash.

"I believe we told you the last time that we call you and tell you where to meet," Detective Dominguez said over his shoulder. "It ain't the other way around. It's not like we've got—"

"Shut up," Ricky said. "I don't have time for this shit. We've got stuff to take care of and we don't have a lot of time to do it."

He could see Dominguez's eyes go wide in the rearview mirror. The detective sputtered for several seconds. "The fuck!" he shouted, now fuming. "Did this piece of shit just tell me to shut up?"

"Dominguez, don't start," Detective Ramsey said.

"You're lucky I'm driving, you son of a bitch," Dominguez shouted, pointing at Ricky's reflection in the mirror, "or I'd come back there—"

"Stop," Ramsey said, once again acting as the mediator. "Just stop! He's right. We're wasting time with this bullshit and we need to get back to the station." He turned in the passenger seat and glared at Ricky. "What is it? You made it sound like you needed us to come right away. Whatcha got?"

"Dolla is doing everything I said he would. He's pimping out girls again. He shot up the Institute and killed two kids because my friend won't help him get his smuggling operations started back up. He almost killed a man who's like a brother to me. Y'all have to act *now*. No more bullshitting around. You need to arrest him and make it stick this time! You should have enough evidence now. It's time to do this!"

"Ricky, I know you're upset. We get it," Ramsey said calmly. "But we told you before that we can't just—"

"Nope." He shook his head. "I'm not listening to that shit anymore. You're gonna do it. You're gonna arrest his ass and put his whole fuckin' crew in jail. No more excuses."

"You get a load of this bullshit?" Dominguez asked Ramsey, jabbing his thumb at Ricky. "This is what happens when you treat these animals like they're regular people, Eddie. They start making demands and giving out orders like they mean something."

"They *do* mean something," Ricky said through clenched teeth. "Because if y'all don't do this, I'm out. I'm not fuckin' cooperating anymore."

"Wait. Wait one damn minute!" Ramsey exclaimed. "What the hell are you saying?"

"I'm saying I'm done being an informant. If you can't arrest him now, this shit is over."

"If *you're* done being an informant, then *we're* done protecting that bitch and that kid of yours!" Dominguez shouted.

"You really think I trust that he isn't gonna find her or our kid sooner or later if he's still walking the streets? You really believe I'd leave that shit up to *y'all* to protect them for the long term?" He sucked his teeth. "You haven't protected any of the other witnesses. You couldn't even protect a school filled with kids! It'd only be a matter of time before he'd kill them both. Dolla better go down, and he better do it if not today then tomorrow, or I'm blowing this shit up. *You hear me?* If I gotta confess everything to him . . . if I gotta tell him what I've been doing for almost a year, so fuckin' be it! But I'm not playin' your games anymore!"

"This is insane. If you confess everything to him, he'll

kill you on the spot," Ramsey argued. "You know that, Ricky."

"*And?* It's better than the slow torture of watching everyone I care about get picked off one by one," Ricky said—and he meant it.

He had thought about what he was going to say today to the detectives, the promise and the threat he would make, even before he got here. Jamal had almost been killed, now Derrick. And who's to say their lives still weren't under threat. Skylar was dead and so was her mom, along with all of the other women Dolla Dolla used to pimp out. Derrick's student had been killed in jail and two more kids had been killed only yesterday. This had all happened in less than six months. The body count was stacking up and accelerating at an alarming rate. Ricky wasn't going to sit around anymore watching the chaos from the sidelines. He knew he had to do something drastic. All his options had been taken away.

For once, Dominguez went quiet. Ramsey did, too. They drove in silence for a minute or two before Ramsey gradually nodded. "Fine, we'll talk to the lieutenant," he said.

"No!" Ricky bellowed, pounding his fist on the back seat. "No more fuckin' talking! I told you—"

"Conducting a raid like this isn't some shit we can authorize or do all by ourselves, Ricky," Ramsey insisted. "We'll show him the evidence. We'll tell him what you said. We'll tell him that you mean it . . . that it has to be done right away."

"You better," Ricky said. "You've got three days."

"*Three days?*" Dominguez squeaked.

"You heard me! Now pull the fuck over. I'm not havin' you drop me off on some random street corner where I have to walk a quarter of a mile back to my damn car."

Dominguez skidded to a halt at the light and Ricky stepped onto the sidewalk. He slammed the door behind him and watched as the sedan pulled off, hoping to God that they weren't bullshitting him yet again. He hoped they could finally do something this time around.

He didn't want to consider the alternative if they didn't.

Chapter 34

Derrick

Derrick sat on the edge of the hospital bed, gazing out the window at the parking lot several stories below. It was good to finally be out of a hospital gown, to be wearing his own clothes, but he still felt drained physically and emotionally.

"You're all set, Mr. Miller," he heard his doctor say behind him, making him turn slightly on the bed.

He found a short, Indian man in a lab coat with brown skin and warm eyes. A stethoscope dangled around his neck and a clipboard was in his hands.

"You're clear to be discharged today," the doctor said. "Just make sure you take care of those wounds, take your meds, and have plenty of rest. No work for another couple of weeks. I mean it! Follow up with your doctor as well."

Derrick nodded. "Yes, Dr. Anand."

"Do you have someone who'll be taking care of you in the meantime? So you can take it easy?"

Derrick nodded again. "My mom said she'll handle it.

She's picking me up today. In fact"—he glanced down at his wristwatch—"she should be here soon."

"Good to hear. You take care of yourself, Mr. Miller."

"I'll try, Dr. Anand."

Derrick watched as the doctor left his hospital room, then turned back around to gaze listlessly out the window. He sighed.

He'd lost Cole—and now two more boys. He had been in the hospital and hadn't been able to share the tearful news with the families, though he felt like it was his duty, his responsibility to do it himself.

Derrick planned to hire additional guards for the Institute and had asked for police to sit in squad cars around the property, but he knew that would only do but so much. With Dolla Dolla still on the loose, they were all still at risk. He could still pick them off one by one. Ricky had promised he would finally take care of the problem, but Derrick knew his friend was limited in what he could do. Ricky had good intentions and usually got good results, but this feat might be beyond even him.

The only solace that Derrick took in all this was that Morgan hadn't been harmed. After he'd woken up, he'd seen her lingering on the periphery of the hospital room, behind his mother and the rest of his relatives who hovered over him. He'd tried to call out to her, to get her attention, but she'd disappeared into the hall. Now that she knew he would survive his wounds, he imagined she was safely on a flight back to Atlanta. At least nothing could happen to her there.

He glanced at his watch again, wondering where his mother was. He was getting impatient. The wheelchair he was supposed to sit in as he exited the hospital already sat in the corner waiting for him, though he really didn't need it. Frankly, he could walk out himself, but the hospital staff wouldn't let him do it. He still needed someone to push the damn thing.

"Ma, where the hell are you?" he muttered.

"Are we ready to go?" he heard a familiar voice call out.

Derrick whipped around again and found Morgan strolling into the hospital room. She was holding one of his jackets in her hands.

"You got everything you need?" she asked, glancing at the plastic bag that sat on the bed beside him. "I brought you a coat. I thought you might need one since it's a little chilly today. Almost in the fifties, and I know how you are about the cold."

He narrowed his eyes at her. "W-what . . . what are you doing here?" he asked, almost with disbelief.

"I'm here to take you home. Your mom's at your apartment right now getting everything ready for you. She wouldn't let me do that," she said with a rueful laugh, holding out his jacket for him to put on. "But she let me pick you up, so I guess I should be happy with that."

"But I thought you were headed to Atlanta," he said dazedly. "I thought you were already on your flight there."

She shrugged. "Yeah, well, there's been a change of plans. I know you'll need someone to help you for a while before you can go back to work. I have nowhere to be now that I've officially quit my job, and this way your mom doesn't have to take any days off from her job to do it. She and I talked it over. It seemed to make sense."

"You're gonna take care of me?" He still stared at her, confused. "You don't have to do that."

"I *know* I don't have to, Derrick."

"Then why are you?"

She lowered his jacket and took another step toward

his hospital bed. "Because you risked your life for me. Because I owe you big, though I know I'll never be able to repay you for it."

His shoulders sank. He had hoped she was staying for another reason—that she had finally forgiven him, that she wanted to be with him again. But he guessed he would have to be happy with that answer. Derrick nodded.

"Okay, well, thanks . . . for everything—again. I guess we should head out," he mumbled.

She offered his jacket to him again and he tried to raise his arm to put on one of the sleeves but he winced in pain at the movement.

"Let me help you," she whispered and eased the jacket onto his arm, then his shoulder. When they finally got it on, she adjusted his collar and patted it gently. He could see there were tears in her eyes.

"What's wrong?" he asked, frowning.

She bit down hard on her bottom lip as tears streamed down her cheeks. She tightened her grip on his jacket collar. "You scared the shit outta me! I thought . . . I thought I lost you. I thought I lost you!" He was caught off guard when she looped her arms around his neck. She squeezed him so tight that his wounds started to hurt, but he didn't tell her to let go. He didn't want her to let go. "Don't ever do that shit to me again!" she sobbed into his ear. "I love you so much! So damn much! I don't know what I would do if anything happened to you, baby."

She finally loosened her hold around him and gazed into his eyes. Her face and green eyes had gone red. Snot was sliding down her nose, but she had never looked more beautiful to him.

"I love you, too," he whispered.

He brought his mouth to hers for a long, hard kiss that

didn't erase all his sadness, but it came pretty close. A few minutes later, they gathered his things and managed to get him into his wheelchair. Fifteen minutes later, they were in her car, headed back to his apartment—the one they had found together. But this time, they would try their best to make it a home for them both.

Chapter 35

Ricky

"Hey, handsome! Why you sittin' over here all by yourself?"

Ricky looked up from his drink and found a scantily clad woman with big brown eyes and big tits smiling down at him.

She was one of the many girls working the room at Dolla Dolla's party tonight. The drug kingpin was in a celebratory mood. This was the fourth party in the past two weeks.

Why shouldn't he be celebrating? Ricky thought morosely.

Dolla Dolla was winning. He was back in business and he had vanquished all his foes. And it looked like no one was going to stop him.

The deadline Ricky had given Detectives Ramsey and Dominguez was drawing to a close; it officially ended today. They still hadn't done the raid. Dolla Dolla still hadn't been arrested for the latest murders.

Who am I kidding? Ricky thought. With the expensive

lawyers Dolla Dolla had hired, even if he was arrested again, he'd probably beat that rap, too.

"Mind if I sit down?" the woman asked, lowering herself onto Ricky's lap.

"Actually, I kinda do," he said, stopping her mid-motion. He shook the ice in his glass and gave her a withering glance.

She rose back to her stilettoed feet and cocked a dark eyebrow at him. "Looks like someone's in a bad mood."

"The worse mood ever, honey."

She trailed her long nails along his beard line. She was smiling again. "I could help with that, handsome."

"I doubt it," Ricky said, hoisting himself up from his chair. He handed her the glass. "Can you take care of this for me?"

Her pleasant façade evaporated. She glared at him. "Do I look like a damn waitress?" she yelled.

He didn't answer her. Instead, he decided to look for Dolla Dolla, wondering if he was in his bedroom again. Though Ricky wasn't sure what he would do when he found him.

The part of him that continued to wear the mask planned to stroll in there, give Dolla Dolla a dap, and tell him he was leaving the party. He'd rave about what a good time he'd had but, regretfully, he had to head home for the night. But the other part of him that was tired of wearing the mask, who just wanted to rip it off, planned to do exactly what he'd threatened the detectives that he'd do. He wanted to spit in Dolla Dolla's face and tell him about every betrayal he'd committed against him in the past year. He wanted to tell him to go ahead and kill him, but he hoped one day Dolla Dolla got what he deserved and rotted in hell.

By the time Ricky strolled down the hall and found

Dolla Dolla not in his bedroom but in a study filled with bookshelves but no books, where Dolla Dolla sat at a grand oak table, smoking a cigar and playing cards—Ricky still hadn't made up his mind what he was going to do. When he entered the room, Dolla Dolla looked up.

"Hey, Pretty Ricky!" he boomed, taking the cigar out of his mouth. "We almost done this round. You wanna play, nigga? I'm tired of beaten they asses!" He then let out a rumbling laugh.

"I told you that I don't play spades," José lamented in his thick accent, slapping down his cards. "It is a stupid American game!"

"It's only stupid 'cuz your ass is losin'," Dolla Dolla argued before turning to Ricky again. He gestured to the table. "Come on. Take his spot, Ricky. Show 'em how it's done."

Ricky opened his mouth, then closed it. He was torn as to what to say next.

Dolla Dolla stared at him quizzically. "You okay, Ricky?"

Before Ricky could answer, he heard a thud and shouts farther down the hall.

"The hell," Ricky murmured, turning in the direction of the sound, wondering if a fight had broken out in the living room.

That's when all the lights went out in the apartment. That's when all the screaming started.

"Get down! Get down on the ground!" someone yelled in the dark.

Ricky knew instantly that it was a cop who'd said it. Only a cop gave orders like that.

He dropped to his knees and closed his eyes when the flash bangs went off, creating a strobe-light effect that was as disorienting as it was meant to be. He coughed as the hallway filled with smoke.

Smoke bombs, his addled mind registered.

So Detectives Ramsey and Dominguez had convinced their lieutenant to finally conduct the raids. Too bad they hadn't told him in advance; he would have appreciated a heads-up. But this raid seemed worse than the one they'd conducted at Club Majesty almost a year ago. He'd remembered the chaos and the screams as the people ran for the exits, but he didn't remember hearing gunshots. He hadn't run the risk of getting killed back then like he was tonight.

Ricky heard more popping sounds, but this time, it wasn't the flash bangs. A bullet whizzed over his head. Then another. Ricky crouched against the wall and opened his eyes, squinting though the dark and the smoke, praying to God he didn't get shot.

He caught figures in the dim light coming through the floor-to-ceiling windows of the study. They looked like men in SWAT gear. He saw the burst of light as they fired their weapons. He also saw a burst of light coming from the opposite direction. Dolla Dolla's men were firing back.

"Shit," Ricky said under his breath, crouching even lower. He was almost on his stomach.

"Dolla! Dolla!" one of the men shouted, "Come on! This way!"

Ricky raised his head slightly and watched as Dolla Dolla charged out of the room with two hulking figures on each side, bracing him and protecting him as they ran to the back bedroom. He stared at them curiously. Why the hell were they going back there? It was a dead end.

He started to follow them, to crawl on his hands and knees in that direction, but was roughly shoved aside by the men running out of the study.

"Get out of my way!" someone yelled before rushing past him and heading in the opposite direction—straight into the gunfire. Ricky heard more bullets and more screams. He heard a crunch and a thud. He cringed at the sounds that made him feel like he was watching a horror movie with the volume turned up to an ear-splitting level.

He continued to crawl toward the back bedroom and felt his hand graze over something cool and metallic. He traced his hand over it again and realized it was a handgun. One of Dolla Dolla's bodyguards must have dropped it in their haste. He considered leaving it there on the hardwood floor where he'd found it, but something told him to pick it up. He might need it later, though he wasn't sure why.

He soon reached the master bedroom and again, the open windows and bright lights from the city landscape helped him to see a little in the dark. He could see Dolla Dolla and two of his bodyguards running toward the bedroom's walk-in closet, which confused the hell out of him.

Were they planning to hide out in here until all of this was over? It didn't seem like a very smart plan since the cops would likely comb the entire condo from top to bottom. They'd find Dolla Dolla and his men eventually.

Ricky went from all fours to a slight stoop as he rounded the four-poster bed. He watched through the open closet door as the men shoved and threw aside wool and fur coats, suits and shirts, revealing yet another door leading to God knows where.

"Faster! Faster!" Dolla Dolla ordered. "Move that shit! They comin'."

So Dolla Dolla had constructed a means of escape in his condo. Of course, he had. But if he got away, this would never end. Dolla Dolla would rebuild or continue his operations somewhere else. He'd hurt more people, *kill* more people. Ricky couldn't let that happen.

"Stop!" Ricky yelled, holding up the handgun, pointing it in their direction. "Stop and hold your hands up!"

Dolla Dolla and his two guards did as he ordered. They stopped and turned but stared at him, bewildered, when they realized who had given the order. One of them even stepped out of the closet.

"Ricky, what the fuck are you doin', man?" the bodyguard hissed.

"Stop! All of you. Get down on the ground," he said, still pointing the gun at them.

"This nigga's gone crazy." One of them laughed, then reached for the door handle.

Ricky raised the gun and fired into the air, making them all jump, making them halt. "I said come out of there and get down on the ground," he repeated. "Do it now!"

Dolla Dolla emerged from the closet, narrowing his dark eyes at him. "You telling me you a undercover cop?"

Ricky shook his head. "No, I'm no cop, bruh."

"Oh, so you a snitch then." Dolla Dolla sneered. "That's worse than one of them bitch-ass pigs! You was the nigga workin' for the cops all along. Weren't you?"

"Get down on the ground, Dolla," Ricky repeated slowly, not answering his question, not feeling any need to. "I'm not gonna say that shit again."

His heart was beating so fast he swore it was going to pound its way out of his chest. He had to hold the handgun with both hands to steady it because he was shaking so hard, now kicked up with fear and adrenaline. But he wasn't afraid of getting killed; he was terrified at the prospect that if he did this wrong, Dolla Dolla would get away.

In the dim light, Dolla Dolla's face turned into something Ricky didn't even recognize as human anymore. It had been morphed by pure rage.

"Kill that nigga!" he growled, pointing at Ricky.

But Ricky fired before either of the guards could reach their weapons. One managed to get it out of his waistband only to take a bullet to the head before he could even fire it. The other got his shirt up, only to realize a gun was no longer at his waist. Ricky was holding it and he fired a bullet into the bodyguard's chest, dead center.

As they both crumpled to the ground, Dolla Dolla and Ricky stared at one another, surrounded by the soundtrack of gunfire, shouts, and screams that seemed to be getting closer and closer as the SWAT team made their way down the hall.

"You gonna do me like this after all I did for you?" Dolla Dolla asked, having the nerve to sound hurt.

"After all you *took* from me," Ricky said through clenched teeth. "And you were only gonna keep takin'!"

"You ungrateful li'l bitch!" Dolla Dolla shouted before charging at him.

Ricky fired once, twice, three times before Dolla Dolla finally came to a stop only inches in front of him, holding his chest and gurgling on the blood pooling in his gaping mouth. Ricky had to take a few steps back to keep Dolla Dolla's limp body from landing on top of him like a fallen sequoia. As the man Ricky had known and had been shackled to since he was damn near fourteen years old thumped to the floor, Ricky dropped his weapon, feeling a wave of fatigue wash over him. Another flash bang went off, making Ricky close his eyes. Smoke filled the master bedroom and he coughed as he dropped to his knees. More gunshots rang out.

"Get down! Get down! Drop your weapon," a voice shouted as the cops charged into the bedroom.

"I don't have one!" he shouted back as he was roughly shoved to the rug.

"You got it. You got it!" he told the cop, to let him know he wasn't going to struggle.

He had no reason to. The fight was over. Dolla Dolla was dead.

Chapter 36

Derrick

Three months later . . .

"Right corner pocket," Ricky called out. "If I make this shot, the game is over for you, nigga!"

Derrick blew air out of his inflated cheeks and leaned on his pool cue. "Just take the damn shot and stop talkin' shit!"

Ricky laughed and did as he ordered. Of course, the nine ball sailed into the corner pocket like he'd said, winning him the game. He did a brief victory dance.

"So you beat a dude who still can't hold a pool cue the right way because he was shot twice," Derrick said dryly, holding back a smile. "You really gonna Milly rock to that?"

Ricky rolled his eyes. "Bruh, you were shot three damn months ago! How long you gonna whine about it?"

"I didn't know mentioning I got shot twice was whining!"

"Bitch-ass nigga," Ricky murmured with a grin before taking a sip from his beer.

The truth was that Derrick's wounds had mostly healed.

Morgan had made sure of that. She had treated him like an invalid for almost two weeks and then watched over him like a hawk when he finally returned to the Institute, making sure he didn't push himself too hard. She could do that because she was working there again, too, resuming her position as carpentry instructor. He found comfort in her being in the same building during the day and in bed beside him at night. She had also helped him find a new line of funding for the Institute—other former clients of hers at the artist cooperative where she used to work, wealthy patrons looking to invest in a good cause. Thankfully, this time he didn't blow it by losing his temper and making a scene. The Donovans were gifting the Institute a cool million dollars, and Derrick was hoping to use the money to make some badly needed renovations, buy equipment, and hire additional staff.

"Come on," Derrick said, laying down his pool cue. "I'm hungry. Let's finally get somethin' to eat."

Ricky nodded. "Sounds like a good idea. I won, so I guess you're treatin'. Right?"

Derrick chuckled as they strolled out of the sports bar's pool hall into the adjoining restaurant. "Yeah, I'll buy you some nachos. I guess I owe you."

Derrick meant that in more ways than one. He owed Ricky for finally taking care of Dolla Dolla, too. He hadn't asked for the details. Ricky said Dolla Dolla and a few of his bodyguards had been killed during the raid at his Kalorama condo back in September. They hadn't been able to dodge all those bullets flying everywhere, with the flash bangs and the smoke bombs going off.

"So how the hell did you make it out of there alive if all of them got taken out?" Derrick had asked.

"Don't know," Ricky had said. "Guess I just kept my head down."

But Derrick had seen something in Ricky's eyes that let

him know that wasn't true, or at least, it wasn't the *full* truth. There was more to the story of why Ricky had survived and Dolla Dolla hadn't, but Derrick didn't question him about it anymore. Dolla Dolla was gone. His cohorts were in jail or on their way there soon once the trials started. That's all that mattered. The only issue that remained unanswered was whether Ricky would also be serving time in prison in the near future. He had told Derrick not to worry about him; he had worked out a deal with the prosecutor. But Ricky still hadn't revealed what that deal was, claiming it was confidential. Would Ricky be serving only a couple of years in prison? Ten? *Twenty?* The question was eating away at Derrick, but he tried not to let on that it was. For now, he would enjoy his time with his boy.

They took one of the free booths near the back of the restaurant and were quickly greeted by a pretty waitress in a referee uniform that included a whistle dangling from a lanyard around her neck. She asked for their orders.

"I'll have the jalapeño burger, medium well," Derrick said, glancing at the menu.

"I'll have the foot-long chili dog with fries. Oh, and can you get us the nacho starter?" Ricky asked.

The waitress nodded. "Absolutely! Will this order be on one check or two, gentlemen?" she asked, looking between them both.

"Oh, you can put it all on one," Ricky said smugly with a nod, then pointed to Derrick. He leaned back against the booth's leather cushion. "He's paying."

"Gotcha!" she chirped. She then tucked her pad into her apron and walked away.

Derrick glanced at his cell phone and saw a message from Morgan.

Just got back from the gym. Gonna take a shower, slather myself in baby oil, and turn the lights down low. Will be waiting for you when you get home.

Derrick grinned and started typing.

**Lookin forward to it. I'll be home in a little more
than an hour.**

"I saw that smile," Ricky said, taking another drink from his beer bottle as Derrick set his cell back on the table. "Your lady texted you?"

"Yeah, I told her I'd be leaving here in an hour."

"I'm glad y'all were able to work that shit out." He nodded thoughtfully. "I like you with her. She brings out your good side. You definitely don't bitch as much as you used to."

Derrick laughed. "Well, the right woman will do that."

"That she will," Ricky said, raising his beer bottle in salute. "Cheers to Morgan."

Derrick raised his water glass and clinked it against Ricky's beer. He took a sip of water then sobered. He tilted his head. "You miss yours?"

"Miss my what?" Ricky asked, lowering his bottle.

"Your woman, bruh. Simone."

At the mention of her name, Ricky's face changed. Again, Derrick saw something in his eyes—a pain and longing that almost made him wince.

"Every damn day," Ricky whispered, dropping his gaze to his bottle. "I miss Miles, too. He'll be seven months old next week. Kinda hard to believe that."

"The cops can't tell you where they are now? Even though Dolla is gone?"

Ricky shook his head. "I knew when I made the deal that I might not see them again. But it was the price I'd pay to keep them safe." He shrugged. "It is what it is."

Derrick couldn't imagine it, never being able to see Morgan or their child ever again, knowing they were out there somewhere in the world living their lives without him. It would eat him alive. He didn't know how Ricky could stand it.

A few minutes later, the waitress brought their nachos, then their meals. Both men dug in. Ricky took a bite of his hot dog, wiping chili from his lips, but he paused mid-motion. His eyes widened. "Oh, shit," he sputtered with a mouth full of food.

"What?" Derrick asked, licking ketchup from his fingers.

"If you want to keep enjoying your burger, don't turn around, okay?"

Derrick raised his brows. "*Huh?* What are you talking about?" he asked, doing exactly what Ricky told him not to do. He glanced over his shoulder.

"Damn, nigga, you can't follow instructions?"

Derrick's eyes landed on a table of women who were all laughing and enjoying their dinner. One of them rose from her chair and did a little shimmy that made the others laugh even harder. Derrick lowered his fingers from his mouth when he realized who it was.

"Melissa?" he said, louder than he'd intended.

Hearing her name, she glanced at their table. When she recognized them, her mouth fell open in shock. "Derrick? Ricky? Hey!" she said.

They both watched as she murmured something to her table companions and walked toward their booth.

"Oh, man," Ricky said behind his napkin. "She's comin' over."

Derrick watched as she approached.

It was surreal to now view a woman, whom he had been in love with for almost twenty years, with the fondness of an old friend, one of the most important friends he'd ever had. He was relieved to see that Melissa looked happy. She practically glowed and was downright beautiful as she pushed up the sleeves of her teal sweater. She held up her hands in mock defense.

"Wait, you aren't gonna throw something at me, are you?" she joked. "You're not gonna start swingin' again, Dee?"

Ricky threw back his head and burst into laughter while Derrick rolled his eyes.

So she still had the same sarcastic sense of humor. Of course, she did.

"You weren't the person I was swingin' at the last time we saw each other, Lissa," Derrick said.

"All the same," she quipped, dropping her elbows to their table, leaning casually in the restaurant aisle. "I want to make sure we're cool now."

"We always were," Derrick said.

It's just Jay who I hated, he thought, but didn't say it aloud.

"I'm glad to see you're doing better, Dee. Did you get my flowers?" she asked.

"Yep, I did. The card, too. Thank you."

He had hidden the card from Morgan, tossing it as soon as he got it. He didn't want to bring up an old argument. He was with Morgan now, not Melissa, but he didn't want to give his girl any reason to question that by seeing Melissa's sweet, heartfelt note wishing him all the best. He didn't want Morgan to think there was any remote chance of them rekindling their old relationship.

Melissa now looked from him to Ricky. "So how have you guys been? What have you been up to?"

"A little bit of this, a little bit of that," Ricky said. "You know how we are."

"Yeah, I can imagine," she murmured, side-eying Ricky, giving him a knowing smile.

"What about you? What have you been up to?" Derrick asked.

"Oh, nothing big! Trying to get the kids in my class to focus even though we're only two weeks away from Christmas. Keeping nine-year-olds' attention is hard enough without having to compete with Santa, but I'm getting through it. At least I have our vacation to Belize to look forward to after the holidays. We're headed there in late December, early January, before school starts up again. I'm excited because I've never been there!"

"*Oh?*" Derrick glanced at the table where Melissa's friends were still talking and laughing with one another. "You going on a girls' trip to Belize? Is Bina going with you?"

"Uh, no," she said, tucking her hair behind her ear. He liked big natural hair on her. "It's not a girls' trip. I'm . . . I'm going with Jay. He's treating me to a getaway after a tough school year and to celebrate getting his new job."

Ricky did an audible intake of breath that sounded like *oof* before raising his beer bottle back to his lips. Derrick's easy smile disappeared.

"So you're still with Jay?" Derrick asked, narrowing his eyes.

Melissa nodded. "Yeah. We're still together."

"Oh," he said flatly. He glanced at Ricky, who was pretending to stare at the license plates decorating their booth wall.

"Look, Dee," she began, shifting back from the table and dropping her hands to her hips. "I know how you feel about Jay and my relationship with him. I know you don't think the best of him right now but—"

"And I never will."

"*But*," she said louder, talking over him, "he loves me and he goes out of his way to make me happy. After how our relationship went down, I thought you would be happy for me . . . that I found someone else."

"Yes, I want to see you happy, Lissa. Of course, I do! But did it have to be with my best friend? My boy?"

"Oh, please! Don't get self-righteous on me. I didn't cheat on you like you cheated on me, Derrick Miller. Jay and I got together *after* you and I broke up. And you guys weren't even friends by that time. You weren't even speaking to each other!"

"But he saw us from the beginning. He knew what we were to each other. But he still slid right in there and went after you *before* we broke up. That nigga was dead-ass wrong!" He turned back to Ricky. "Come on, bruh! Back me up!"

Ricky shook his head and took a bite of one of his fries. "Nope. I'm staying out of this."

"He was wrong. You were wrong. So what, Dee?" she said, flapping her arms. "We're all okay now. You've moved on. I've moved on. That doesn't mean you guys can't put that all behind you. That doesn't mean you can't be cordial to each other. Maybe it's finally time for you guys sit down and . . . you know . . . talk. Work out your differences."

"*Are you kidding?*" Derrick barked out a cold laugh. "I'd rather eat shit than say hi or goodbye to that nigga."

Her face fell. "Really, Dee?"

"Yes, really! I mean . . . would you like me to set up a meeting between *you and Morgan?*" he asked. "Maybe you two can have lunch sometime. Go shoppin' together."

"No, thank you, smartass." She crossed her arms over her chest. "I have no interest in ever seeing that woman again, but unlike you with Jay, I don't plan to beat her ass on sight. I refuse to let myself be bogged down with that kinda energy."

"Well, you're a better person than I am."

"*Obviously!*" Melissa slowly shook her head. "Oh, well, I tried. But if you're gonna insist on staying in your feelings, there's nothing I can really do about it." She waved. "It was nice seeing you guys. Have a merry Christmas. Happy New Year. Have a nice life, Dee."

She then turned around and headed across the restaurant. It looked like she was going to the ladies' room.

Derrick turned back to face Ricky, who was staring at him.

"What?" Derrick snapped.

"Hey! I ain't say nothin'!"

"I know. You just sat there while she was defending Jay the whole time, when you and I both know what he did was some shit!"

"I'm not getting in the middle of a fight between you and your ex, Dee. I ain't that type of nigga. You can handle yourself, and besides . . . I think you were being kinda hard on her considering everything that happened."

"*What?*"

"I'm just keepin' it one hundred with you, bruh," Ricky said before taking a bite of his hotdog.

Derrick grumbled to himself. "I wasn't being hard on *her*. I was being hard on *him*, because he deserves it!"

"Whatever, man," Ricky said before wiping his mouth. "It's up to you." He slid out of the booth.

"Where you goin' now?" Derrick asked.

"To take a piss! Damn! I need your permission?"

Derrick ignored his sarcasm and watched as Ricky walked toward the bathroom. He then sighed and returned his attention to his meal, though he didn't have much of an appetite anymore.

Chapter 37

Jamal

Jamal was trying to concentrate on his laptop screen and take notes, but the cat purring on his leg and the television blaring in the background weren't helping.

He was at Melissa's place tonight and trying to catch up on his work as the new domestic policy director at the political foundation that had hired him months ago. It was work he usually preferred to do in the tranquility of his own home office, with jazz music playing in the background. But he had decided to come here tonight because he hadn't seen Melissa all week. He'd missed her—her conversation, her smell, and her laughter. He'd missed making love to her and listening to her snore softly in her sleep. He'd forgotten, though, that she liked to keep her apartment noisier than a busy train station.

Jamal typed a few more keys but abruptly stopped when he felt something whack him on the back of the head.

"Oh, excuse me. Pardon me," Melissa said with a laugh as she shifted and hit him again with her butt. The laptop fell off his lap, nudging Brownie aside. The cat mewled in protest before hopping to the living room floor and walk-ing off to slumber in a corner on his cat bed.

"I'm sorry. I'm so clumsy. Did I disturb you?" she asked in a high-pitched voice, bumping him again. This time in the cheek. "Huh? *Huh?* Am I disturbing you?"

Jamal grabbed her hips to hold her still and nipped her ass through the cotton of her yoga pants, making her yelp. He dragged her over the sofa arm and onto his lap. She squealed.

"Stop! Stop!" she shouted between giggles as he held her close, kissing her neck and bare shoulder. "I was just trying to get your attention!"

"Yeah? Well, now you've got it." He reached over her to the coffee table to grab the remote and turn off the tele-vision. He tossed the remote aside and gave her a quick peck on the lips, then another. "So now that you do, why don't we—"

"I wanted to get your attention *to talk*," she said, pulling her mouth away from his and clasping his face in her hands. "I've been talking to you the past five minutes. Did you hear anything I said?"

He frowned.

"I take that as a no."

"I couldn't hear anything over the TV!"

"Well, I said I spoke to Derrick yesterday."

Jamal's heart lurched to a stop before quickly starting up again.

"You spoke to Dee?"

She nodded. "Yeah, I saw him at a restaurant. We talked for a little bit."

Jamal eased Melissa off his lap onto the cushion beside him. He took a deep breath, telling himself silently not to freak out.

Melissa could speak to Derrick. Jamal wasn't the type of guy who would ban his girlfriend from having any contact with her exes. He wasn't that territorial. But a part of him knew that Derrick wasn't your average ex. Melissa had been with the guy off-and-on for twenty damn years and they hadn't ended on healthy terms. Derrick and Melissa had history—and history could lead to nostalgia and nostalgia could lead to regret and that could lead to . . .

Don't freak out, he told himself again when he could feel his mind and his heart racing. *Just listen to what she has to say.*

"Okay?" he said, nodding, trying his best to sound casual. "And how . . . how is he?"

She shrugged. "He seems okay . . . good, actually. Ricky was there, too. I spoke to them both and told them I think it's finally time for *all* of you to meet up and talk to each other. To see if you can reconnect."

Jamal stared at her, now dumfounded. "Are you kidding?"

She laughed, shook her head, and slumped back against one of the sofa pillows. "That's *exactly* what Dee said."

"Baby, the last time I saw that man, he punched me in the face!"

"Because he was upset!" She winced. "And he still kinda is, frankly."

"Which underlines my point."

"His anger has less to do with us being together and more with him feeling you betrayed him."

"That's the same damn thing!"

"But it's been months since then. I told him he was wrong for hitting you, and, in some ways, I think he knows it. I told him you make me happy and that he should be happy for me, considering everything that went down. The fact that the guy who makes me happy happens to be you, shouldn't bother him."

Jamal narrowed his eyes at her. "And what did he say?"

"I can't remember exactly." She winced again. "But it

was something along the lines of he'd rather eat shit than talk to you."

Jamal sighed. "Look, Lissa, I'm glad you guys spoke. It sounds like you two are in a much better place than you were months ago, I guess. But it sounds like he still feels the same damn way about me as he did then. There is no way in hell Derrick and I are going to meet up for dinner and drinks. It's just not gonna happen!"

She inclined her head, reached out, and rested a hand on his leg. "You miss them, honey. I know you do. They were your boys! And despite all that's happened and all the mess Derrick was talking, I think they miss you, too."

Jamal lowered his eyes.

She was right; he did miss Ricky and even Derrick, despite the rancor between them. They had been his buddies, his confidants, and the closest thing he'd ever had to siblings his entire life. Jamal had no idea when he'd uttered the words *It's time to break ties* to them at Ray's more than a year and a half ago what it'd really meant. He had no idea what would happen after, either.

"When I went to the bathroom, Ricky pulled me aside and said he's willing to try to get you guys together again to talk if you're willing to do it," she said. "I told him I'd ask you."

Good ol' Ricky . . .

Who would've known the dude in their crew who had always seemed the most jaded would have the biggest heart. When the chips were down, more than once Ricky had proven he was willing to put all his anger aside to help a brother out, to help Jamal. He was the one who finally got Mayor Johnson arrested, after all. But Jamal doubted Derrick would be as benevolent. Stubborn, pissed-off Derrick wouldn't be willing to let bygones be bygones.

He raised his eyes and sighed. He scrubbed his hand over his face and began to shake his head. "Look, if Ricky wants to meet again one-on-one, I'll do it in a heartbeat. But bringing Dee into this . . . I just don't think it's a good idea, Lissa."

"But I do," she whispered, leaning forward.

"Why?"

She loudly exhaled. "Because . . . because sometimes I feel like something is still hanging over us. Like for you, there's still a question mark."

"What do you mean?"

She licked her lips and paused like she was trying to find the right words. "I love you, Jay. You know that, right?"

"Of course!" *It took you a while to figure it out, but finally you did. Thank God*, he thought.

"So why did that look cross your face when I said I spoke to Dee?"

He blinked in surprise. "What look?"

"You know the look."

"No, *what look*? I don't know what you're talking about, baby!"

"The look you have when you're waiting for a cancer diagnosis. The look you have when you're waiting to hear if a jury found you innocent or guilty. It was a look like you were waiting for a shoe to drop. Like I was gonna say Dee and I were back together again!"

"I don't know what you're talking about," Jamal lied. "I think you're reading more into this than you should."

"I'm over him, Jay. I can say that for sure now. But I don't know if *you're* over everything. The beef and animosity between you and Dee needs to end for us to be good."

"But we *are* good!" he insisted, clutching her hand. "He doesn't have a damn thing to do with us!"

She pursed her lips. "I'm not sure if that's true. I'm not saying you have to be tight again. It might be kinda weird if you were. I'm just saying I think if you talk to him, it could give you some . . . some closure. You know?" She kissed his cheek. "Are you willing to try? For me?"

He let go of her hand, closed his eyes, and grumbled.

Damn it, why couldn't she ask him for something simpler, like a night out on the town or jewelry or a designer handbag? With the six-figure salary he was making now at the think tank, he could buy her something nice, something expensive. Plenty of his past girlfriends would be appeased by that. Bridget certainly would.

"What do you think?" Melissa persisted. She kissed him again and nuzzled his cheek. "Will you call Ricky to set something up?"

Jamal gradually opened his eyes. He leaned back and met her gaze. "If I agree to this—I'm not saying that I will—but *if* I agree to meet up with Ricky and Dee, and I show up there and it goes left, I'm out. Okay? I'm not going there to get yelled at or jumped."

Melissa chuckled. "Understood." She wrapped her arms around him and pulled him close. "I'm so proud of you, honey."

"Yeah. Yeah. Yeah," he muttered against her lips, kissing her back. "Just remember this when I ask you for something."

"*What?* What have you asked me to do that I haven't done?" she exclaimed.

"I asked you to wear that thing I got you."

She scrunched up her nose. "Oh, come on! It was *so* cheesy! And it barely covered my . . ." She sucked her teeth and laughed. She threw back her head and groaned. "Okay, fine. Fine! I'll wear it tonight."

He raised his brows. "Really?"

"Yeah, really," she said as he eased her back onto the sofa cushion.

"You know I would've done it just for the lingerie," he whispered before snaking a hand up her tank top.

She laughed. "Then why'd you have me bother with the whole damn pep talk?"

He didn't answer her question. He kissed her instead and fondled her breast, and all talk about Derrick, Ricky, and everything else ended.

Chapter 38

Jamal

Jamal took a deep breath before pushing open the glass doors to Ray's Bar and Lounge. When he stepped inside and the smell of smoke and liquor filled his lungs, he was hit with a wave of nostalgia. He remembered the many nights he, Ricky, and Derrick had spent here laughing and drinking. He remembered the stories and the chiding. He'd thought those days would last forever, but of course, they hadn't.

"Well, look what the cat dragged in!" Ray rasped from behind the counter.

Jamal smiled and gave the old man a dap. "What's up, Ray?"

"I haven't seen your ass in a while," Ray said. "Where you been?"

"I've been around. Just been busy." Jamal glanced over his shoulder and spotted Ricky sitting at their usual booth, the one that practically had their names written on it.

He noticed that Ricky was sitting alone. Derrick wasn't here yet, which was odd; Jamal was usually the late one.

"You'd be late to your own funeral, Jay," Derrick used to joke.

But Jamal was usually punctual when it came to every other aspect of his life: business meetings, doctors' appointments, and dates. For some reason, he had never been on time when he was supposed to meet up with Derrick and Ricky. He'd always made them wait for him.

Because I never treated them like they were important, he now thought forlornly. *Because I never thought our friendship was important.*

He regretted that now.

"You head on over. I'll bring your whiskey on ice," Ray said, snapping him out of his malaise.

"Thanks, Ray," Jamal murmured before strolling toward Ricky. "What's up?"

"What's up, nigga?" Ricky said, rising to his feet, holding out his hand.

It started as a dap but Ricky quickly pulled Jamal in for a hug. When he did, Jamal was overwhelmed with another wave of emotion. This time, it wasn't nostalgia. It was more than that. It was the distinct sensation of returning to something familiar, like throwing on your favorite hoodie but twenty times more intense. There was something comforting and reassuring about it.

He thumped Ricky on the back and smiled up at his friend. "What you been up to?"

"A little bit of this, a little bit of that," Ricky said, releasing him and sitting down again. "Thanks for coming, man. You told me you were gonna do it, but I was hoping you wouldn't back out at the last minute."

Jamal took the other side of the booth. "Like you said—I told you I would come. I wouldn't back out." He glanced around him. "Are you sure Dee didn't though? I notice he ain't here."

"He's coming. He's just running a little behind, that's all," Ricky said before raising his beer bottle to his lips.

"You sure? Maybe he decided this shit is just too much and skipped it. I mean, this isn't going to be easy . . . us all hashing out things."

Ricky lowered the bottle from his mouth back to the table. They both nodded at Ray as he set the whiskey glass in front of Jamal and shuffled back to the bar counter.

"Yeah, about that," Ricky began. "Uh . . . I-I didn't tell Dee you were gonna be here tonight."

"*What?*"

"I didn't tell Dee you were—"

"Yeah! I heard you the first time!" Jamal cried. "Why the hell didn't you tell him? I thought we were all meeting up!"

"We are. It's just that two of us know that—and one of us doesn't."

"I thought you liked Ray, Ricky. Is there a reason why you want to see bottles thrown at the walls and tables flipped over in here?"

"Jay, don't exaggerate. Dee ain't gonna do all that!"

"Really? You sure?"

"Yeah," Ricky said, thought for a second, and shrugged. "Mostly."

Jamal sighed. He seriously contemplated getting up and walking out. He wasn't here for an ambush. But he didn't get the chance to exit stage left. They both looked up when the door to Ray's opened again. Derrick stepped through, then halted mid-step. When his gaze settled on Jamal, his face changed. His brow lowered.

Ricky rose to his feet. "I know you weren't expecting this shit, but give it a chance, Dee!"

"You one dirty motherfucka, you know that, Ricky?" Derrick said menacingly, pointing a finger at him.

"No, I'm a *well-meaning* motherfucka. Just chill!"

Derrick shook his head. "I'm not doing this. I'm not doing this shit!" He turned around like he was about to head out the door.

"Dee, stop acting like a bitch and come on, man!" Ricky lamented.

"*A bitch?*" Derrick squeaked, looking both surprised and pissed off.

"Yeah, a bitch! Y'all been doing this shit for too long and I'm tired of it. Enough is a fuckin' 'nough! Let's just deal with it! Come over here and chop this shit up. Once and for all!"

Derrick seemed to hesitate. He looked at Ricky and Jamal and back again. Meanwhile, Ray was staring uneasily at all three of them while he dried a shot glass.

"Yeah, okay," Derrick finally muttered before striding to their booth. He loudly dragged over a chair from a nearby table and sat down. He stared at Jamal. "What you gotta say to me?"

Jamal loudly exhaled. "Really, Dee?"

"Yeah, really. You've got no problem doing shit behind my back. I wanna know what you have to say to my face."

"I'm not here for this," Jamal said.

"Then what are you here for?" Derrick challenged.

"*The truth?* I came here to make Melissa happy."

"Oh, look at you!" Derrick cried sarcastically. "Trying to be all considerate for your girl. Too bad the only way you could get that girl was by sliding in and stealing her from someone else, you shady motherfucka."

Jamal shook his head and took a sip from his whiskey glass. "I didn't steal her. You cheated on her. She dumped you. She moved on."

"But you were waiting in the wings, right? You even made a play for her when we were still together, Jay. That was fucked up!"

Jamal nodded. "I did—and yes, that part was fucked up," he admitted, shocking even himself.

Ricky's eyes widened. Derrick's glower eased, though it didn't disappear completely.

"So you're admitting you were wrong?" Derrick asked.

"With that part? Yeah. I was wrong. I was selfish. I ran for something that I'd wanted for a long time. I didn't think about you and how you would feel. I didn't care."

Ricky tilted his head. "So . . . you were wrong," he repeated slowly. "And now you wanna apologize to Dee, right?"

Jamal nodded. "Yeah, I'll apologize for that part."

"Why do you keep saying, *for that part*?" Derrick snapped. "What's with the damn caveats? Why not just apologize and stop playin'?"

"Because I know you want me to apologize for being with her—and I'm not. I can't! I love Melissa. I have for a long time. I'm sorry how I went about pursuing her, but I'm not sorry about the result. I'd be lying to you if I said that I was."

Derrick let out another bitter laugh. "See! See, that's why I can't fuck with you. That's why you're as good as dead to me, nigga. You're still selfish as hell! Nothing's changed with you!"

"Come one, Dee. That ain't fair," Ricky said. "Jay just apologized to you for—"

"And why the fuck do you keep defending his ass?" Derrick charged, turning on Ricky. "Do you remember how all this started? He told you to kick rocks! Not me! I had your back! He said hanging out with you was a liability for him."

"And I was wrong for that, too. I realize that now, and I apologize," Jamal said. "But my mind-set was different back then. I thought I didn't have a choice. I thought—"

"You always had a choice, Jay! You had a choice with that just like you had a choice when you started fuckin' my ex!"

Jamal slumped back against the booth cushion and stifled a groan. So they were back on this again?

"You keep acting like you had to do that shit just because you liked her," Derrick argued. "There are dudes who like women all the time, but they don't fuck 'em! They hold back!"

"*You* didn't," Ricky said softly.

"What?" Derrick asked, turning his glare on Ricky.

"I said you didn't hold back. How you gonna lecture Jay for going after Melissa, when you went after Morgan? You had a choice, too, and you made it. And you didn't care about the consequences."

"Yes, I did!" Derrick shouted. "I agonized over that shit! You know that. I didn't want to hurt Melissa."

"But you *did* hurt her, Dee." Ricky raised his hands. "Come on, bruh! We *all* went after women we knew damn well we shouldn't have. We knew what we were doing, but we were willing to take the risk. Jay is no different than you or me."

Derrick fell silent. For the first time, he looked like he was considering Ricky's words, letting them sink in.

Even Jamal hadn't thought to approach it from that angle. He nodded in appreciation at Ricky's insight. Once again, his old friend had surprised him.

Derrick obviously hadn't considered Jamal had felt compelled to pursue Melissa much like Derrick had felt compelled to go after Morgan, or Ricky had been unable to let go of Simone—despite all logic that told all three men to do the opposite. They were all in the same boat.

"So instead of punishing him or wanting to beat his ass, why don't you just own up to your shit? You of all people should know where he's coming from," Ricky said.

Derrick slumped back in his chair. He still hadn't uttered a word. He squinted at Ricky. "Since when did your ass turn into Dr. Phil?"

Jamal burst into laughter. "Not Dr. Phil. Shit! Iyanla Vanzant. I was waiting for him to break into a speech about civil rights and slaves."

"Ricky Vanzant," Derrick muttered, laughing, too.

"Oh, fuck the both of y'all!" Ricky said, waving them off.

Pretty soon, all three men were laughing—hard and loud.

Jamal hadn't laughed this much in quite a while. The joke wasn't even that funny, but tears still came to his eyes. Even Derrick was slapping the table. Ricky was doubled over in the booth.

When they stopped, Jamal looked around the table. "Damn, that felt good."

Derrick slowly nodded. "It did."

They met gazes. Jamal was surprised to discover that in that moment, all the pain, anger, and resentment from the past two years had eased out of him. He wondered if Derrick felt the same. None of them could change the past, and they would probably never go back to what they had been before, but Melissa had been right about one thing: He felt lighter now.

"Shit, I need another drink," Ricky muttered, holding up his empty bottle. "Dee, you gettin' somethin'?"

"Yeah," Derrick said, nodding again. "I guess I will."

They stayed for another three hours. The conversation stayed light. There was no mention again of Melissa. They didn't talk about Dolla Dolla's death or Mayor Johnson's conviction. They just joked and laughed.

"I'm glad we did this," Ricky said. "I knew if we all chopped it up, we could make it right."

"We still got a ways to go though. I'll be honest with you, Ricky," Derrick conceded.

"I ain't expect a miracle, bruh! I just wanted y'all on better terms before I go," Ricky said.

Jamal squinted. "Go where?"

Ricky took a drink from his bottle and lowered it back to the table. He sighed. "The hearings start next week. I agreed to testify in the federal trial and that could last a few months. After that, I'm going away for a while. It's part of the deal I worked out."

"*Away?*" Derrick raised his eyebrows. "You mean to jail?"

"For how long?" Jamal asked simultaneously, now panicked.

They had finally reconnected and now Ricky had to disappear to prison.

What kind of bullshit is this? Jamal thought.

"I can't go into detail, but I'm gonna be away for a while. A *long* while." He stared down at his bottle, no longer meeting their gazes. "You do the crime, you gotta do the time, right?"

"You risked your life to help them," Derrick began, almost sounding hurt. "You did all that shit and then they're gonna—"

"Hey," Ricky said, finally looking up, "it is what it is! I just wanted to give y'all a heads-up. I'm not gonna be here anymore to referee and I wanna know y'all are good. Y'all ain't coming to blows anymore, right?"

Derrick pursed his lips. "Yeah, I'm good."

Jamal nodded. "I was always good."

"Good," Ricky said, thumping the table. "So that's the end of it."

"No, it's not the end of it!" Jamal insisted, feeling like he had just stumbled into a funeral. "We've lived in the same city . . . we've known each other since we were twelve years old. We've been like brothers—whether we were together or fighting, and now you're just . . . you're just . . ."

He couldn't find the right words to express the overwhelming sense of loss he was feeling right now. He looked at Derrick to see if maybe he could pick up his string of thoughts and make it make sense, but Derrick looked away, like he was in pain, too.

"You just gonna disappear. I know what you gotta be going through. I don't want to put any more burden on you, Ricky, but I can't hide the fact that I'm . . . I'm gonna miss you, man," Jamal said.

Ricky slowly smiled. "Well, shit! It ain't like I'm dying. I'm not even leaving tomorrow!" He playfully slapped Jamal's shoulder. "You got tears in your eyes and shit! Goddamn!"

"Shut up, Ricky," Jamal muttered, making his friend laugh. Derrick laughed, too.

"Come on, y'all! No more depressing stuff. Let's keep this party goin'! Let's shut down this joint," Ricky said.

Jamal gave a forlorn smile and wondered if this was the last time they would ever get to do this. He couldn't believe it, but he really was starting to feel a little choked up. "Whatever you want, Ricky."

"That's what I want." Ricky waved his hand. "Eh, Ray, we need another round!"

Ray nodded. "I got you."

Chapter 39

Ricky

Four and a half months later . . .

Ricky stepped through the airport's automatic doors onto the sidewalk. Though it was late April, he was immediately hit in the face with the cold, crisp mountain air. It slapped him with a wallop, almost sucking the air out of his lungs.

He had taken the red-eye from Dulles to Denver International Airport. With transfers, the entire flight had taken about seven hours. He was exhausted and should probably have headed to an airport hotel to sleep for a few hours, shower, and shave, but he didn't want to waste any time doing that. Now that he was in the same town as Simone and Miles, he didn't want to waste another minute getting back to them.

He walked to the line for those waiting to get a taxi and was relieved to see only two people standing there, which meant he wouldn't have to wait long. He adjusted his duffel bag on his shoulder, which contained all the belongings the feds had allowed him to take with him before he left town. He hadn't even been allowed to say goodbye to Derrick and Jamal, though the truth was that he had tried to prepare his friends for his abrupt departure. Unfortunately, they believed he was headed to prison, not to a new place and identity in Denver. But again, that had been one of the dictates of the witness protection program: ending all connections to the life he'd had before. It had been painful to do it, to walk away from them. The only solace he took in this was that at least he was walking *toward* something; he was returning to his family.

"Where you headed?" the attendant asked when Ricky finally reached the front of the taxi line and a mini-van pulled up to the curb.

"East Yale Avenue," Ricky said.

That was the address Detective Ramsey had given him, slipping it into his pocket on the last day of the trial.

He had been surprised when the detective did it, especially after the feds broke the news to him that he and Simone wouldn't be reunited.

"That's not how the program works, Ricky," his lawyer had told him. "Whatever promises those cops made to you, they couldn't follow through. They can't tell you where they've sent other witnesses."

But Ramsey did tell him, probably risking his badge to do it. Yes, he had helped the detectives for a year. Yes, what he'd given them as an informant had helped them land several criminals and put all of them in jail—including Dolla Dolla's business partner, José Palacios, who'd had to be muzzled during his trial because he kept shouting out, cursing Ricky while he was on the stand. But Ricky had thought his relationship with the detectives had been all business. Or, as was the case with Detective Dominguez, a hate-filled relationship that they only maintained because they had to. He certainly never thought of them as friends.

So when Ramsey had not only gone out of his way to find out where Simone lived but also relayed that info to Ricky, it had touched Ricky deeply. He'd wanted to thank the detective but didn't have the chance. After his last bit of testimony, he had to climb into a police car and was driven to the nearby jail, only to exit the cruiser and climb into a blacked-out sedan two hours later after shaving off his beard and changing his clothes. He then headed straight to the airport to buy a ticket with a photo ID that showed his new name, Jared Bryant.

Ricky now climbed inside another vehicle—a cab that would take him to Simone's home.

"First time in Denver?" the driver asked a few minutes into their drive.

"How'd you guess?" Ricky asked.

"No offense . . . but you don't really look like you're from around here," the driver said.

"None taken," Ricky replied as he stared out the window at the passing scenery.

The driver leaned slightly in his seat to gaze at him in the rearview mirror. "You here for business or for pleasure?"

"Pleasure, I hope."

"*You hope?*" The driver barked out a laugh. "Why don't you know for sure?"

"*I* know why I'm here . . . but I don't know if everything will turn out like I hoped," he said, honestly.

The driver nodded. "I know how that goes. Whenever I go on vacation, I'm never sure if they're gonna screw up my reservations or lose my luggage. But it usually works out okay. I'm sure it will for you, too, pal."

"Here's hopin'," Ricky muttered as he stared at the mountains in the distance.

Forty minutes later, the driver drew to a stop in front of a series of garden apartments.

"You're here!" the driver called out.

Ricky dug through his wallet and gave him several bills, including the tip.

"Thanks!" the driver said with a smile. "And good luck to you, pal!"

"Thank you," Ricky said.

Ricky climbed out, taking his duffel bag with him, and slammed the cab's door shut. He listened as the taxi pulled off, and stared down at the address written on the paper. It didn't take him long to find her apartment. He climbed the stairs and looked for her apartment number. When his eyes landed on it, 404, he hesitated. Ricky stood frozen in front of the apartment door.

He wanted to knock but part of him was afraid of what lay on the other side. Thanks to the investigation and the trial, he and Simone had been apart for almost a year. That was a lot of time. Much could have happened in the interim. Simone could've found a new man. Or she simply may not be in love with him anymore. Maybe she wouldn't be happy when she saw him. Maybe she'd see his arrival in Denver as an unwelcome surprise.

Enough with the maybes, he silently told himself.

He couldn't stay in this damn hallway forever. And he had traveled so far, waited so long. Whatever happened, however she reacted, he would just have to accept it. But he was knocking on the door—regardless.

Ricky took a deep breath, raised the steel knocker over the peephole, and banged it twice.

He heard footsteps, then Simone's voice shouting to someone. He heard the door unlock and then it swung open.

Simone stood in the doorway in an oversized purple sweater that hung off one of her bare shoulders and a pair of gray leggings and rainbow socks. Her cell phone was tucked between her ear and her shoulder, a set of electronic instructions was in one hand, a plastic spatula was in the other. She looked like the frazzled mom that she probably was now.

When he saw her, he breathed in sharply. He wasn't prepared for how beautiful she was. His memories hadn't done her justice.

"I'll get you more eggies, honey!" she shouted distract-edly down the short hallway of her apartment, trying to be heard over a kid's cartoon soundtrack playing in the background. "Mommy just has to answer the door. I bet it's the guy finally coming to fix the . . ."

Her words drifted off when she turned back around and saw Ricky standing in the hallway. Their gazes met and her mouth fell open in shock.

He gave a sheepish smile. "Hey, Simone," he said.

Simone screamed. She dropped her cell phone from her ear. The spatula and booklet of instructions fell to the floor. She ran straight for him. He had to drop his duffel bag to catch her. He almost collided with the hallway wall when she fell against him and wrapped her arms around him. He didn't get a chance to say anything. Not *hello* or *how have you been?* She kissed all his words away—and sobbed as she did it.

"Oh, my God!" she whispered against his lips. "I missed you so much, baby!"

He threw his arms around her and kissed her back, letting her warmth and softness cover him like a blanket. He had missed this, too, all of this, and the sensation of having it again after he had waited so long and been through so much almost made his knees buckle.

"Mama!" he heard a little voice call out. "Mama!"

Simone leaned back from Ricky. She sniffed. "Mommy is right here," she called over her shoulder. "I'm comin'. Don't worry, honey!"

"I'll be damned," Ricky murmured in wonderment. "He knows how to talk now?"

He knew time had passed since he'd last seen Miles, but in his mind, the little boy was still a squirmy, cross-eyed infant.

She nodded and laughed. "He says a few words here and there, though it's still a lot of babbling and gibberish. *He* knows exactly what he's saying, though I don't most of the time." She chuckled and unwrapped her arms from around Ricky and nodded toward the open door. "You wanna see him?"

Now overcome with brand-new emotions, Ricky didn't trust for the right words to come out so he only nodded. He grabbed his bag and she grabbed his hand, tugging him inside. She shut the door behind them and reached down to grab her cell phone.

"Hey, Steph," she said into the phone, "let me call you back . . . Yes, I know you heard me scream. Sorry if I scared you but I swear, everything is okay. I just was a little surprised . . . Okay . . . Okay. Talk to you soon." She then pressed the button to hang up and looked up at him. "That's Steph. She's my friend. I met her in my mommy group."

He nodded vaguely but he was barely listening. He was going to see Miles. He was going to see his son.

"Just so you know," Simone continued as they walked down the hall, "I'm Deidre now. Not Simone. It's Deidre Wilkins. That's the name they gave me. And Miles is Miles Wilkins. They let him keep his first name. I requested that."

"I'm Jared Bryant," he said, making her pause.

"Jared?" She slowly looked him up and down. "Your beard is gone now. Makes you look like a different person. I guess the new name suits you." She then stood on the

balls of her feet and kissed his cheek. "Pleased to meet you, Jared."

"Pleasure's all mine, Deidre," he whispered.

"You can set that down here and unpack later," she said, gesturing to his duffel bag.

He did as she ordered. She then tugged his hand again and they rounded the corner, revealing an eat-in kitchen. A television sat on the granite counter, playing the cartoon that Ricky had heard in the hallway. Staring at the television was a little boy in a high chair. He had curly hair just like his mother's but skin closer to a lighter shade like his father's. When Ricky entered the room, the boy turned slightly in his high chair. His face and bib were smudged with applesauce. He stared at Ricky and quickly broke into a little grin, revealing four tiny white teeth.

"Dada!" he called out and clapped his chubby hands.

Ricky gaped. He looked at Simone. "He . . . he remembers who I am?"

She squeezed Ricky's hand. "He's said goodnight to a picture of you on my cell almost every day of his life. I'm surprised he recognizes you without the beard though."

"You really showed him a picture every day?"

She lowered her eyes. "I wasn't supposed to keep it but I . . . I couldn't let it go. I couldn't let you go, Ricky."

Ricky leaned down to kiss her again but paused when their son shouted. "Eggy! Eggy, Mama!"

They both laughed and turned to face him.

"I guess I better go make him those eggs." She released Ricky's hand. "He's not gonna let up. He's persistent like his daddy."

"I'll sit with him while you do that." He walked to the table and pulled out a chair beside Miles's high chair while Simone made her way to the stove.

"Dada!" Miles said again, slapping his tray. "Dada! Dada!"

Ricky reached up and loosened the straps of Miles's high chair. He raised him out of it then lowered the boy onto his lap. He was heavier than Ricky thought he would be. Solid through the middle.

"Hey," he whispered as Miles reached up and grabbed his cheek with his sticky fingers. "I used to call you 'li'l man,' but now I think I'll call you 'big guy.' You're gonna grow up to be a linebacker, aren't you? You gonna make your daddy proud."

"Dada!" Miles said again.

"Can I make you some eggs, too? Have you eaten breakfast?" Simone asked.

He glanced up at her. She was taking a carton of eggs out of the refrigerator and placing them on the counter. He looked down at his son, who was hopping up and down on his lap.

He never thought he would have this again, that he would *ever* have this. His girl, his son, his family. His odyssey was finally over. He was home.

"Yeah, I'll take some eggs. Scrambled, please," he muttered, kissing Miles's brow.

"Coming right up!" Simone said, placing a pan on the burner.

Get the whole story on the
Branch Avenue Boys
In
IN THESE STREETS
And
KNOW YOUR PLACE
Available now from
Shelly Ellis
And
Dafina Books
Wherever books are sold

DISCUSSION QUESTIONS

1. Derrick insists to Morgan that even though he had his outburst at the education benefit when he saw Jamal and Melissa together, he no longer wants to be in a relationship with his ex. Do you believe him?

2. When their midwife, Mary, sees the news about the murders after Simone gives birth, Ricky decides to tell her the truth about what happened and trust her with their secret. Would you have made a similar decision or gone on the run again?

3. After Jamal is shot and Derrick discovers Cole is the culprit, he decides to go to Jamal to plead Cole's case but aborts his mission when he sees Jamal and Melissa together again. Do you think he made the right decision to leave the hospital to avoid conflict, or was he taking the easy way out? Should he have gone back later and spoken to Jamal anyway?

4. Ricky agrees to work as an informant again in exchange for Simone and their son, Miles, being put in witness protection. Did you believe the cops would hold up their end of the deal?

5. Jamal decides to reveal his feelings to Melissa and tell her his emotions haven't changed from before. She tells him she's not ready to fall in love again. Is she being selfish, or is she being honest and a good friend to him, like she assures him she is?

6. Derrick ultimately decides to reject Dolla Dolla's offer to use the Institute for his operations, even though it will put his life and the lives of the boys and teachers at the Institute at risk. Were you surprised by his decision?

7. Ricky tells the detectives that if they don't arrest Dolla Dolla soon, he's going to blow their entire investigation and tell Dolla Dolla everything. Did you believe he would really do it? Why or why not?

8. Both Derrick and Jamal are surprised by Melissa's suggestion that they try some form of reconciliation. Were you also surprised by her suggestion? Do you agree with her reasoning?

9. Derrick, Jamal, and Ricky decide to let bygones be bygones and stay civil, but they also agree that things can never go back to the way they were before. Do you think they will ever have the potential to become true friends again?

10. Have the Branch Avenue Boys changed or switched personalities since the beginning of the series? How have they each evolved as men?

Connect with U s

Visit us online at
KensingtonBooks.com
to read more from your favorite authors, see books
by series, view reading group guides, and more.

for sneak peeks, chances to win books and prize packs,
and to share your thoughts with other readers.

facebook.com/kensingtonpublishing
twitter.com/kensingtonbooks

Tell us what you think!

To share your thoughts, submit a review,
or sign up for our eNewsletters, please visit:
KensingtonBooks.com/TellUs.